# *The Nightmare Begins...*

Wyrdrune hated flying because he knew all too well how easily something could go wrong, if not with an exhausted pilot adept, then with an overtaxed air traffic controller, whose eyes would start to cross after sitting hunched over for several hours, staring at all the tiny planes circling in a miniature holding pattern inside a crystal ball. Wyrdrune's nerves were already badly frayed from the transatlantic flight, and now the careening limo, skimming along way too fast merely three feet or so above the ground, was finishing the job of unnerving him completely.

"Could we please slow down a little?" he said.

"We are almost there," Jacqueline said impatiently.

Before long they were pulling up in front of the Dorchester Hotel and the doorman was escorting them out. They checked in and found that among the rooms Jacqueline had reserved for them was the same room that Modred had disappeared from. As they signed the register, Wyrdrune picked up a complimentary copy of *The London Times*. The headline read, "RIPPER STRIKES AGAIN!"

THE WIZARD OF WHITECHAPEL

Also by Simon Hawke

**The Wizard of 4th Street**

Published by
POPULAR LIBRARY

# THE WIZARD OF WHITECHAPEL

## SIMON HAWKE

**POPULAR LIBRARY**

An Imprint of Warner Books, Inc.

A Warner Communications Company

**POPULAR LIBRARY EDITION**

Copyright © 1988 by Simon Hawke
All rights reserved.

Popular Library®, the fanciful P design, and Questar® are registered
trademarks of Warner Books, Inc.

Popular Library books are published by
Warner Books, Inc.
666 Fifth Avenue
New York, N.Y. 10103

Cover illustration by Dave Mattingly

 A Warner Communications Company

Printed in the United States of America

First Printing: September, 1988

10  9  8  7  6  5  4  3  2  1

For Adele,

with thanks for a decade of working together.

Here's to the next ten.

# PROLOGUE

London had changed little in two hundred years. It was hard to believe he'd been away so long. The neatly bearded blond man with the gold wire-rimmed glasses sipped an unblended Scotch as he stared out the window of his suite in the Dorchester Hotel. He was wearing a white silk shirt with lace trim and an elegant, high-collared black suit. It was a cool, early-autumn evening, and through the open window he could hear the orchestra playing in the pavilion in Hyde Park. He lit a cigarette and removed his coat, revealing the black 10-mm semiautomatic he wore in a shoulder holster under his left arm.

People and fashions come and go, he thought, but the city always stays the same. Like Rome and Venice, London was a city that stubbornly resisted change. Londoners took great pride in their city's history. They cherished the buildings that dated back hundreds of years. They installed blue plaques on houses where famous people had once lived. 48 Doughty Street had been the home of Charles Dickens; 34 Tite Street boasted Oscar Wilde; Thomas Carlyle had once kept lodgings in Cheyne Row. Londoners took meticulous care of their ancient monuments and statues and fastidiously restored their old mansions, mews, and churches, maintaining a tangible connection with their

1

noble past. But the artifacts of London, from its Tudor architecture to its Victorian gas lamps to the nightmarish Bauhaus office buildings of the Windsor Era, were mere novelties to him. He remembered a much older England, when London had been little more than a thatch-roofed village eclipsed by that great stone monument to the roaring ego of his father—a castle fortress known as Camelot.

Almost two thousand years had passed since Modred first left England at the close of the sixth century. Back then, he never thought he would return. They had all believed him dead, all except Morgana, who had never given up. And now she, too, was gone. England held nothing for him anymore, and yet he had come back once again. It had always been that way. Years would pile up into decades, decades into centuries, and he would find himself once more inexorably drawn back to England, to see what new generations had accomplished and what, if anything, remained of the England he once knew.

He had known since childhood that he was descended from the Old Ones, but he had never truly known just what that meant until his first century had passed and he still looked like the wild young boy who had brought down a king. He had aged since then, although extremely slowly. Now, within two hundred years of his second millennium, he looked like a man of forty. There were streaks of gray in his blond hair and beard. The tinted, gold-rimmed glasses were an eccentric touch. He didn't really need them, but they gave him a clerical, antiquarian look that was often usefully deceptive. His body was lean and well muscled, his reflexes and instincts as sharp and quick as ever.

His grandmother, Igraine, had been a human, as was his paternal grandfather, Uther. As a result, when Uther raped Igraine, the issue—Arthur—was a normal human child. But his maternal grandfather, Gorlois, the Duke of Cornwall, was of the Old Race, and Modred's mother had inherited the genes and eldritch powers of the Old Ones. Morgan Le Fay had been a half-breed, as was Merlin.

They both had the same blood running through their veins. Neither of them was completely human.

Morgana herself did not know what she was till she met Merlin and he became her teacher. Merlin had told her the secret of her past and instructed her in the mystic arts of thaumaturgy, but he never suspected her true purpose. Her boundless ambition and her lust for vengeance had consumed her and contaminated everything she touched. She seduced her own half brother, Arthur, and gave birth to Modred. Through him she had brought down Arthur's kingdom, but when it was over, she had been left with nothing. She could take no satisfaction in the bitter irony of Arthur being destroyed by his own son. The spoils of her vengeance were denied her. There had been no kingdom she could rule through Modred, because without Arthur, the kingdom fell apart and there was no Modred to try to hold it all together.

With Arthur dead, the poison had gone out of Modred. He remembered Lucas and Bedivere standing over him as he lay upon the battlefield, impaled on his father's spear, and he heard Bedivere saying flatly, "He is done." Then they had left him lying there and went to help their king, but Arthur did not survive his wounds. Modred had been certain that he would die of his as well. At that moment he had longed for nothing quite so much as death, and yet his body lingered, clinging stubbornly to life in a way that no merely human body ever could.

He remembered lying on the corpse-strewn field of battle, looking up at the darkening sky as the ravens feasted all around him, his body flushed with agony, tears of despair flooding his eyes. He grieved for the waste his life had been, never suspecting how much life was still ahead of him. It was as if the hate that fueled him all his life had spilled out with his blood, and now he was an empty vessel, lying shattered and discarded on a field of broken dreams.

He had dragged himself away to heal and then had left

England, to live first as an itinerant bard, then as a thief, and finally, having no other marketable skills, he became a mercenary. It was a line of work for which he was eminently suited. He fought without passion or ideals and with no thought for principles or morals. He knew only too well that even a knight like Lancelot could be destroyed by passion, and a woman pure as Guinevere could betray her own ideals. Modred had seen how easily principles could be perverted and morality manipulated. He had known the self-righteous hypocrisy of Camelot, where might made right and adultery was tolerated so long as the appearance of virtue could be maintained. He wanted no part of chivalry or honor. He cared even less for love and glory. The consuming emotions of his youth were banished utterly, to be replaced by the ruthless pragmatism of a black knight errant ruled only by cold logic.

He traveled the world and watched it change throughout the centuries. He became the consummate master of invisibility, living many different lives under countless aliases, hiding his vast wealth and his true identity in an impenetrable cloak of secrecy. He made his way by means of his physical and intellectual powers rather than thaumaturgic skill. His mother's training and the natural gifts he had inherited from her had made him an adept, but magic was Morgana's way, and Merlin's. Modred wanted no part of it.

Yet the choice was never really his to make. He had learned that he could not escape his destiny. He rubbed his chest and felt the hardness of the small ruby embedded in the skin over his heart. He unbuttoned his lace-trimmed shirt and glanced down at the enchanted runestone set into his chest. It was glowing softly.

He did not know why it had started glowing, or why it throbbed the way it did. It seemed to pulse like a small heart.

He emptied the bottle of Scotch, picked up the phone, and ordered another sent up from room service. He rubbed his chest once more. It felt sore from the strangely throbbing runestone. He felt an intense anxiety that he could not define. He did not understand what was happening, and it worried him. He lit another cigarette. Smoking and drinking were destructive human vices, yet they had no visible effect upon him. At one point or another he had done just about every self-destructive thing a man could do. It was as if he had been playing a game with Death for all those years, daring the Grim Reaper to come and try to claim him. Many times the Reaper had almost done just that, but Modred had always managed to elude him. He had started to believe that he was indestructible, but Merlin's death at the hands of the Dark Ones had firmly convinced him otherwise. If Merlin could be killed, then he could die as well. That knowledge had given life a sharper edge. That, and the knowledge that he now had a purpose that was greater than his own survival. A quest, of sorts, not unlike Galahad's relentless search for the Holy Grail.

Modred smiled as he thought of his old tutor. He finally understood him how, after all these centuries had passed. Galahad had known that a man could not define himself through his relationships with others. He had understood that his identity was not bound up with his father or his mother, nor with his fellow knights, nor with his king. It was to be found somewhere within himself, and it was there that Galahad had searched with an anguished desperation, looking for that essence of himself, seeking to define his soul. In the end he found his Holy Grail, but the quest had killed him. Now Modred wondered if he was the darker side of Galahad, and if his own unholy quest would lead to the same end.

As he stared out at the sun setting over the city, he drew deeply on his cigarette and wondered how a cat burglar, a bumbling warlock, and a professional assassin could possibly hope to succeed where Merlin himself had failed. As if in response, the runestone embedded in his chest flashed and sent a searing pulse of energy flowing through him like an electric current.

He doubled over, clutching at his chest and grimacing with pain. Suddenly the hotel room became somehow *transparent*. He could see through the walls, floors, and ceiling to a galaxy of stars. The light around him drained away, and he heard the sound of distant, mocking laughter. Then it was over and the pain was gone, as quickly as it had come. He stood once more in the hotel room, the walls around him solid, his face flushed, his skin warm and damp with perspiration. He leaned against the wall, shook his head, and blinked his eyes to clear his vision. The gem set into his chest was strobing brightly.

"What the devil is happening to me?" he said, as if asking the living gem that had become a part of him.

There was a knock at the door.

"Room service," said a voice outside the door.

Unsteadily Modred walked over to the door and opened it. The waiter came into the room, stooped over to push the serving cart that held several covered dishes, a pot of tea, a small basket of bread, and a vase holding a single yellow rose.

"I didn't order dinner," Modred said. "I asked for a bottle of Scotch. You must have the wrong room."

The room service waiter straightened up, and Modred found himself staring at a grinning, worm-infested skull with green fire glowing in its empty eye sockets.

Instinctively he jerked back and drew his pistol in a lightning-swift motion. He fired three times, point-blank, at the fearsome apparition. The figure literally collapsed. With his gun still in his hand, Modred cautiously approached the pile of smoking clothing on the floor. He gingerly lifted up the waiter's jacket. The hideous skull was lying on the floor beneath it. There was only the skull, cracked and brown with age, and nothing else. As he stared down at it a snake crawled out of the left eye socket.

A hollow, echoing laugh boomed forth from the skull's gaping jaw.

And then the skull *exploded,* shattering into a thousand bright blue shards of shimmering, glowing crystal that spun around the room in arabesques and coalesced into a whirlwind funnel of blue fire, encircling him and sucking all the air out of his lungs, spinning him around and around, faster and faster and faster, and then the maelstrom sucked up into itself and disappeared, taking him along with it.

There was a loud, insistent banging on the door.

"*Sir*! Sir, are you all right? Sir, what's going *on* in there? What is that *noise*? What are you *doing*? *Sir*! *Sir*!"

The room service waiter tried the knob and found that it was open. He took one step inside and froze. The room was empty, but it looked as if a tornado had passed through it. It was totally destroyed.

"*Bloody hell!*" the waiter exclaimed, staring at the wreckage with stunned disbelief. Then he shook his head and squinted. For a moment he could have sworn that the walls inside the room had become somehow insubstantial. It seemed as if he could see through them to a galaxy of stars. And then he heard the distant sound of malevolent, ghostly laughter.

The bottle of Scotch crashed to the floor as the waiter took off running down the hall.

# CHAPTER ONE

As Wyrdrune passed the Washington Square fountain, the white-faced mime fell in step behind him. Wyrdrune was preoccupied, deep in thought as he walked with his shoulders hunched and his hands shoved into the pockets of his brown Inverness coat. A wide-brimmed brown felt hat was pulled low over his forehead. He didn't notice the mime walking close behind him, burlesquing his stride, his posture, and his facial expression. It was only when he heard the eruption of laughter from the people who had gathered to watch the mime that he stopped and looked up, puzzled. The mime, playing to his audience, didn't notice Wyrdrune stop and walked right into him.

Wyrdrune turned around, frowning, and the mime backed off a pace, exaggerating surprise, then he once more fell into Wyrdrune's attitude, duplicating his posture and his frown. Wyrdrune folded his arms and stared at the mime with a wry expression. The mime mirrored him, enjoying the laughter of his audience. Wyrdrune unfolded his arms and took one step toward the mime. The mime quickly backed off a couple of paces, threw up his hands in an exaggerated expression of alarm, and then "constructed a wall" between himself and Wyrdrune. He mimed, pressing his hands up against the invisible wall, indicating that Wyrdrune couldn't touch him. The audience loved it.

"Fine," said Wyrdrune, scowling, "Have it your way." He mumbled under his breath and gestured at the mime, then turned and walked away.

Behind him, the smile slipped from the face of the mime as he suddenly felt a *real* invisible wall before him. He spun around, stretched out his hands, and encountered another invisible barrier. Frantically he felt all around him, his alarm growing as he realized that he really *was* trapped inside an invisible box. The audience laughed louder and louder at his antics.

"He sure makes it look as if he's really in a box, doesn't he?" one man said to his companion.

"Yeah, he's really good," the woman replied.

"*Help!*" the mime shouted desperately. "*For God's sake, somebody help me!*"

The audience laughed as he seemed to mime shouting for help and hammered, panic-stricken, on the invisible walls with his fists. No one could hear him through the invisible box, which extended straight up into the air for ten stories and was open at the top, so he wouldn't suffocate for the three hours he would remain in there until the spell wore off.

"Hey, warlock," said Kira as Wyrdrune passed the hot-dog stand. "Over here."

She stood next to the vendor's cart with her hands in the pockets of a black leather jacket with chain-mail trim. She had on tight yellow trousers and high black boots. She wore her dark hair short, swept back sharply at the sides and down low over her forehead at a rakish angle. She was long-legged, athletically trim, and pretty in a slightly feral-looking way.

"You said in front of the *arch*," said Wyrdrune in an irritated tone. "This isn't in front of the arch. This is in front of the *fountain*."

"My, aren't we in a shitty mood today," she said. "I got

hungry, okay? So sue me." She turned to the hot-dog vendor and said, "Gimme one with the works."

The vendor, a sepulchral-looking black man with large gold earrings and a shaved head, ladled chili over a hot dog covered with sauerkraut, relish, onions, peppers, and grated cheese. Just looking at it made Wyrdrune's stomach churn.

"I saw that," Kira said, gesturing toward the imprisoned mime, who was growing more frantic by the minute. "You should be ashamed of yourself."

Wyrdrune's lower lip dropped down in a sneer. "I hate mimes."

Among the crowd gathered to watch the mime was a skinny old man walking a land squid on a leash. The land squid was reaching out with its tentacles and deftly lifting wallets out of people's pockets, then handing them to the skinny old man, who dropped them in his purse. Over by the arch, a group of young black kids were street-dancing with a rapper box. As it danced and spun around on its chunky little legs, the box was improvising a fast-paced rap to the beat booming from its speakers. One of the kids slipped a whooshboard underneath the box, and it took off on a wild, gyroscoping course, finally smacking into the side of the arch, where it fell off the board and lay on its side, going, "Uh-huh, Uh-*huh!* Uh-huh, Uh-*huh!*" Wyrdrune wondered if Merlin had ever thought that it would come to this when he'd brought back magic to the world.

Kira took the hot dog and bit into it with gusto. A great glob of condiment slop dripped down onto the sidewalk. "Mmm," she said.

Wyrdrune shook his head. "It beats me how you stay in such terrific shape eating that garbage," he said.

She turned to the hot-dog vendor. "Man's got no taste," she said.

"This from a woman who uses twelve-year-old Scotch to wash down nachos," Wyrdrune said.

Kira shrugged. "There wasn't any beer." She held her

hand out for her change. The hot-dog vendor froze, staring wide-eyed at the gleaming sapphire embedded in the palm of her right hand.

"Whatsa matter, you never seen jewelry before?" she said. She snapped her fingers twice. "Come on, sometime today, all right?"

The vendor counted out her change, then did a double take as she suddenly vanished into thin air. Wyrdrune had disappeared as well.

"Magic users," the vendor mumbled uneasily. He quickly made a warding gesture with the forefingers and little fingers of both hands extended, crossing his arms right over left, then left over right, then he quickly opened up his cart and checked his cash to make sure it was still there.

Wyrdrune reappeared in his railroad flat on East 4th Street with a pop of displaced air. He took off his coat and slouch hat and threw them down on the couch. He was wearing loose-fitting, multipocketed brown trousers, a light brown warlock's cassock, and high-topped red leather athletic shoes with blue lightning stripes. A bright green emerald was embedded in the center of his forehead. The runestone was partially covered by his shoulder-length, curly blond hair.

"Right," he said, "now what did you . . . ?" He glanced all around the room, but Kira was nowhere in sight. He squeezed his eyes shut. "Oh, no. Not *again*."

There was a sharp, insistent rapping at the window. Kira was standing outside, on the fire escape.

Wyrdrune exhaled heavily with relief. He hurried over to the window and opened it. He extended his hand to her and helped her in, then his eyes grew wide and he gasped, stiffening with pain as she squeezed his hand in a bone-crushing grip. "Aah! *Aaah! Kira! Stop! Please. . . .*"

He went down to his knees, then clutched his hand to his chest protectively as she released him.

"*Ow! Damn,* you're strong! It feels like you broke it!"

"Next time I *will* break it, so help me!" she said, glaring at him furiously. "Six more inches to the right, you bird-brain, and you would've dropped me on the sidewalk!"

"I'm sorry! It was an accident. . . ."

"That's what you say *every* time! What the hell is wrong with you? Why can't you learn to cast one lousy little tele-portation spell without screwing something up? What've you got against cabs, anyway?"

"*Oy, gevalt!* Enough already with this *mishegoss!*" A spindly-looking straw broom came swaying into the room on its bristles. It had thin, rubbery arms with four fingers on each hand, and its matronly voice seemed to be coming from somewhere near the top part of its handle, although it had no mouth. It had no hips, either, but that didn't stop it from putting its hands were its hips might have been if it had hips. "Arguments, arguments, always with the arguments! Always with the yelling! A person would think you two were married! What is it *this* time?"

"You want to know what it is? I'll tell you what it is," snapped Kira. "I'm getting sick and tired of being popped into closets and dropped into dumpsters and teleported onto fire escapes and—" She broke off and rolled her eyes up at the ceiling. "Will you listen to this, for cryin' out loud? I'm explaining to a *stick!*"

"Well! Excuse me for living," the broom said huffily. "Is that gratitude, I'm asking you? I work around here till I could *plotz*, scrubbing my fingers to the bone, cooking, cleaning, ironing, washing out somebody's skimpy little black panties who never wears a bra, but I won't mention it, and now all of a sudden I'm not good enough to talk to?"

"She didn't mean it, Broom," said Wyrdrune, sighing heavily. "She's just upset."

"Upset?" The broom turned to Kira. "You want upset? *Five* bristles I lost today, Miss Hoity-toity, but do I shout at *you* when you come home?" The broom turned back to

Wyrdrune and wagged a spindly finger at him. "And as for you, Mr. Wizard, with your *farpotshket* spells, you should be more careful before somebody gets hurt! Pay attention to what you're doing with all this *meshuggah* popping and poofing all over the place. Why you can't take a bus like a normal person, I'll never understand. So we're finished with the yelling now? Yes? Good. There's fresh coffee and some hot apple strudel on the table. Sit! Eat! And now, if you'll excuse me, 'the stick' has to go and do your laundry."

As the broom swept out of the room Kira shook her head and shucked her leather jacket. She plopped down onto the couch and put her feet up on the large wooden cable spool that served as a coffee table. She was wearing a wide chain-mail and leather belt and a skintight, sleeveless black tunic, sheer enough to leave nothing to the imagination. "You could've had a nice cat for a familiar," she said wryly, "but no, not you."

"Never mind the broom," said Wyrdrune, going into the kitchen to pour them both some coffee. "Did you learn anything from Makepeace?"

Dr. Sebastian Makepeace, a professor at New York University, was one of Modred's contacts in New York. Aside from teaching courses in pre-Collapse history, he was also somehow connected with government intelligence. He knew Modred by the code name Morpheus and the alias Michael Cornwall. He had no idea who Modred really was.

"No, Makepeace hasn't heard a thing," said Kira. "I take it you didn't have any luck, either?"

Wyrdrune shook his head. "Nobody's seen him, nobody's heard from him. And it took me all day just to find out that much. Even knowing who his people are and the proper procedures and recognition signals, trying to get any of them to talk is next to impossible."

"I know what you mean," she said. "Makepeace was suspicious as hell, and Modred had specifically *told* him about us. He's a weird guy, that Makepeace."

"Modred's got his people trained real well, no question about that," said Wyrdrune. "What makes it difficult is that none of them know any truly essential information. Most of them are only message drops. And none of them knows who he really is. To some he's John Roderick; to others he's Michael Cornwall or Mikhail Kutozov or Antonio Modesti. It just goes on and on. I don't know how I ever kept it all straight. In fact, I'm not even sure I did."

"What do you mean?"

"Have you ever heard of Phillipe de Bracy?"

She frowned. "No, I don't think so." Then she brightened. "Oh, sure, it's one of Modred's aliases. He uses it in France when he—"

"How did you know that?" Wyrdrune asked, interrupting her, watching her intently. "Did you *remember* that just now, or did you all of a sudden simply *know* it?"

She stared at him. "What are you saying?"

"I'm saying that I think your first response was the correct one," he said. "I don't think you ever heard that name until I mentioned it just now and your runestone filled in the blanks."

"But . . . no." She frowned and shook her head. "Are you *sure*?"

"Think carefully," said Wyrdrune. "Did you ever hear that name from me before?"

She bit her lower lip, concentrating. "I suppose I must have, I—"

"Don't suppose. Do you remember me or Modred *ever* mentioning that name?"

She shook her head. "Well, if you put it that way, no, I don't remember, but just because I don't remember doesn't mean it didn't happen."

"I *never* mentioned that name to you before," Wyrdrune said emphatically, "because until a short while ago I didn't even *know* it. I had called every single contact of Modred's I could think of, and I'd run fresh out of ideas. And then, all of a sudden, I realized that Modred also used the name

Phillipe de Bracy. And the moment I realized it, I also knew who Phillipe de Bracy's contact in Marseilles was."

"Jacqueline Monet," said Kira. Her eyes grew wide. "My God, you're right! I didn't know that until just now! It's like those dream visions the runestones gave us." Nervously she moistened her lips. "You think it's Modred trying to get in touch with us?"

"Why didn't he use the mind link?" Wyrdrune said.

Kira had no answer. She remembered Modred's words to them the last time he had communicated with them telepathically.

*"We've hurt them, and they've fled to hide and lick their wounds. As long as we remain alive, they'll never be as strong as they once were. They'll be vulnerable. We'll find them. And when they're ready, they'll try to find us."*

"That's what the dream was all about last night," she said softly.

They had both awakened abruptly in the middle of the night, at the same time. Each of them had had a dream where they sat up in bed and saw the wall across the bedroom from them, where a bookshelf stood, transformed into a bare wall constructed of huge blocks of mortared stone, dark and damp and ancient. Large iron rings were set into the wall, and Modred hung from them in chains. He was bare-chested, sagging down, and the vision was so real that they could hear the chains clink as he moved weakly, raising his head to look directly at them. The runestone over his heart was glowing faintly. He opened his mouth to say something, and at that moment the vision abruptly faded away and they both awoke, sat up in bed, and stared at each other. The both had had exactly the same dream, and they knew that it was no coincidence.

Kira swallowed hard. "They've got him, haven't they?" she said.

Wyrdrune took a deep breath and let it out slowly. "I'm afraid they do," he said. "But where?"

"They've got him," Kira said again, as if she were trying to make herself believe it. "And now they're after us."

Billy Slade kept hearing voices. This worried Billy a great deal, especially since he had never taken drugs or gotten drunk or even suffered a strong blow to the head. He had no idea if there was any history of insanity in his family, because he had never known his family. He didn't even know what his ethnic background was. Looking in the mirror didn't help much. He was either a very light-skinned black or an Hispanic, he couldn't tell for sure. Maybe he was Italian. For all he knew, he might be part Jamaican. Or perhaps he was a Creole. And it also looked like maybe there was a little Asian in there somewhere, Indian or Oriental. *What the hell,* he thought, *they threw a bit of everything into a blender and I was what came out.*

He was small and wiry, with attractive, delicate features that gave him a slightly androgynous look. His lips were thin and had a natural tendency to drop down a little at the corners of his mouth. His nose was straight and blade-edged, almost elfin, and his cheekbones were high and pronounced. His eyes were dark and almond-shaped, Eurasian-looking, and his eyebrows had a thin, graceful arch. He was, in fact, insufferably pretty, so he tried to cultivate a mean look to offset it. His dark hair was worn very short on the sides and luxuriantly thick and long in the center, descending in a ponytail down the middle of his back, almost to his waist. It had the appearance of a horse's flowing mane. He dressed in the manner of a tatterdemalion thug—scuffed black army boots, a long-fringed jacket sewn from pieces of recycled leather in various shades of black and brown, and patched military fatigue trousers, crudely altered to fit his considerably less than military size. He habitually wore thin, black, studded leather gloves with the fingers cut off, and beneath his jacket his thin black tunic was soiled and torn.

He had run off from one foster home after another until

he was finally placed in a community school, a polite British euphemism for reformatory, but he had run off from there as well, and for the past several years he'd been living on the streets of Whitechapel. He was thirteen years old. And he was hearing voices.

Actually it was one voice in particular. He knew it wasn't his, because his own voice hadn't changed yet. The thought occurred to him that perhaps he was possessed. He thought he'd rather be possessed than crazy, because at least possession was something that came in from the outside and maybe you could fight it. Crazy was the mind coming apart from the inside, and he didn't see what the hell he could do about that. So, with a certain draconian logic, Billy was hoping that his problem was a demon.

The first time it happened, he was looking in a mirror, brushing out his "do," and suddenly his eyes went very wide and a strange, deep, cultured-sounding voice came out of him and said, "Oh, my *God*!"

For a moment Billy wasn't sure where the voice had come from, and he turned around quickly, thinking someone was behind him, but there wasn't anybody there. A second later the voice was there again.

"No, back here, you guttersnipe! Look in the mirror!"

He turned back and looked into the mirror and realized with a shock that *he* had said that. He saw his own lips moving, as if of their own volition.

"Oh, *no*!" said the strange voice. "This can't *possibly* be happening! I won't *allow* it! I won't *stand* for it!"

Billy squinted at his own reflection in the mirror. "'Ere!" he said belligerently. "Who in bloody 'ell you *talkin'* to?"

Then he blinked twice, shook his head as if to clear it, and stared back uncertainly at his reflection in the mirror. "You're talkin' to yourself, Slade, you bleedin' twit. Come on, pull yourself together! Stop it!"

And then a deep groan suddenly escaped him. "Ohhhh,

God! First that miserable, squirrel-infested oak tree, and now *this!*"

"'Ey!" Billy said, frowning angrily at his reflection in the mirror. "Who the bleedin' 'ell's *in* there?"

There was no response.

"Gor', I'm crackin' up, I am," said Billy, turning quickly away from the mirror and hurrying out into the street.

For a while the voice did not return, but Billy couldn't shake the certain feeling that he was being watched, that someone was constantly looking over his shoulder, eavesdropping on him. At night he had strange dreams, and when he awoke, he was often tired. He had the sense that someone had been using his body while he was asleep. He took to drinking coffee by the gallon and staying up until he collapsed from exhaustion. He began avoiding mirrors. He became nervous, irritable, and high-strung. He flinched every time he heard a deep voice speak.

The young toughs who made their living in the street did not think that he was paranoid, because they did not deal in sophisticated concepts such as paranoia. They marked the change in him and simply decided he was loony. And having decided this, they started referring to him as "Loony Slade" on every possible occasion, a development that Billy took strenuous exception to. He was taking strenuous exception to it in an alleyway one afternoon, despite the fact that he was both outnumbered and outsized by five older boys.

He had delivered an eloquent kick to the essentials of the first one, got in a fast lucky shot to the nose of a second, and then inevitably things had turned against him. They had bloodied his mouth and bruised his eye and cut his ear and pummeled him down onto the ground when out of nowhere a deep voice had cried out, "Stand off, you miserable little troglodytes, or you'll regret it!"

The young street toughs didn't notice the strange, wild cast to Billy's eyes; otherwise they might have taken heed of the warning. They were momentarily taken aback by the deep voice, turning and looking behind them until they realized it was Billy who had spoken. Then they recovered quickly, driven by a simple, elemental urge to take out their aggressions on someone who was weaker.

"Wot's that ya called me, ya sodding little bastard?" the largest of them said, snarling and leaning down toward Billy menacingly.

Billy was half lying, half sitting, his back against the alley wall, blood running from his mouth and nose. But his eyes blazed with a cold, preternatural rage. That gaze should have warned them off. That *voice* should have warned them off. The sound of it should have told them that they were faced with something far beyond the norm, but all they saw was someone who was smaller than they were, someone who was down and bleeding.

"You heard me, you loathsome little pismire," Billy said with a voice far older than his years. "Stand off or suffer the consequences!"

"'Ere, listen ta him, 'ey?" the gang leader said, grinning at the other boys. "Must've 'it 'im in the throat. 'E sounds like me bleedin' grandfather!" He turned back to Billy. "Consequences, it is? I'll give ya bloody consequences, ya little wanker. . . ."

He drew his foot back to give Billy a savage kick in the ribs, but Billy stretched out his arm, fingers splayed wide, and a crackling bolt of cobalt-blue thaumaturgic energy leapt from his hand and struck the gang leader squarely in the chest. It hit him with such force that he was picked up and hurled back against the alley wall. He dropped down to the ground, senseless. The other young toughs stared at Billy with stunned disbelief. Blue sparks were dancing in his eyes like electric fire. The boys turned and fled back down the alleyway as fast as their feet would carry them.

The blue firestorm in Billy's eyes dimmed, then went out. He slowly picked himself up off the ground and wiped the blood from his mouth with the back of his hand. He stared down at the motionless form of the gang leader.

"What in the bleedin' blue blazes did I *do*?" he said with awe. Then he snorted at his unintentional pun. "Blue blazes? Right, that's a bloody good one! Gor', what the 'ell's 'appenin' to me?"

And then the deep voice spoke again, only this time it was in his mind. *"If you're going to use the King's English, lad, try not to speak it as if your mouth were full of soggy biscuits. A blue-arsed Pict would sound more intelligible than you!"*

"Oh, Lord." Billy moaned, putting his hands up to his face. "I'm done! I've lost it, sure!"

*"If you're referring to that pathetic little undeveloped organ that you call your mind, no, you have not lost it, so calm down. You're beginning to hyperventilate."*

"Ayper-wot?"

*"Hyperventilate, you little bog trotter. It means . . . oh, never mind! Try to relax before you give us a nervous breakdown. I know it's hard to believe, but you are not going insane, I promise you. You're not imagining this. Unfortunately I really am here, inside you."*

"Who *are* you? *What* are you? Are you the devil, then?"

*"Well, I've been accused of that, but I can assure you that I am most emphatically* not *the devil. My name is Merlin Ambrosius, and I am—or perhaps it would be more correct to say I was—an archmage. As to how this disaster came about, I'm afraid that will take a good deal of explaining, so please pay close attention. I don't want to repeat myself."*

As Billy limped home, Merlin began to tell him a strange and terrifying story. There had been a time, he said, before the dawn of history, when another, older race of beings had lived on Earth. They had left behind only traces of their presence—in the ruins of ancient Egypt, among the crumbling temples of the Incas and the Mayans, in the huge stone idols of the Pacific islands, and in the forgotten shrines of Kali in the mountains of the Hindu Kush. Primitive humans had worshiped them. They were the terrible deities of Egypt, the gods of Greece and Rome, the avatars of India. The Arab tribes knew them as the djinn. Native Americans knew them as Kachina. And to the Celts, they were known simply as the Old Ones.

There were signs of them in the mythology of every human culture. Warriors who were immortal yet who could be killed in battle; supernatural beings who could become invisible or transform themselves into other creatures, sometimes terrible, sometimes benevolent. Werewolves, vampires, witches, spirit beings who could mate with mortals, all such tales had their beginnings with the Old Ones. They had considered humans an inferior race, and they used them for performing labor. And because life energy was one method of utilizing thaumaturgic principles, the Old Ones had used the humans in their magic rituals as well.

The more powerful the spell, Merlin explained, the more energy it required. Such was the price of magic. But while there were many spells that used energy in such a way that it could be replenished, others depleted it completely. And if the source of energy was another living being, that being was destroyed. The human sacrifices of the druids and the Aztecs, the ritual killings of the Thugee cult, the barbaric rites of the Egyptian Pharaohs, all were practices that grew from memories of these ancient thaumaturgic rituals. Necromancy. The sorcery of death. Black magic.

But as time passed, many of the Old Ones came to believe that it was cruel and wasteful to use the humans in this way. They came to feel that life energy should be conserved and nurtured, and that energy used for magic should always be replenished. This, Merlin said, was the beginning of white magic. Yet there were still those among the Old Ones who were unwilling to give up all the power they controlled. To increase their power further, they slaughtered humans by the thousands. It led to competition for the human resource. It led to war. A war more terrible and devastating than any war humans had ever fought.

It survived in human legends as the Ragnarok. The Götterdämmerung. The Twilight of the Gods. In the end the white faction had emerged victorious. Although the white mages were able to subdue the necromancers, whom they called the Dark Ones, they were unable to destroy them. So the ruling council of the white mages devised a spell to contain the unrepentant Dark Ones for all time. They gave their lives to empower the incantation, imbuing their own life energies into the symbols of the spell.

"Three stones, three keys to lock the spell,
Three jewels to guard the Gates of Hell.
Three to bind them, three in one,
Three to hide them from the sun.
Three to hold them, three to keep,
Three to watch the sleepless sleep."

"'Ey, that's nice, I like that," Billy said. "'Ere, I got one. There was a bird whose name was Sherry, she thought she 'ad a golden—"

"*Please! We're talking about spells, not infantile limericks!*"

"Well, all right, guv, don't get yer cock up."

"*God, why me?*" said Merlin.

"'Ey, look, I didn't ask to 'ave you in there, y'know. Go on, then. Finish the story. It's not like I could get up an' walk out, anyways."

Merlin sighed and continued. The keys to the spell, he said, were three enchanted runestones—a sapphire, an emerald, and a ruby. And when it was done and the white archmages had infused their life spirits into the symbols of the spell, the youngest and the last of the ruling council of white mages, a sorcerer named Gorlois, stood alone in the vast underground cavern that would be the prison of the Dark Ones for all eternity.

He placed the runestones inside a small brass box, which he then placed inside a golden chest. He placed the chest upon the lip of a stone ledge high above the deep pit to which the Dark Ones had been consigned. The chest he sealed with a spell and fixed in place so that it could not be moved. The pit he surrounded with a warding pentagram, and then he sealed up the cavern, burying the entrance beneath tons of stone. He then took off his sorcerer's robes, never to put them on again. He left them where they fell and went out to join the others of his kind, the few who had survived and scattered all throughout the world.

"What 'appened to 'em?" Billy said.

*"If you'll kindly refrain from interrupting, I will tell you,"* Merlin said.

"Sorry."

*"That's all right."*

"It's just that I ain't never 'ad no archmage in me 'ead before, y'know? Takes gettin' used to."

*"So does your grammar,"* Merlin said wryly. *"Now, then, where were we?"*

"Old Gorlois and the rest of the Old Bleeders done scattered after they fixed the Darkies," Billy said.

*"I think I understand now,"* Merlin said morosely. *"You're a punishment from God."*

"Yeah, an' you're probably a bloody case o' indigestion," Billy said. "Get on with it."

Billy had the sense that Merlin was slowly counting to ten. A moment later he continued with the story.

The few remaining Old Ones soon learned to conceal what they were if they wanted to survive. They hid among the humans and interbred with them, producing children who often displayed unusual abilities, abilities that in future years would be referred to as "paranormal." Abilities that these children also soon learned to conceal, because the Old Ones and their descendants were mercilessly hunted down.

The hunt had continued through the centuries, said Merlin, even when the true reason for it was no longer remembered clearly. Anyone who was even slightly different was immediately suspect. The persecution of the druids, the extermination of the Aztecs, the Spanish Inquisition, the Salem witch-hunts, the efforts of Fundamental Christians to suppress the quest for knowledge . . . the old fears remained deeply embedded in human racial memory.

Gorlois was one of the few who had survived the persecution of his race. He traveled far from the Euphrates Valley, where the Dark Ones had been entombed, making his way to a cold and windswept island in the north. There he took a human wife from a tribe known as the De Dannan. She bore him a son named Merlin.

" 'Ey, that's your name," Billy said.

*"It was me, you young idiot."*

"So this Gorlois bloke was your old man, then?"

*"Brilliant deduction."*

"Well, bleedin' Christ, 'ow the 'ell was I supposed to know? I thought this all 'appened a long time ago!"

*"It did happen a long time ago. Almost two thousand years ago, in fact!"*

"Gor', y'don't tell me!"

*"If you don't stop interrupting, I won't tell you!"* Merlin said irately. *"Now I've forgotten where I was again!"*

"An' you told me to pay attention," Billy said. "Old Gorlois went an' got 'imself a bird an' she 'atched you."

*"She didn't hatch me, I was born in the conventional manner,"* Merlin said stiffly.

"Right, right, get on with it."

Merlin counted ten once more, a bit more slowly this time, then explained that because his mother was a human, time passed more quickly for her than it did for Gorlois, and when he could no longer bear to watch her growing old, Gorlois left her, vowing never again to take a human wife.

"Fine chap, your old man, 'ey?" said Billy.

*"Yes, indeed, he was a bastard,"* Merlin said. *"My poor*

*mother died of a broken heart. But as the years passed, Gorlois forgot his vow. He had lived with humans for so long, he had become vulnerable to their weaknesses. He succumbed to human passions and to human flaws. A lust for power and possessions grew in him, and he took another wife, a beautiful young Welshwoman named Igraine. She bore him three daughters—Elaine, Morgause, and Morgana."*

One day, Merlin continued, smitten by the beauty of Igraine, a savage knight named Uther—aided by a spell cast by Merlin—took on the appearance of Gorlois and had his way with Igraine, then killed Gorlois in battle. In this way, Merlin said, he had revenged himself on Gorlois for abandoning his mother. Not long afterward Igraine gave birth to Uther's son, who was named Arthur. Arthur grew up to become the King of Britain, with Merlin as his adviser. And Morgana, who was half-sister to both Arthur and Merlin, came to Merlin and asked to be his pupil. She learned well and she learned quickly. She used her powers to ensorcle Arthur and seduce him, and so Modred was conceived.

"What, you mean she did it with 'er own brother?" Billy said.

*"Half brother,"* Merlin said. *"Still, you're quite right, it's the sort of thing that simply isn't done. However, Morgana never bothered with such things as morality and ethics."*

As Modred grew, Morgana—who had become known far and wide as the sorceress Morgan Le Fay—passed on to him the knowledge she had learned from Merlin. She prevailed upon the finest knights in the kingdom to teach him the skills of physical combat. And then she brought him to Camelot, to take his place among the Knights of the Round Table.

Arthur was always formally correct around him, but little more than that. He flinched visibly whenever his son came near him, and when they spoke, Arthur was always stiff with discomfort, distant in his tone. Modred was his shame, his sin come back to haunt him. And as Morgana had planned, Modred's bitter pain at his father's rejection of him laid the groundwork for her plot. Merlin had revenged himself on Gorlois through Uther, and now Morgana would revenge herself on Uther's son through Modred. And as for Merlin, who had brought about her mother's ruin and her father's death, Morgana had made other plans.

As his pupil she had learned all that she could from him, not only of his thaumaturgic knowledge, but of his strengths and weaknesses as well. She took on pupils of her own, and from them she selected a young witch called Nimue, whom she had chosen for her elfin, sultry beauty and her descent from the De Dannan tribe. Under Morgana's guidance Nimue embarked upon a carefully conceived plan of seduction, and when Merlin was distracted and weakened by their lovemaking—

Billy chuckled. "You old—"

*"Never mind,"* said Merlin. *"Wizards need a little companionship, too, you know."*

"Are you sure it was just 'er company you 'ad in mind?" said Billy, grinning.

*"Are you quite certain that you're only thirteen?"* said Merlin.

"I'm old enough to know better an' young enough not to give a damn," said Billy. "Get back to the story. Sounds like we're gettin' to the good part."

*"I've forgotten where we were again."*

"Some bird 'ad you distracted," Billy said.

*"Yes . . . I'll say she did,"* said Merlin. *"And she was a far more clever little witch than I ever gave her credit for."*

Nimue cast a spell upon him, making him fall into a deep sleep. Morgana then had Merlin placed into the cleft of a giant oak tree, and there she sealed him up, to sleep within a living tomb. While Merlin slept, immured in the enchanted tree, the world was once more plunged into bar-

barism. Kingdoms rose and fell. The Dark Ages passed and the Renaissance began. With the birth of the Industrial Age came the rise of technology, which reached its zenith with the Nuclear Age. Then came the Collapse, when the power-hungry technocrats exhausted the weary world's resources and the machines had finally stopped. The world was once more plunged into darkness until the spell that had held Merlin prisoner was broken and he returned to bring back magic to the world.

*"I ended the Collapse by fusing magic with technology, with thaumaturgy as the new energy base,"* explained Merlin. *"In the years since I awoke, I've established programs of thaumaturgic study so that now every nation has a college of sorcerers in at least one major university. The world had forgotten the ways of magic, and I wanted to bring it back to them. They had forgotten so much. I wanted to teach them how to live in harmony with the natural forces of the world. But I had overlooked one thing. The world may change, but fundamentally human nature will remain the same. One of my most gifted students could not be content with carrying on the honorable traditions of the white mage. Rashid wanted more. He wanted power. And as his feet began to stray from the rightful path, his way brought him ever closer to the Dark Ones."*

"But I thought they were dead an' buried," Billy said.

*"Buried but not dead,"* said Merlin. *"The Dark Ones do not die. They must be killed. Over the centuries they have fed off the evil deeds that men did, and little by little they grew stronger, until they were able to reach out and seize Rashid and take his soul. They brought him under their control and led him to the place where they were buried. By now Rashid had become a wealthy man, and he financed an archaeothaumaturgic expedition to unearth what he thought were enchanted relics. And, in a sense, that was exactly what he found. He removed the enchanted runestones from the golden chest within the warding pen-*

*tagram, and thus he opened up the way for the Dark Ones to escape."*

"An' did they?" Billy said, caught up in the story, not noticing how people stared at him as he walked down the street, talking to himself.

*"Not right away,"* said Merlin. *"They were still weakened from their eons of confinement and they needed to gather their strength. Rashid had lost the runestones, and they knew that so long as the runestones still existed, they could never attain their full power."*

"So they 'ad to destroy the runestones first," said Billy.

*"Exactly,"* Merlin replied. *"Only the runestones were not so easy to destroy. Remember that the life force of the ruling council of white mages was contained within them. Yet, by themselves, the runestones could do little, so they needed to chose champions, three people with whom they could unite, so that they would become the avatars of the old white magic. And since the enchantment of the runestones was built upon the living triangle, the runestones chose three descendants of the three daughters of Gorlois. A young warlock named Wyrdrune, descended from Morgause; a thief named Kira, descended from Elaine; and Modred, for Morgana's son still lived."*

"Gor', so it all comes full circle, then!" said Billy. "But I still don't understand what all this 'as to do with me. Why 'ave I got you inside me 'ead?"

*"Billy, do you know what the word* reincarnation *means?"* asked Merlin.

"When someone comes back from the dead as someone else, right?"

*"Something like that,"* Merlin said. *"This may be difficult for you to understand, but there is a metaphysical relationship between life cycles and the natural forces in the world. New souls enter the world all the time as old souls leave, but often it takes many lifetimes for a soul to complete its cycle. Sometimes a soul comes into the world and blazes brightly, igniting a shining light that illuminates all*

*those who came in touch with it long after that soul recedes into the darkness. Other times a life cycle is completed before the soul can finish the work it had to do."*

"So it comes back again as someone else," said Billy. "'Ey! Wait a minute—"

*"We tried to stop the Dark Ones from escaping, Billy,"* Merlin continued. *"We failed. We destroyed some of them, but many managed to escape. And in the struggle I was killed."*

"No," said Billy, shaking his head. "Oh, no, don't tell me . . ."

*"My work is not yet finished, Billy, and it appears that I have been reincarnated into you. It's not supposed to work this way, but I think I know why it happened. You are descended from Nimue, lad. I am your great-great-grandfather, Billy, some twenty-five times removed."*

"Sweet bleedin' Jesus!" Billy said. "You mean I'm stuck with you for the rest o' me *life?*"

*"It had to be one of my descendants, Billy, so that I could use your inherited abilities to bring my powers to full strength. The Dark Ones must be stopped. I needed to come back, lad, and I had nowhere else to go."*

# CHAPTER TWO

Whitechapel, originally part of Stepney, was now a crowded suburb of the sprawling City of London. The chapel after which the district had been named, the parish church of St. Mary Whitechapel, known simply as St. Mary's, dated back to the fourteenth century. For hundreds of years Whitechapel had been the home of poor tradesmen, dockworkers, and immigrants who lived in squalor in its congested, fog-enshrouded, mazelike courts and alleys. But the district was perhaps most famous—or infamous—for the legendary Whitechapel Murders of 1888, the grisly work of Jack the Ripper.

During the latter part of the twentieth century, and well into the twenty-first, much of the area had been redeveloped. Numerous office buildings were constructed, as well as some apartment buildings, but as the economy faltered in fits and starts until the inevitable Collapse, construction projects were started and abandoned and then started once again by new developers, with the result that the area had become a surreal cacophony of architectural styles. Here would be a monolithic tower made of steel and glass, there a ferroplast cluster of geometric shapes rising up like some mutant stalagmite, dwarfing a Victorian courtyard at the end of a narrow alleyway.

Many of the buildings were abandoned. A few had been picked up by speculators, but the reasons for the cheap purchase prices soon became apparent. Few of the buildings were in any stage resembling completion. Most were little more than shells, with such things as plumbing and environmental systems either incomplete or not installed at all, rendering the structures virtually uninhabitable. None of the windows opened. They were there to see out of, not to let in breezes. What little had been done on the interior of the buildings had been gutted during the Collapse. Still, this did not prevent the desperately poor from seeking shelter in them, and it was difficult, if not impossible, to clear the often savage squatters out and keep them out long enough to effect any improvements. And what would be the point? It was hardly the sort of neighborhood that would attract desirable tenants.

So, for the most part, Whitechapel had been left in limbo, a gloomy, post-apocalyptic urban jungle. The half-finished modern buildings jutted up into the sky like pieces of dark, broken quartz, vertical purgatories to which the lost souls of the city were consigned. At night fires could be seen burning on many of the floors behind the dark glass walls, most of which had been broken for ventilation, leaving the large panels veined with cracks resembling giant spiderwebs. Sometimes the fires would get out of control, and before long an entire building would be burning like a torch. The fire brigades usually would refuse to go inside the burning building. Anyone who came out would be rendered cursory assistance, but those who had been trapped inside were on their own. The brigade's sorcerer adepts would call up a cloudburst to wet down adjacent buildings and keep the flames from spreading, and chances were, if the inhabitants survived, that many of them would continue to make their homes inside the smoking ruin. A short distance away was London, elegant and stately, but to those who lived in the dark and deadly urban war zone that was Whitechapel, it was like another planet.

In some respects things hadn't changed very much at all since 1888.

It was unlikely that Joey Lymon had ever heard of Jack the Ripper. It was unlikely that any thought more complicated than one associated with the seven deadly sins had ever crossed his mind. Make that six deadly sins. Joey Lymon had no pride.

Joey was a very uncomplicated young man. He was not particularly stupid, nor was he particularly smart. He had a certain innate shrewdness that had allowed him to survive for twenty-two years, an ability to scratch out a subsistence living one way or another, something that was no mean feat since the spectacular failure of Britain's experiment in enlightened socialism. What made life difficult for Joey was his surpassing ugliness.

At an age when his sexual hormones were in full roar, Joey could make Medusa turn to stone. He was tall and gangly, thin as a stick, and he moved with spastic motions, like a spider with Parkinson's disease. He had a nervous tic at the corner of his mouth, and his nose was always running. His hair was lank and dark and greasy, and his skin had an unhealthy, sluglike pallor. He had warts and pimples that were so pustulant and so profusely scattered all over his face and body that he looked as if he were a victim of some grotesque fungus. His eyes were bloodshot and his teeth were rotten. He had lice, and he smelled worse than a week-old road kill. Even the rankest whores in Whitechapel fled at his approach. It had always filled him with self-loathing when that happened, but lately he had begun to direct that loathing outward, toward all the women who looked at him with such disgust, especially the whores of Whitechapel.

Given the circumstances, it was Joey Lymon's tragic fate to have a sex drive three times as strong as any ordinary man's. He would stand in the shadows, chewing on his lower lip, desperately trying to work up his courage, feeling awful, dirty, *ugly* . . . and when he could no longer bear it, he would accost some prostitute. He often tried to pick the oldest and most unattractive ones on the theory that they would be equally as desperate as he, but invariably they would recoil from him in disgust or, even worse, they'd laugh at him. It made the hate within him grow and grow until he thought that it would make him burst. And the time came when he could not contain it any longer.

Her name was Mary Spring, but Joey didn't know that. He'd been standing in the shadows for close to half an hour, watching her, trying to work up his nerve. *Just once,* he thought, *just once so I could know what it's like.* Perhaps then these awful yearnings that filled him with such shame would go away. Maybe this one would be different. In the time that he'd been watching her, no one had passed by. It was late, and a thick fog had descended. Anyone with any sense would be inside by now, hiding from the predators who roamed the streets at night. She was shivering, yet she was still displaying as much of her emaciated body as she could, hoping to attract some customers. She obviously needed money very badly. Perhaps she could not afford to turn him down.

"Evenin', luv," said Joey, stepping up to her and trying hard to sound casual. "Nice night for a stroll, eh? 'Ow's about—"

Mary recoiled from him in disgust. "'G-wahn wif ya!" she shrilled. "Git out of it, ya ugly brute! Gorblimey, what a bloody stench—"

Without thinking, Joey uncorked a right cross at her jaw and dropped her like stone. He stood there, quivering with fury, his fists clenched, and he felt like giving her a savage kick in the ribs for good measure before he left, but then another idea occurred to him. He quickly looked around, picked the unconscious whore up by the ankles, and dragged her into a dark alley.

He quickly tore off all her clothing. So what if she was unconscious? He'd have her, anyway, leave her to come to naked in the alley. It would serve her right, he thought.

Maybe he'd even wait around till she came to and pound on her some more, make her beg for it, beat some of that bloody arrogance out of her.

"Serve the bleedin' bitch right if I killed 'er," Joey said, the hate boiling up within him.

"Why don't you?" a soft voice behind him said.

Joey gasped and spun around, the color draining from his face.

About twenty feet away, near the mouth of the alley, stood a strikingly good-looking man dressed in elegant evening clothes with a generous amount of lace at the throat and cuffs. A long, dark coat was thrown over his shoulders. He was clean-shaven, with an angular jaw and high cheekbones. His mouth was wide and sensual, his green eyes had a mocking, knowing look. His hair was flaming red, full in the front, and swept back at the sides. He slowly sauntered toward Joey, a wry smile on his face.

"Go on," he said, casually lighting a cigarette. "Kill her. You know you want to."

"'Ere, stay back, you!" yelled Joey, panicking. "You stop right there! You stay away from me!"

The red-haired man stopped momentarily and smiled in a friendly manner.

"No need to be afraid, Joey," he said. "I won't harm you. In fact, I understand exactly how you feel."

"You just 'old it right there!" Joey said, backing away from him. "Who are you? 'Ow'd you know me name?"

"I know a lot of things about you, Joey," said the red-haired man. His eyes seemed to see down to the very depths of Joey's soul. "I know how you were abandoned by your mother, and that you grew up in a foundling home. Alone. Unwanted. I know how you've been made to suffer all your life, simply because you don't look the same as others. I know all about the painful taunts, the innumerable beatings, those countless expressions of disgust and loathing, the comments made not quite out of your hearing"— the red-haired stranger looked down at the unconscious

Mary Spring—"and the rejection, even by such as these," he added softly.

Joey trembled as he listened to the red-haired stranger catalog his life. His jaw hung slack and his breathing became labored. His entire world had become centered around the red-haired stranger's luminous, compelling gaze. He heard nothing but the lilting, haunting sound of the red-haired stranger's voice. He couldn't speak. He couldn't move.

The red-haired stranger sadly shook his head. "This slut would degrade herself for the price of a cheap drink, with anyone, anyone at all . . . only not with you."

Joey was on the verge of tears.

"And *why*?" the red-haired stranger continued, looking deeply into Joey's eyes. "What do they know of you, of what you think, of what you *feel*? What do they care? Outward appearance is the only thing they see. You could have a heart as black as pitch, a soul a thousand times more loathsome than a rotting, maggot-ridden corpse, yet give you pleasing features, a charming manner, and an easy smile, and they would come and lay their whole world at your feet. Very well, so be it. Behold . . ."

The red-haired stranger made a languid gesture and an ornate, gilt-framed, full-length mirror appeared mounted on the alley wall. It seemed to glow faintly. Startled, Joey glanced at it, and his breath caught at what he saw reflected there.

It was the face of a young man of stunning beauty, with flowing, wavy, jet-black hair and classic, darkly handsome features. The mouth was full and sensual, the teeth were dazzlingly white and perfect, the chin was firm and slightly pointed, the cheekbones prominent, the jawline graceful, the skin without a blemish. Intense, dark eyes looked back at him with a knowing, blatantly sexual expression.

"Is that what they all want, you think?" the red-haired stranger said as Joey stared, transfixed, at his reflection in the mirror.

He slowly brought his hand up to his face, staring as the handsome image reflected in the mirror did the same. He shook his head slowly as he traced his jawline and felt the smooth skin of his cheek.

"That isn't me," he said, and he gasped with surprise at the sound of his own voice. It had become deep and melodiously masculine, the diction perfect, a voice that spoke of elegance and breeding. "It doesn't even *sound* like me," he said. He shook his head and stared at the red-haired stranger with awe and disbelief. "You're a wizard!" he said. "I've never met a real wizard. Who are you? What do you want from me?"

The red-haired stranger smiled. "What does it matter who I am or what I want? The important thing, Joey, is what *you* want."

"You're no wizard," Joey whispered. "You're the Devil!"

The red-haired stranger chuckled. "Suppose I were," he said. "At least I understand you, Joey. At least I care. What has God ever done for you?"

Joey mouth was dry. "It's my soul you're after, isn't it?"

"No, Joey," the red-haired stranger said. "Not yours." He glanced down at the unconscious prostitute. "Hers."

He made another graceful gesture, slowly sweeping his arm out, palm open, and Joey saw an array of lethal-looking steel blades appear upon the ground, razor-sharp and gleaming, spread out upon a soft, black leather roll-up case.

Mary Spring moaned softly and began to stir.

"She deserves it, Joey," said the red-haired stranger softly. "She and all the others like her. All the ones who've hurt you. All the ones who spread their filth, preying like parasites on all those who are unloved, on all the poor souls who did not receive the gift of beauty and must live alone and unwanted in the world. They've already made their choice. They chose hell, Joey. And you're the one who's going to send them there."

"I'm the one," said Joey in a dull voice.

The red-haired stranger was no longer there, but his words came to Joey like a whisper on the wind.

*"Give her to me, Joey. Send her black soul straight to hell."*

Joey suddenly found himself holding the smooth, ebony handle of a long, sharp, gleaming blade.

Mary Spring moaned once again, and her eyelids fluttered open. She saw the blade descending and she screamed—

Dr. Sebastian Makepeace was a very large man, but he moved with surprising agility for his size. He weighed three hundred pounds and stood six feet six inches tall. He came striding across the park, carrying a shapeless briefcase and puffing on a big cigar, his Dickensian gray hair streaming out from beneath his black beret, his ankle-length black leather overcoat unbuttoned and billowing behind him like a cape. he made straight for Wyrdrune and Kira like a juggernaut, knowing people would make way for him. When anything that big comes bearing down on you, you make way.

He came up to them where they stood by the fountain and stopped directly in front of them, towering over them both like a mountain.

"Hello, my dear," he said to Kira, after first taking the cigar out of his mouth. He had a booming voice that any stage actor would have envied. He took her hand and made a small bow. "Thank you for coming so promptly." He put the cigar back between his teeth and glared at Wyrdrune. "You must be young Wyrdrune. We've spoken on the phone."

"No, sir, I don't think we have," said Wyrdrune. "You spoke to Kira before."

"Quite right, quite right," said Makepeace gruffly. His eyes narrowed beneath his bristling eyebrows. "What's your truename? I must be sure, now."

"Karpinsky," Wyrdrune said.

Makepeace grunted. "First name?"

Wyrdrune hestitated. "Melvin," he said. "But no one ever calls me that," he quickly added. "I go by my mage-name."

"Of course you do, Melvin," Makepeace said, and Wyrdrune grimaced sourly as he realized that Makepeace was probably never going to call him anything else. "You mind removing your hat?"

Wyrdrune complied with his request. Makepeace squinted at the runestone and grunted. "One can never be too careful. Tell me, does Morpheus have one of those little gems as well?"

"Yes," said Wyrdrune, putting his hat back on.

"What kind?"

"A ruby."

"Where?"

"Over his heart. Are you satisfied now, or do you want me to produce my birth certificate?" said Wyrdrune wryly.

"One can never be too careful," Makepeace said. "Humor me, okay? What does the name Appollonius mean to you?"

"A sentient hyperdimensional matrix computer that was hijacked while en route to Langley," Wyrdrune said. "Morpheus used it to raid classified data banks. It was destroyed in a fire when the late Shiek Al'Hassan hit the Park Avenue penthouse Morpheus was renting under the name John Roderick. That's one of the reasons he's the *late* Shiek Al'Hassan. Any more questions?"

Makepeace grunted. "No, that will do. I'm quite satisfied."

"Wouldn't it have been simpler just to have Kira vouch for me, since she'd already passed your muster?"

"Perhaps, perhaps," said Makepeace, "but on the other hand, you might have been holding her at gunpoint or some such thing. Or she might have been under a spell to force her cooperation. You never know. Possibilities abound. I'm a careful man, Melvin. Morpheus pays me to be careful, pays me handsomely. Now what is it I can do for you?"

Wyrdrune and Kira exchanged glances. *"You* called *us,"* said Wyrdrune.

Makepeace grunted. "Ah, yes, yes, so I did. Slipped my mind for a moment." He sat down on the edge of the fountain, took out a huge purple handkerchief, and mopped his face with it. "You'll have to excuse me, it's been a long day. The morlocks are trying to yank my tenure once again. Looking for loopholes so they can get me. Accusing me of incompetence, teaching my classes drunk. *Hah!* *Rubbish!* I can teach twice as well drunk as any of those morons can sober. My lectures are always packed! *Packed,* I tell you! Those bastards are just jealous because I publish more than they do, and I'm popular with the students. Why—"

Wyrdrune cleared his throat. "Uh, Dr. Makepeace? Can we get to the point, please?" He glanced at Kira. She shrugged.

"The point?" said Makepeace, looking up at them, his eyes bloodshot. "Ah, yes, of course, the point, the point." He looked at Kira. "You asked me to call you if I heard anything."

"You've heard from him?" said Kira anxiously.

"Well, no, not exactly, not exactly," Makepeace said, shifting his immense weight slightly and reaching into his pocket for his steel cigar case.

A thin tentacle came up out of the fountain, wavering like a stalk, reaching stealthily for his pocket. Makepeace's hand brushed the tentacle as it was reaching into the very pocket he was going for. He leapt up with a roar and plunged both arms into the fountain up to his elbows, snarling with the cigar butt clenched between his teeth. The water in the fountain churned, and several tentacles came out, wrapping themselves around Makepeace's neck. Still holding on to the creature with one hand, Makepeace tore the tentacles away, then yanked the squid up out of the water and proceeded to batter it savagely against the wall of the fountain. A short distance away, a skinny old man with a large purse hanging from his shoulder started to walk away quickly. Makepeace spotted him.

*"Hey! Come here, you!"*

The old man started running.

*"Get back here, you old fruit!"* hollered Makepeace at the top of his lungs, throwing the dead squid after him. It sailed through the air and hit the old man in the back with a wet smack, knocking him down. He scrambled up again and took to his heels in a panic, glancing over his shoulder fearfully.

"Damn dips are everywhere," growled Makepeace, wiping his hands on his coat as he watched the old man recede into the distance. He held his right arm out to the side and snapped his fingers. The skinny old man's purse appeared dangling by the strap from his right hand.

"You're an adept!" said Wyrdrune.

Makepeace turned around and knitted his brows at him. "I am *not* an adept," he said stiffly. "I'm a fairy."

"You're a *what*?" said Wyrdrune.

"A fairy, a fairy! What are you, deaf?"

"You mean . . . you don't like women?" said Kira.

"Not *that* kind!" said Makepeace. He growled. "God, I *hate* that! I *like* women, all right? I *love* women! I crave women *constantly*! I am *not* gay! I am a *fairy*!"

"Whoever heard of a three-hundred-pound fairy?" said Wyrdrune.

"I also like food," said Makepeace, his eyes narrowing to slits. "You want to make something of it?"

"Noooooo," said Wyrdrune, "I don't think so. I . . . think . . . we'd better go."

"Wait a minute," Kira said, "we haven't heard what he's got to tell us."

"Kira, the man says he's a fairy."

"So?"

"A six-foot-six, three-hundred-pound fairy?" Wyrdrune lowered his voice. "Kira, the man is a banana."

"What, you can be a warlock and he can't be a fairy?" she said.

"Fairies are tiny, supernatural beings who flit around like hummingbirds on gossamer wings and hang out with Peter Pan," said Wyrdrune. "If this guy's got wings, they must've come off a pterodactyl!"

"I heard that, Melvin," said Makepeace, scowling and pointing an accusatory finger at him. "You know, a thousand years ago they would've burned you as a witch. They would've said you communed with spirits and ate babies! They would've said you were afraid of silver and could be burned by holy water! They would've said all sorts of nonsense because they didn't *know* any better!"

His face started turning purple. His eyes bugged out. His voice kept rising until it reached a maniacal crescendo.

"Who the hell *told* you that fairies are tiny creatures who have wings?" he screamed. "Where did you get that crap? Hans Christian Andersen? The Brothers Grimm? *Walt-bloody-fucking-Disney*? What the hell do *you* know about fairies?"

"Right. That's it. We're leaving." Wyrdrune took Kira by the arm.

"*Don't!*" she said, jerking away from him. "You're *not* going to do it to me again! I don't give a damn even if he does say he's a fairy! He could say he's Snow White for all I care! We're going to listen to what he has to say!"

"Kira, for God's sake—"

"Listen to her, Melvin," Makepeace said. "You're going to need my help."

Wyrdrune stopped and glanced at him sharply. Makepeace stood there with his arms folded, staring down at him imperiously.

"This had better be good," said Wyrdrune, pointing at him. "Otherwise you're going to wish that squid had drowned you in the fountain."

Makepeace raised his bushy eyebrows. "Are you threatening a fairy?"

"All right, I'm going to count to three, Tinkerbell," said Wyrdrune, scowling at him. "One . . ."

"You're awful sure of yourself, aren't you?" Makepeace said.

"Two . . ."

"What the hell. Go ahead, kid. Take your best shot."

"That does it. *Three!*"

Wyrdrune gestured at him violently with both hands . . . and nothing happened. He frowned, mumbled a spell under his breath, and repeated the gesture. Nothing.

"Was *this* more or less what you had in mind?" said Makepeace, and Wyrdrune suddenly started to float up into the air.

"*Hey!*"

He rose until he was about six feet off the ground, then Makepeace took a deep breath and blew it out at him. Wyrdrune started to spin in midair like a pinwheel, faster and faster and faster.

"*Aaaaaaaaaah! Put me downnnnnnnnnnnnnnnnnnnnn!*"

"Certainly," said Makepeace.

Wyrdrune went down with a splash into the fountain. Kira stifled a laugh as he got up shakily, water streaming from him. Several passersby had stopped to watch when Makepeace levitated him, and now others had joined them. The crowd was enjoying the show.

"What the hell are *you* looking at?" Wyrdrune shouted at them.

"Uh, Dr. Makepeace, I think it's time we took this someplace else," said Kira.

"I think you're right, my dear," said Makepeace. As Wyrdrune climbed out of the fountain, Makepeace inhaled deeply and blew out at him again. Wyrdrune yelped as a fierce, hot desert wind hit him, blowing so hard that it almost knocked him off his feet. He grabbed the side of the fountain as the hot, hurricane-force wind howled around him, until he stood there, completely dry, gasping for breath. The onlookers gave Makepeace a polite round of applause.

"Thank you, thank you," Makepeace said, bowing to them. He turned back to Wyrdrune. "Come on, kid. No hard feelings. I'll buy you a beer."

Lovecraft's on MacDougal Street was a small and relatively unpretentious bar for the neighborhood. The lighting was dim, the tables were rickety, the tablecloths were black, and the candles were all set in white ceramic skulls. The bartenders and waitresses were all dressed in black and made up to look like zombies, with huge circles of heavy black eye shadow that seemed to drip down onto the cheeks painted on their faces.

"You come here often?" Kira said, looking around at some of the other patrons dubiously.

"The place has a certain decadent charm," said Makepeace. "It's a popular literary hangout. Everybody in here looks either dead or depressed. Makes the writers feel at home."

A slinky, black-clad young waitress set two pitchers of beer and two glasses down on the table. She bent over and gave Makepeace an affectionate kiss, and he patted her on the bottom.

"Ah, thank you, Morticia," he said, sighing contentedly as he picked up one of the pitchers and drank straight from it. Kira poured a beer for herself and Wyrdrune from the other pitcher. Wyrdrune looked shell-shocked.

"I don't understand," he said. "Why didn't my spell work? How'd you manage to turn it around on me?"

"Simple, Melvin," Makepeace said. "You were thinking impure thoughts. You intended to use your power in a petty, spiteful manner, and the runestones weren't going to allow that. What kind of person attacks a fairy, for God's sake?"

"You *know* about the runestones?" Wyrdrune said, staring at him.

"Of course I know about the runestones," Makepeace replied irritably. "What did you think I thought they were, costume jewelry?" He quaffed half the pitcher in what seemed like one swallow and belched profoundly. "Modred told me the whole story."

"Modred? Then you know everything!" Wyrdrune shook his head in astonishment. "I can't believe he told you."

"Oh, really?" Makepeace said, glaring at him. "And why not? You can't see why Modred would share his secrets with some wacked-out academic, a schizoid sorcerer who's slipped a cog or two and thinks that he's a fairy?"

"No, I didn't say that . . ." Wyrdrune began, hesitantly, though it had been exactly what he was thinking.

"Look, get this straight," said Makepeace, leaning toward him and putting his hands down flat on the table. "I'm *not* a wizard or a sorcerer. I'm *not* some neurotic thaumaturgy professor who's teaching history because he's going senile and can't keep his goddamned spells straight anymore. I'm a sprite. A spirit being. A fairy, got that? *A fairy! A fairy!*"

His scream was loud enough to rattle the glasses in the overhead racks. The waitress came over to their table and stood looking down at Makepeace with her hands on her hips. She spoke to him as if to a small child.

"Now you *stop* that right now, Sebastian! If you don't behave yourself, I'm cutting off your beer!"

"Morticia, my love, you tell them, okay?" said Makepeace, giving her a pleading look.

"He's a fairy," said Morticia patiently, looking at them with a wry expression and rolling her eyes.

"There, *see*?" said Makepeace.

"I'm getting a headache," Wyrdrune said, shutting his eyes and rubbing the bridge of his nose.

The waitress left, shaking her head with resignation.

"Dr. Makepeace, about Modred . . ." Kira said.

"Yes, yes, of course," said Makepeace. "That's what I called to talk to you about."

"Something's happened to him, hasn't it?" said Kira. "I can feel it."

"I'm afraid it has," said Makepeace. "I had a dream about him last night."

Wyrdrune glanced up at him sharply. "What kind of dream?"

"I dreamed he was being kept a prisoner somewhere, chained up in some kind of a dungeon," said Makepeace.

"We had the exact same dream!" said Kira. "I *knew* it! I *knew* he was trying to send us a message! He's tried to reach you the same way!"

"That doesn't make any sense," said Wyrdrune. "Why would he send us dreams? Why wouldn't he simply get in touch with us through the mind link?"

"Mind link?" said Makepeace, frowning. "You have some sort of telepathic link with him?"

"Well, I guess he *didn't* tell you everything, did he?" Wyrdrune said sarcastically.

"Will you settle down?" said Kira. "What's wrong with you?" She turned to Makepeace. "The runestones somehow allow us to communicate telepathically, even over great distances," she explained. "Modred seems to have better control over it than we do, maybe because he's a naturally more powerful adept. He can form the mind link with us at will, but we can't always do it anytime we want to, the way he can."

"Hmm," Makepeace said with a grunt, rubbing his chin thoughtfully. "Perhaps that's because his descent from the Old Ones, through Gorlois, is more direct than yours."

"Jesus, you know that too?" said Wyrdrune.

Makepeace closed his eyes wearily. "Melvin, give it a rest, will you, please? I'm not just anybody, you know."

"Yeah, I know," said Wyrdrune sourly. "You're never-never land's answer to King Kong."

Makepeace glared at him and started to twitch at the

corner of his mouth. A low, rumbling growl came from deep down in his throat.

"Will you *stop*?" said Kira. "I've about had it with you two! We haven't got time for this!"

Makepeace took a deep breath and let it out slowly. "Of course. You're absolutely right, my dear. However, young Melvin, irritating though he may be, does have a good point. If Modred can establish a mind link with you at will, why hasn't he? And it would seem that some sort of mind link would be necessary for him to send a telepathic dream image, even briefly, and I have never had such contact with him before. Neither has Jacqueline."

"Jacqueline?" said Wyrdrune. "Jacqueline Monet?"

Makepeace nodded. "She called me this morning. We've never spoken to each other before, you understand. We didn't even know each other. Modred was always very careful to keep his contacts separate, but she found out about me somehow—she said she suddenly just *knew*—and so she called me. She had a similar dream."

"What the hell is going on?" said Wyrdrune, baffled.

"Wait, there's more," said Makepeace. "Her experience was slightly different. She remembered more of the dream than I did, or she was given more of it. She said that Modred was in England."

"England?" Wyrdrune said. "How did she know?"

Makepeace shook his head. "I couldn't really get that part of it straight. It wasn't a very good connection. But she seemed absolutely certain that he was in England, being held prisoner by one of the Dark Ones. Somewhere in or around London."

Kira nodded. "I don't know why, but it sounds right." She glanced at Wyrdrune. "I can't explain it, but suddenly I'm *sure* he's there."

"None of this makes any sense at all," said Wyrdrune, shaking his head, "but I have the same damn feeling. I can't explain it, but the minute he said London, it just *felt* right."

"That settles it, then," said Makepeace, getting up from the table. "We're going to London. I'll make arrangements to have one of my colleagues take my classes. I'll meet you back at your place in about an hour."

"Whoa, wait just a minute there, Sebastian," said Wyrdrune. "What do you mean, *we're* going to London? Who said *you* were coming?"

"You're going to take on the Dark Ones all by yourselves?" said Makepeace. "Even Modred couldn't handle them alone. What makes you think you could?"

"Because together the three of us are infinitely stronger than we are apart," said Wyrdrune. "If you know about the runestones, then you know why that's so."

"Yes, the three of you together make up the living triangle," said Makepeace gruffly. "But before you can unite your forces, first you must get to Modred. And without him, any fairy can drop you in a fountain. *Hah*! *Ha-ha-ha*!" He threw several bills down on the table and walked out of the bar, cackling crazily.

Wyrdrune stared after him. "That man is certifiably bughouse."

"But Modred obviously trusted him," said Kira.

"Did he?" Wyrdrune said.

"What do you mean?" she said. "How else could he have known all that?"

"I don't know," said Wyrdrune, scowling. "I just can't figure it. Maybe Modred confided in him before he went off the deep end. Maybe Modred figured it wouldn't matter what he knew, because who the hell would believe a guy built like a gorilla who goes around saying he's a fairy?"

"Or maybe he really *is* a fairy," Kira said.

"Yeah, and I'm Queen of the May," said Wyrdrune. "Has it occurred to you that he might be the opposition?"

Kira's eyes grew wide. "Makepeace? I can't believe it! You think he's under their control?"

"It's possible," said Wyrdrune. "Think about it. The minute you start looking at it that way, everything starts to fall into place. It's even possible that he could be one of them himself. Makepeace could be a necromancer. One of the Dark Ones."

# CHAPTER THREE

Billy Slade was less unhappy when he merely thought that he was going crazy. In retrospect, he now thought that going insane was something he could learn to handle. Having a legendary archmage reincarnated in him was something else again. It might have been interesting if he'd simply inherited the mage's powers, but unfortunately Merlin's personality had been part of the package. And Merlin seemed intent on taking full control anytime it pleased him. And *that* didn't please Billy one damn bit.

After the set-to with the five toughs in the alley, Billy had started walking home while Merlin explained to him about the runestones and the age-old struggle between white magic and necromancy. Billy had listened, fascinated, until he suddenly realized that he had absolutely no idea where he was going. Merlin had taken over surreptitiously, and by the time Billy realized he wasn't in complete control, he was in a truly nasty neighborhood, indeed. A place he didn't like much, even in the daylight.

"'Ere, where're we goin'?" he said, stopping suddenly and looking around, alarmed. "This ain't the way! Where the 'ell'd you bring us to, old man?"

*I would appreciate it if you could refrain from calling*

49

me 'old man,'" said Merlin. *"There's no reason for us to continue staying in that hovel you've been living in. It's filthy, cramped, and rat-infested. It's not a fit place for a human being to live."*

"An' you think this is?" said Billy, looking up at the dark, foreboding, tower of black glass looming over them like some gargantuan, obsidian tombstone. "If you think I'm goin' in there, you're out of your bloomin' mind! There ain't nothin' but freakin' screamers in that place! They'll tear me bleedin' 'eart out and 'ave it cooked for supper!"

*"They will do no such thing,"* said Merlin. *"Now come along."*

Billy involuntarily took three steps forward before he could make himself stop. One foot lifted up to take another step, but with a determined effort Billy planted it back down.

"I ain't goin' in there," he said obstinately.

*"Now, Billy, don't be difficult."*

"I ain't gettin' meself killed for the likes o'you," said Billy. "'Ey, if I get it, you get it, too, y'know."

*"Nobody's going to 'get it,' all right?"* said Merlin. *"In fact, you've already been in there before."*

"I 'ave? Go on, I 'ave not! When?"

*"When you were sleeping,"* Merlin said, patiently. *"I have . . . or perhaps I should say we have been here before. We have living quarters on the top floor."*

Billy frowned. "We do?"

*"We do. The people in there know us and won't bother us. Now come along, it's getting chilly out here."*

Billy sighed. "I don't know about this. . . ."

*"Trust me,"* Merlin said. *"You have nothing to fear. I will protect you."*

Billy swallowed hard, took a deep breath, and allowed Merlin to guide his steps into the building.

There were no front doors. They'd been smashed off long ago. The entrance led into a dark courtyard lobby with a large fountain in the center. There was no water in the fountain. Instead a small refuse fire was burning in the fountain basin, and there were several dark figures gathered around it, warming themselves. Billy hesitated.

*"Have no fear,"* said Merlin.

"Yeah, easy for you to say."

Trying hard to calm himself, Billy bit his lower lip and moved forward. His mouth felt dry. He could feel his heart beating faster and faster and his breath growing short. The figures gathered around the fire looked up at him as he approached, the firelight illuminating their coarse and dirty features. One by one they stood as he came closer, and Billy saw that one of them was holding a piece of iron rod. Another held a heavy piece of wood like a club. Another reached into his pocket, and Billy almost bolted when he saw the long knife blade gleam in the firelight.

*"Steady, lad, steady,"* Merlin said.

His heart hammering with fear, Billy came closer, his fingers closing around the flick knife in his pocket. He stepped out of the shadows. The moment the firelight caught his features, an immediate change took place in the ragged men. Several of them backed away at once. The one with the knife quickly put the blade away and hurriedly pulled off his filthy cap, contritely holding it before him in his hands as he inclined his head toward Billy. His whole body took on a servile posture.

"Beggin' yer pardon, me lord," he said, to Billy's complete and absolute astonishment, "we didn't rek'inize ya at first."

He stepped aside, bowing and scraping, and Billy went past him, amazed at his reaction. The savage derelicts outnumbered him; they were all armed and more than twice his size, yet they had given way before him. He moved past them into the darkness, toward the elevator banks.

"They don't work, you know," said Billy. "They 'aven't worked for years. No power. We'll 'ave to take the stairs."

The elevator doors slid open soundlessly. The light in the ceiling of the elevator came on.

"Right," said Billy. "What do *I* know?" He stepped inside the elevator, and the doors closed behind him with a whisper. "Where to?"

*"Push the top button,"* Merlin said.

"What, the one with no number on it?"

*"That's right."*

Billy pushed it and the elevator began to rise swiftly.

"Can anyone use this lift, then, or just us?" asked Billy.

*"Just us,"* said Merlin. *"It's spellwarded. It won't open for anyone else, and only we can make it run."*

"That's cozy," Billy said. He watched the lights over the door changing swiftly. The elevator was traveling at an astonishing rate of speed. There was almost no sensation of motion. And then it stopped at the penthouse floor and the doors opened.

Billy couldn't believe his eyes. He stepped out of the elevator onto a soft, thick, handwoven Persian carpet. The huge penthouse living room opened out before him, softly illuminated with indirect lighting. The dark glass wall looked out over the glowing nightscape of the city. The center of the living room was dominated by a sunken conversation pit containing a wraparound sofa upholstered in soft black leather and a gleaming mahogany coffee table. The walls were lined with bookcases holding hundreds of ancient, leather-bound tomes with titles written in many different languages. Among them Billy recognized Arabic, Old English, Old French, Chinese, and even Aramaic, though he knew none of those languages and had no idea how he could tell what they were. There were several old, iron-banded, wooden chests placed around the room, as well as bizarre bronze sculptures, primitive wood carvings, and a stuffed owl fixed to a perch. In the corner was an ornate wooden desk covered with scrolls and parchments. There was a pipe rack on the desk, as well as a wooden humidor and a human skull with the top of its cranium removed so that it could hold a glass ashtray. A small, square-shaped personal computer with thaumaturgically etched and animated chips also stood atop the desk. As Billy entered, it stood up on chunky little legs and marched across the desk, turning to face him.

"Did you get me a modem?" it asked. It had a voice that sounded the way people's voices sound when they inhale helium.

"No," said Merlin, speaking through Billy. "I didn't have a chance."

"I need a modem."

"I know that."

"How do you expect me to work without a modem?"

"Will you stop pestering me?" said Merlin. "There aren't even any phone lines in this building. How do you expect to use a modem?"

"There isn't any power, either, but I notice you got the elevator and all these lights working just fine. You got power for your damn Gordon Lightfoot tapes—you can't get me power for a modem?"

"That's different. I understand about generating electricity; it's a relatively simple spell. But I don't understand the first thing about computers."

"What's to understand? You get a modem that functions on the same principle as a radiophone. I can take care of the rest. I don't know why you get so intimidated by technology. It's not as if I'm asking you to write me a new program, for God's sake. This is simple stuff. A child could do it."

"Archimedes, you are becoming very tiresome," Merlin said wearily. "I'll work on it, all right?"

"What's to work on? You—"

"Archimedes . . ."

"All right, all right, just don't blame me if I can't get anything done, that's all."

Merlin sighed. "Whoever came up with the idea for

computers, anyway? And I thought crystal balls were temperamental—"

*"You'ad me bring all this stuff up 'ere while I was sleepin'?"* Billy said, interrupting him. *"No wonder I was so bloody tired when I woke up!"*

"You did not actually bring all these things up here physically," Merlin explained. "I teleported them here magically. Some of these things were salvaged from the fire when my house burned down, others came from storage, and some were in my office at the college in Cambridge, Massachusetts. However, the exhaustion that you felt was a direct result of energy expended thaumaturgically."

*"What the 'ell does that mean?"*

"It means that magic use exacts a price in energy," said Merlin. "In other words, the more magic you use, the more it takes out of you, and the more time you need to recuperate. Ordinarily, teleporting these things here would have been effortless for me, but I hadn't counted on the fact that you're not physically mature yet. Your body simply won't take the same amount of stress that an adult body would be capable of handling, especially an adult body accustomed to the strains placed upon it by magic use."

*"So what you're sayin' is you worked me 'alf to death an' then sat back an' left me to feel it all. Well, thanks ever so bleedin' much!"*

"You're quite right," admitted Merlin. "That wasn't very fair to you. However, I didn't have much choice. We're pressed for time and I had to hurry things along."

*"Why? What's the rush?"*

"Lives are at stake," said Merlin earnestly. "Many lives. Something monstrously evil has been loosed upon the city. I can feel it. And it's up to you and me to stop it, Billy. If we can."

Joey Lymon discovered something strange after he murdered Mary Spring. For a little while the act of killing somehow made the dirty, shameful feelings go away, while at the same time giving him a profound sense of relief and satisfaction, a feeling that he had done something important and correct. And he knew that what he had done was right. He had eliminated a source of temptation from the world. He had made sure that Mary Spring's body would never tempt anyone again.

Afterward he had looked for the redheaded stranger, but there had been no sign of him. There was some money in the roll-up leather knife case. And there was a card, engraved on fancy white rag stock, with an address handwritten on the back. The front of the card read, "Lord Nigel Carfax."

Perhaps he really was the Devil, Joey thought, and part of him was terrified, but another part didn't care. For the first time in his life he could walk down the street without having people recoil from him in disgust. He could enter a pub without having anyone stare at him—except the women, but they no longer stared at him the way they used to. Now there were invitations in those stares. And he despised them for it. He downed his pint, wiped his mouth, and ordered up another, all the while staring at the card lying before him on the bar.

His hand was shaking as he picked up the card and turned it over, reading the address. Mayfair. Of course, he thought, where else would a bloody lord live? There was no question but that he would have to go. The card was not an invitation, it was a summons. A command. He had no choice. He'd have to go, and he could not delay.

"'Allo, ducks. Buy a girl a drink?"

He looked at her and she mistook his smoldering gaze for passion. She leered at him and pressed up against him, her hand rubbing the inside of his thigh. She moistened her lips and winked at him.

"I 'ave a place not far from 'ere," she said suggestively.

Well, thought Joey, perhaps he could delay a little while. Lord Carfax would understand.

* * *

Terri Clancy was heartachingly beautiful. She had long, raven-black hair and blue-gray eyes so light that they seemed to give off a silvery glow. Her skin was flawless, her nose was slightly turned up at the end, and her mouth full and sensual. She was long-legged and narrow-waisted, and her breasts were large and firm. She could do more to arouse a man with a slight lowering of her eyelashes than most any woman could do with her entire body. She had a walk that made men bump into lampposts and women loathe her on sight. It was as if her every curve had been purposely designed to provoke the maximum amount of lust. Terri knew this, of course, and had learned to take advantage of it at an early age.

Many men made the mistake of thinking that a woman as beautiful as Terri could not be especially intelligent, since the obsessive cultivation of beauty and the painstaking emphasis on its display were superficial preoccupations that did not require much intelligence at all. But Terri was different. Terri was both extremely beautiful and highly intelligent. She catered outrageously to the sexual imaginings of men . . . the better to destroy them.

In many respects Terri Clancy was the exact reverse of Joey Lymon. She despised men because of the effect she had on them. A tragic childhood of physical abuse and emotional neglect had left her with an empty heart and a twisted mind. She wanted to be loved, but she didn't really know what love was. She dreamed of finding the man who would want her for herself rather than the way she looked, but she felt the only way she'd ever know if she had found him was if he proved to be immune to her considerable arsenal of charms, so each man who came into her life was struck with a barrage of sexual temptation, the likes of which had not been seen since Salome had danced for Herod.

And, predictably, since men are only men, and paragons of virtue such as Galahad are few and far between—one comes along every two thousand years or so—the men that

Terri met invariably succumbed to her allure. It didn't take much, either. A knowing smile. A lingering, suggestive look. A slow, deliberate moistening of the lips. A show of leg, a slight display of cleavage; it really was absurd how little it would take to make a man's brain turn to oatmeal and his hormones rage out of control. And having thus proved once again her innermost conviction that all men were basically scum, Terri would proceed to lay waste to their lives.

She left a long trail of broken marriages and bankrupt businesses, of men who turned to drink or were convicted of embezzlement or fraud or theft, all for her sake. She brought men to an intimate acquaintance with their baser selves and set their feet irrevocably upon the path to self-destruction. And with every male thus brought to justice, Terri grew wealthier and more embittered. Then, one day, she finally found the man she had been seeking all her life. It was her great misfortune that he wasn't human.

He was attentive, charming, cultured, and as handsome as she was beautiful. He was tall, red-haired, and elegantly slim, striking in his appearance and obviously wealthy. At the same time he was so shockingly immune that he regarded her repeated attempts to seduce him with an amused tolerance. And when, in desperation, she had finally accused him of not loving her, of being impotent or homosexual, he had merely smiled and set the trap. She never even saw it coming. He told her that if it was what she really wanted, he would go to bed with her, but only on one condition—that she would give herself to him completely, body and soul.

She had laughed at him. She knew she had him then. He was no different than any of the others. Terri had never met a man she could not manipulate. And she had never known a man who did not become her abject slave once she had taken him to bed. This one had resisted longer than anyone ever had, and she was almost sorry to see the game drawing to a close. She prepared for their assignation like an assassin getting ready for the kill.

She turned down all the lights and lit some scented candles. She put brand-new black satin sheets upon the bed. She chilled a magnum of French champagne and prepared a tray of iced oysters and caviar. She sprinkled the sheets with perfume and lightly touched some behind her ears, in the hollow of her throat, in the crook of each elbow, between her breasts, and in that special place, then she put on her spike heels and her sexiest, sheerest black lingerie, an ensemble calculated to make even the most restrained man drool like a St. Bernard. *We shall see,* she thought as she looked at her reflection in the mirror, *who will belong to whom, body and soul.*

The house was empty and she had given him the key. She checked the time. He was always very punctual. He would arrive at any moment. She smiled, pleased with her efforts, and arranged herself upon the bed in a pose that was guaranteed to make a man's blood boil. Suddenly a chilly breeze blew through the room and the candle flames flickered and dimmed, then flared up, giving off a bright green light. She stared at them, uncomprehending, then gasped when she saw him standing in the doorway to her bedroom.

She had not heard him come in. Suddenly he was simply *there,* standing motionless in the doorway, his flaming red hair blowing slightly in the ice-cold breeze that came sweeping through the room, as if every window in the house were open and there was a storm outside. She shivered, goose bumps standing out all over her, and she tried to regain her composure, to take control of the situation, but she could not tear her gaze away form those burning eyes that seemed to see right down to the depths of her very soul. She tried to speak but couldn't.

He came toward her, but he did not seem to be walking. Incredibly, he seemed to be floating toward her, gliding across the floor until he was at the foot of her bed. His intense gaze never left her for an instant. She was cold. The breeze that eddied around her was freezing, and she was shivering violently, both with cold and fear. He's a sorcerer, she thought, suddenly afraid that she had made a bad miscalculation.

She had always steered clear of adepts before, because she felt they were too dangerous, to unpredictable, but he was still a man, she told herself—not knowing just how wrong she was—and she had yet to meet a man she couldn't handle. Besides, she thought, she had never yet experienced magic used in foreplay. The thought excited her. She moistened her lips and moved on the bed invitingly, her bosom heaving as she breathed heavily, her lips slightly parted, her eyelids lowered . . . and then he suddenly stretched out one hand toward her and the bed burst into flame.

She cried out as the flames rose up all around her. She could feel the searing heat, but though the entire bed was burning, the spot on which she lay remained untouched. She was unable to move, paralyzed with terror, surrounded by a wall of fire. Through the crackling flames she saw him, naked, crouching on the footboard like a cat, the dancing flames reflected in his eyes. For a moment it seemed to her that she saw something else, something dark and terrifying, inhuman. As he leapt, she screamed.

Chief Inspector Michael Blood was not having a good day. Spread out on the desk before him were the daily papers. The headlines were sensational, as usual, only this time he figured in them prominently. WHITECHAPEL MURDERER RETURNS? RIPPER ON THE LOOSE! and, the worst of the lot, RIPPER SEEKS BLOOD! BLOOD SEEKS RIPPER! And that one from the *Times*, no less. Constable Shavers knocked on the door and stuck his head in.

"Sir? It's the superintendent on line one."

"Yes, of course it would be," Blood said with a sigh, putting down his coffee cup. "Very well, thank you,

Danny." He picked up the phone. "Good morning, Superintendent."

"Michael, have you seen the papers?"

Blood winced. It was the sixth or seventh time that morning that someone had asked him if he'd seen the papers. "Yes, sir, I'm afraid I have."

"I've had reporters calling in all morning," said the superintendent. "I've managed to avoid them so far, but I suppose I'm going to have to tell them something sooner or later, so I thought I'd call and find out just what the hell is going on. What *is* this Ripper business, anyway? First I've heard of it."

"It apparently started with the murder of a young prostitute in Whitechapel the day before yesterday, sir, as reported in the press," Blood said. "Her name was Mary Spring. They got that right, at least. Gruesome business. Stabbed with a very sharp knife, possibly a number of different knives, which has led to some conjecture that we may have more than one killer, but there's nothing firm on that at the moment, one way or the other. Several of the papers claim that a man was spotted running from the scene, but frankly I think that's a load of rubbish. We haven't been able to find any witnesses at all. And then yesterday, the body of another prostitute named Annie Saylor was discovered in her flat. Again, stabbed numerous times, apparently killed on the same night as Mary Spring. In both cases the bodies were severely mutilated. In the Saylor case there was blood spray everywhere, internal organs flung about the room—"

"Christ, Michael, spare me the details," the superintendent said. "I'm having breakfast."

"Sorry, sir," said Blood. "I'll have the reports sent to your office. In any case, some bright boy or girl on Fleet Street saw fit to do a bit of homework, and they came up with a series of brutal, unsolved murders that occurred in Whitechapel in 1888—"

"*1888?*" said the superintendent.

"Yes, sir, the so-called Whitechapel Murders, allegedly committed by a man calling himself Jack the Ripper, also known as Saucy Jack and Springheel Jack—"

"Wait just a moment," said the superintendent. "You *did* say 1888?"

"Yes, sir, that's correct. Anyway, to continue, the six victims in those cases were also prostitutes, all except one, and they were all killed within a one-square-mile area of Whitechapel, each body found with a slashed throat and precise, almost surgical mutilations—"

"Michael, for God's sake!"

"Sorry, sir."

"Are you seriously telling me that the papers are making a connection between these two murders of yours and something that happened in the *nineteenth century*?" said the superintendent with disbelief.

"Apparently so, sir. You must admit, there are certain rather sensational similarities—the geographical location; the victims being prostitutes, both murdered on the same night, as happened with two of the original Ripper's victims; the . . . uh . . . murderer's methodology. You can see where an enterprising journalist could draw some rather lurid parallels and indulge in some creative speculation. It does sell newspapers."

"Yes, but really!" the superintendent exclaimed. "I've never heard such a load of nonsense!"

"Perhaps not entirely nonsense, sir," said Blood. "Admittedly, it seems unlikely that some sort of psychopath might have fixated upon a killer from the nineteenth century, but it's not impossible. I've been doing some research, as I'm sure the press has, and it seems that Jack the Ripper was never brought to justice. The Whitechapel Murders became infamous, taking their place in folklore, and apparently there was such a public outcry over the failure to arrest the murderer that the police superintendent at the time was forced to resign."

There was a long silence on the line. Blood cleared his throat awkwardly and continued.

"In any case, sir, it may indeed have started out to be a load of nonsense, as we've had more than our share of murders in that sort of neighborhood before, but with the press picking up this angle, as it were, and playing it up the way they've done, our murderer might very well decide to pick up on it as well, even to the point of adopting the identity of Jack the Ripper. These sort of serial killers are compulsive, and they seem to enjoy all the attention."

"Good God," the superintendent said. "Then by the very fact of making this comparison, the press is contributing to the problem!"

"Possibly, sir," said Blood with slight emphasis on the word *possibly*. He added, "However, with all due respect, might I suggest that it would not be in our best interests to point this out to them?"

"Yes, quite," said the superintendent. He sighed. "Hell. This could become a monstrous migraine for us all. Look, Michael, I'm going to make some sort of statement to the effect that we're giving this our top priority and that you are taking charge of the case personally, highest confidence in your abilities, so on and so forth. Let's dispose of this one with alacrity, shall we?"

"Yes, sir, I'll do my very best," said Blood.

"Good. See that you do. I'm counting on you. Keep my office posted, will you?"

"Yes, sir, of course," said Blood, and he replaced the phone on its cradle.

He grimaced and ran a hand through his short brown hair. Well, that was that. He'd just been appointed official scapegoat. If the Ripper wasn't brought to justice posthaste, it would all come down on Chief Inspector Michael Blood. At least, at thirty, he was still young enough to look for another line of work. His youth had always worked against him before. He knew that many people in the department felt that he was much too young to be Chief Inspector, and even with his mustache he still looked at least five years younger than he really was. "Youngblood." He knew that was what they called him behind his back. He was only too painfully aware of his position. He took great care not to be too authoritarian, not to direct any of his subordinates to do anything he would not do himself. He was careful not to fraternize or flaunt his extensive education. He was uncomfortable about his family background, just as his family was uncomfortable about his choosing police work, which they felt was far beneath him. Yet it was what he'd always wanted, work that was interesting and stimulating, with a new challenge every day. Work that was meaningful.

His father would have preferred him to be a financier, to join the family firm, but Michael had always wanted to be a policeman, ever since his childhood. He'd grown up on swashbuckling adventure stories of the Urban Police Service—the vaunted UPS, with their dark green armored vans—London's paramilitary police organization during the dark days of the Collapse. He could not remember ever wanting to do anything else with his life. His older brother, Ian, could be found in the House of Lords, and younger brother Andrew usually could be found in some house of ill repute, but Michael Blood kept modest bachelor lodgings in Soho, where he could almost never be found unless he was in bed. Alone or, more frequently, with a good book.

"He's a handsome, likely enough lad," his father always said of him before shaking his head sadly and adding, "But he has no damned ambition, none whatsoever."

That wasn't really true. Michael did have one ambition. To be the best at what he did. And if his father could not appreciate that, his superiors at New Scotland Yard could and did. He was the superintendent's fair-haired boy, as some of the senior police officials were always quick to say, and Michael always winced whenever he heard it, especially the telltale emphasis on the word *boy*. Still, that would not prevent the superintendent from throwing him to the wolves if he did not produce results. He stood with his hands clasped behind his back, staring out the window of his office at the city streets below.

"So Michael Blood," he said softly to himself, "you wanted a challenge. Now you've damn well got one. What are you going to do about it?"

Shavers knocked at his office door again and stuck his head in.

"Yes, Danny, what is it?"

"Uh . . ." Shavers cleared his throat uneasily. "There's a . . . uh . . . a lad to see you, sir."

Blood frowned. "A lad? What do you mean, a lad? You mean a child?"

"Uh . . . well . . . sort of a child, I suppose," said Shavers awkwardly.

Blood raised his eyebrows. This was not at all like Shavers, who was normally unflappable. "Sort of a child?" He shrugged. "Well, send him in, then, and we'll see what sort he is."

The door opened and Billy Slade came in.

# CHAPTER FOUR

Jacqueline Marie-Lisette de Charboneau Monet, whose name was pronounced "Zha-kleen" and who preferred *not* to be called Jackie, was in her late forties, yet she had the body of a woman in her twenties. A very fit woman. Despite her athletic build, she chain-smoked unfiltered French cigarettes that smelled like a forest fire and slugged down 180-proof Russian vodka from a silver hip flask she kept in her purse. She wore an expensive, Neo-Edwardian maroon velvet suit with tight trousers tucked into high boots, a high collar and lace trim, all exquisitely tailored to flatter her slim figure. Her hair was dark, heavily shot through with gray, and she wore it shoulder-length, loose and casual. Her voice was a husky, whiskey baritone, only slightly accented; her English was flawless; and she had the manner of a regimental sergeant major. Makepeace fell in love with her at once.

She met them at Heathrow Airport and had a limo waiting to take them to their hotel, the Dorchester in Park Lane. The same hotel Modred had disappeared from. On the way in, between manic puffs on her cigarette, slam-dunks with the flask, and sharply barked commands to the chauffeur to watch what the hell he was doing, she filled them in on what she had managed to discover.

"The last place he was seen was at the Dorchester," she said. "Watch what you're doing, idiot!" (This last remark was to the chauffeur, who was so nervous at having such a volatile passenger that he was having trouble maintaining his levitation and impulsion spells.) "He checked in shortly after noon," Jacqueline continued. "He brought with him only one small suitcase, which he never even unpacked. He ordered a bottle of Scotch sent up to his room, took a long walk, had dinner, returned to his room, ordered another bottle of Scotch, and that was the last anyone ever heard from him."

"What about—" Makepeace began, but she held up a hand to forestall him.

"Wait, there is more." She took out another cigarette, and Makepeace lit it for her. She grunted her thanks, apparently not noticing that Makepeace hadn't used a lighter or a match. He snapped his fingers, and the flame came out of his thumb.

"The room was torn apart," Jacqueline continued, exhaling a long stream of smoke. "Completely destroyed, as if, in the words of one of the hotel staff, 'a hurricane had blown through it.' Overturned furniture, broken glass in all the windows, shattered mirrors, and so on. A room service waiter who was bringing up the whiskey was the first to discover it. He was reluctant to speak with me, since the police had already questioned him, but I gave him some money and he told me that he heard 'echoing laughter' when he came into the room. But there was no one there. Also, he said that for a moment he could see through the walls, the floor, and the ceiling, as if somehow the entire room had become transparent."

"Or as if it temporarily had become a dimensional portal to some other place," said Makepeace, and she glanced at him sharply.

"He said he could look through the walls and see stars floating in space," she said. "He was very frightened by it. He did not tell any of this to the police, and he swore he would deny everything if I told them what he said to me. He had no question in his mind that there was sorcery involved. Oh, and there was one more thing—a discarded room service waiter's uniform was discovered lying on the floor of the room."

"Yes, clearly a visitation of some sort," said Makepeace with a grunt. "He was snatched by some demon, no question about it. Certainly no ordinary man would have been able to abduct him."

"On that I will agree," said Jacqueline emphatically. There was something in her tone that made Kira glance at her with interest. Jacqueline had spoken with a sort of proud defiance, almost as if she were challenging anyone to deny that Morpheus could not be taken so easily. She loves him, Kira thought.

The undercarriage of the car smashed briefly against the ground as the chauffeur lost his concentration in the face of all this talk about demonic visitations. Jacqueline swore at him in French, and though he didn't understand the words, the tone of her voice was clear enough. He redoubled his efforts at maintaining his levitation and impulsion spells, which were relatively undemanding, really, something any first-year warlock could do without much effort, but it was precisely that sort of spell that got people into trouble.

If a transportational adept was easily distracted as, indeed, many of them were, otherwise they would have gone on to more advanced (and thereby more profitable) levels of adept certification, then the vehicle would lose levitation and/or impulsion and crash. This was one of the reasons why most transportational adepts kept their speeds down very low. Another was that collisions were all too frequent.

The best of the transportational adepts became airline pilots, a job with an extremely high pay scale because it took an enormous amount of energy to hold up a plane. The job simply wore out pilots at an amazing rate, not to mention what could happen if they lost control of their levitation and impulsion spells. Many people wouldn't even get on board an airplane unless there was at least one sorcerer along as a passenger on the flight, able to assist the pilot in case of an emergency. For this reason wizards and sorcerers always flew for free, in first class, and a mage was treated as absolute royalty.

Wyrdrune hated flying, because he knew all too well how easily something could go wrong, if not with an exhausted pilot adept, then with an overtaxed air traffic controller, whose eyes would start to cross after sitting hunched over for several hours, staring at all the tiny planes circling in a minature holding pattern inside a crystal ball. Wyrdrune's nerves were already badly frayed from the transatlantic flight, and now, the careening limo, skimming along way too fast merely three feet or so above the ground, was finishing the job of unnerving him completely.

"Could we please slow down a little?" he said.

"We are almost there," Jacqueline said impatiently. Like all the French, she saw driving less as a mode of transportation than as a contact sport.

"It's just that I would prefer to arrive in one piece," said Wyrdrune.

This vote of confidence upset the harried driver even more, and the limo veered wildly before he got it back under control. His collar was damp with perspiration, and he kept glancing at them nervously in the rearview mirror.

"Look, it's all right," Wyrdrune told him. "Just relax. Slow down. We're not in that much of a hurry. We'll get there when we get there, okay?"

Jacqueline glanced at him with a wry grimace but she didn't argue, and the chauffeur flashed him a grateful look in the rearview mirror. Before long they were pulling up in front of the Dorchester Hotel and the doorman was escorting them out, to the chauffeur's immense relief. They checked in and found that among the rooms Jacqueline had reserved for them was the same room from which Modred had disappeared. As they signed the register Wyrdrune picked up a complimentary copy of the London Times. The headline read, RIPPER STRIKES AGAIN!

Chief Inspector Michael Blood was having a nightmare. He was chasing the killer through the streets of Whitechapel. Unfortunately he couldn't see what the Ripper really looked like. The killer always appeared as a shadowy figure in the distance, stalking some unwary victim while Blood ran gasping through the fog-enshrouded streets, his coat flapping behind him as he plunged down one narrow alleyway after another, always seeing the shadowy form of the Ripper turning around a corner just ahead of him. And when he arrived upon the spot, there would be no one there, only a misty courtyard, not a sign of life. He would stand there breathing hard, wildly looking all around him . . . and then a throat-rending scream would ring out, shattering the stillness of the night and echoing through the deserted, foggy streets. And always, each and every time, the victim cried out the same thing, and the sound of it would reverberate like thunder in the night.

*"Michael!"*

Over and over and over, it would echo through his mind. *"Michael! Michael! Michael! Michael!"* And he would start running once again, chasing phantoms in the night while terror-stricken voices called his name. *"Michael! Michael! Michael!"*

He awoke with a cry, sitting up in bed and gasping for breath, then he sighed wearily and rubbed his eyes, wondering what time it was. He groped for the cigarettes on the nightstand, shook one out of the pack, put it between his lips, and struck his lighter. As the flame flared up, it illuminated the tatterdemalion figure of Billy Slade, sitting cross-legged in the chair across the room.

"We really ought to 'ave another talk, y'know," said Billy. "You're out of your depth on this one, Mick."

Blood started, the cigarette falling from between his lips. He dropped the lighter and lunged for the lamp on the nightstand, but when he turned it on, the chair was empty. He looked all around the room, but there was no sign of the boy. He stared at the empty chair for a long moment, then lit the cigarette with a shaky hand.

"Steady, Michael," he said to himself. "Mind's playing tricks on you. You're just overtired, that's all."

Under the circumstances that wasn't terribly surprising. This Ripper thing was occupying all his time, and it was really getting to him. The savagery of the murders was unlike anything he'd ever seen. Then there was that visit yesterday from that poor, demented Slade boy. Apparently it had upset him much more than he had realized, which was a clear signal that his nerves were getting badly frayed.

The poor little bastard had started babbling in an affected deep voice, some sort of nonsense about necromancy and inhuman wizards and being Merlin Ambrosius reincarnated when news of the latest murder had come in and he had rushed out of the office, shouting something over his shoulder to Danny Shavers about seeing to the lad, only when Shavers had gone into the office, the boy had disappeared. Gone out the window, undoubtedly, and climbed down to the street. Those slum kids were like little monkeys. Thorough as ever, Shavers had looked up the lad's record, and sure enough, he had one. He'd been in and out of trouble since he was eight years old. And now, as if his prospects weren't dim enough already, apparently the poor little sod had lost his senses. Thought he was Merlin Ambrosius of all people! Well, why not? The sort of desperate lives these poor kids lived, it would take an archmage to help them.

Blood took a deep drag on the cigarette and got up out of bed. There was no point in trying to go back to sleep. It was almost dawn, in any case. He had felt bad about the boy and he'd pushed it from his mind, so now it had come back just to remind him that there was some unfinished business in that locked file marked "Emotions." That file was getting overburdened. The only problem was, he didn't quite know how to clean it out. You see things on the job every day that would break the stoutest heart, he thought, and you tell yourself that you can take it, that you won't let it get to you, but it's a blade dance all the way. Only you can't dance on the knife edge and expect not to get cut, he thought. At what point do you stop caring and become a cold and heartless machine, as dead as the corpses you see every day? Or do you start to care too much and become paralyzed with agony, unable to think, unable to function, unable to do anything except hurt?

He went over to his desk and poured himself a whiskey from the bottle he'd left there last night. It was half full. He winced, hesitating as he brought the glass up to his lips. He'd started taking a couple of drinks to help get him to sleep, and now he was having a drink to help him get started in the morning. Not a good sign. Not a good sign at all. To hell with it, he thought, and tossed back the Scotch. It felt like fire going down. He held up the empty glass and looked at it with a wry grimace.

"Be careful, Michael," he said to himself. "You like this evil stuff too damned much. you keep this up and it'll be your undoing." He put down the glass and filled it up again. He raised it. "Well, sod it, here's to my undoing."

The second one went down more smoothly than the first. He walked over to the window and raised the shade. The sky was getting gray over the city. The phone rang.

He flinched, and his hand involuntarily squeezed so hard that the glass shattered in his grasp. "*Damn,*" he said, opening one of the bureau drawers and fumbling for a fresh handkerchief while the telephone kept ringing. He wrapped the handkerchief around his bleeding hand and picked up the phone.

"Yes, yes, what is it?"

"Sorry to wake you, Chief Inspector, but I'm afraid we've got another one."

He closed his eyes. "Oh, bloody hell," he said.

"Yes, sir. It certainly is that."

At twenty, Andrew Lloyd Blood was overweight, weak-chinned, and rather pasty, but he made close to ten times the money that his older brother Michael made as Chief Inspector. He was in training for the family business, which meant that he was learning to become a shark, and he was an astonishingly quick study. He was not quite ready for the subtle world of investment banking yet, because those polished predators took carefully selective bites and sheared the flesh off very neatly, whereas Andrew had a tendency to chomp at everything in sight as if in a blood-crazed feeding frenzy. So, appropriately, he had become a stockbroker. Occasionally he even made some money for his clients. However, that was not his chief concern. Andrew was chiefly concerned with making enough money to support his hobby, which was self-gratification. Consequently he was eagerly looking forward to the evening's entertainment, and especially to meeting the mysterious Lord Carfax.

It seemed that everyone who was anyone was talking about him, but no one really seemed to know just who he was. It was impossible to trace the fellow's lineage, which was a pity, Andrew thought. There was no help from anything like *Debrett's* anymore; the whole thing was so corrupt that one could practically rent a peerage for a fortnight these days. A bloody fishmonger could print up cards and call himself Lord Wanking Bumkisser or whatever; even the House of Lords was full of the worst sort of people nowadays. The only way that one could judge anymore was by the way a fellow carried himself, by his manner and his sense of style, and if it turned out later that he was descended from a long line of tradesmen, then one could always harrumph and raise one's eyebrows and say, "How shocking!" and hope that one's own pedigree was not too closely scrutinized.

Carfax, by all reports, was quite the real thing, and if he wasn't, well, then he should have been, which amounted to the same thing, more or less. He was fabulously wealthy and old-school to the core, despite having grown up in India or Thailand or wherever, some damned wog country, but for all that, he knew a thing or two the locals didn't. *Yes, indeed, I'll bet he does,* thought Andrew, *living like some bloody maharaja in Kafiristan or wherever the hell it was he came from.* Handsome, young, elegant, and charming, Carfax was the epitome of what the empire had stood for in the old days, and he was said to give fantastic parties.

Andrew had all this on the best authority. He'd heard it from one of his new clients, a young chap named Joseph Lymon who'd come into a kingly inheritance from an uncle in Los Angeles or something; it didn't really matter because he was a splendid fellow who was well on his way to turning his apparently considerable inheritance into a staggering fortune. He completely disregarded all of Andrew's best advice and insisted on picking his own stocks, which subsequently performed amazingly. In short order, knowing a good thing when he saw one, Andrew had hitched his star to Lymon's, buying when he bought and selling when he sold, and invariably Andrew prospered. Andrew had cultivated a friendship with Lymon, sponsoring him into his club and introducing him to all the right people, and one night Lymon had confessed that he actually received his stock-market tips from a friend of his named Lord Carfax.

This news had electrified Andrew, as he had been hearing fascinating things about the young Lord Nigel Carfax ever since he had arrived in London from Sumatra, or wherever it was he came from. No one really seemed to know, though everyone agreed that it was some far-off, exotic place in the Far East. Or was it the Middle East? No matter, the point was that everyone had heard of him, yet it seemed that few people had actually met him, though some people claimed having been to his parties at his elegant Georgian town house in Charles Street, or at his newly reconstructed medieval castle on the outskirts of London. And stories of these exclusive parties grew more and more fantastic with each telling. Reportedly they were not parties quite so much as orgies, but orgies of a highly refined nature, admitting only the best sort of people and providing only the finest sort of cuisine and entertainment.

And what entertainment! Andrew had heard incredible stories about the women at Lord Carfax's parties. The man was said to have a magnetic personality and a voracious sexual appetite. Society women of Andrew's acquaintance were either scandalized by these stories or slyly claimed to have attended his parties, and even if they hadn't, all of them doubtless wanted to. In any case, it seemed that everyone had been talking for weeks about the party Carfax was throwing that night. It was to be a masked ball. And Andrew, thanks to his good friend, Joey Lymon, had received an invitation!

Andrew had dressed as Napoleon. Joey Lymon had arrived to pick him up dressed in a dark costume with a top hat and a long black cloak with a high collar.

"Who are you supposed to be?" asked Andrew.

Joey had smiled. "Can't you tell, Andrew? I'm the Ripper."

"Oh, I say!" Andrew had exclaimed, chuckling. "What a capital idea! Wish I'd thought of it!"

"Well, we can't have two Rippers at the same party, can we?" Joey said, opening the car door for him.

"No, I suppose not," said Andrew. "Still, I ought to have done better than Napoleon, don't you think? There're bound to be several Napoleons at the party, aren't there? I mean, it's sort of an obvious choice."

"Which may be precisely why most people would shy

away from it," said Joey as the car levitated and started moving forward, floating gracefully down the street, the driver invisible behind the darkly tinted glass that separated the front seat from the passenger compartment. "Chances are excellent that everyone thought it would be an obvious choice, so perhaps nobody made it, which will probably leave you as the only Napoleon in attendance."

"You know, you're right. I hadn't thought of that," said Andrew, feeling better, though still disappointed that he hadn't thought of going as the Ripper.

"Nigel says that people's reactions are really very easy to predict," said Joey. "That's why playing the market is so easy."

Easy! Andrew thought. Good God!

"He says that people are like sheep," Joey went on. "They have a herd instinct, and because of that they're easily led. One only has to understand this and have a basic grasp of the laws of probability, and anticipating market trends becomes a snap."

A snap! Incredible, thought Andrew. He could hardly wait to meet this man. He'd have to make a point to listen carefully to his each and every word. He'd have to see if he could steer the conversation around to these "laws of probability," to see how Carfax saw them. Was it possible that one could apply the same principles to trading in the market as one used in games of chance? Both were a form of gambling, after all, but to think that one could actually apply some sort of system, as professional cardsharps did . . .

"Joey," Andrew said, "you never told me, how did you come to meet Lord Carfax?"

"Oh, we just sort of ran into each other one night," said Joey with a smile. "He really changed my life, you know. Sort of took me under his wing, rather like you've done, Andrew. Lord knows, you've been simply an amazing help to me, sponsoring me and introducing me around—"

"Oh, posh, it was nothing," Andrew said with false humility. "One does what one can to help one's friends, you know."

"Yes," said Joey, "yes, indeed, that's as it should be, which is why I'm so pleased to be able to introduce you and Nigel to each other, to bring together two of my closest friends. I think you'll have a lot in common. You both enjoy the finer things in life, eh?"

"Ah, yes, well," said Andrew, pouring himself a drink from the bar. "One must cultivate one's tastes, mustn't one?"

"Indeed," said Joey.

"Indeed," said Andrew, thinking what a splendid chap young Lymon was, while Joey sat there thinking, What an incredible berk!

They chatted amiably till the car pulled up in front of the elegant stone-faced town house on Charles Street that was the home of Lord Nigel Carfax. Tall, spiked wrought-iron railings surrounded the entrance, and they were admitted through the formidable-looking gate by a liveried footman who carefully examined their invitations before allowing them inside.

They climbed the short flight of stone steps leading to the ornately carved front door with the tall and narrow leaded stained-glass windows framing it on either side. The door was opened for them by a blond girl who made Andrew's eyes bug out. She couldn't have been a day over seventeen, with a peaches-and-cream complexion, freckles dusted lightly across her nose and delightful dimples, the sort of girl one might expect to see in church on Sunday morning in the Yorkshire Dales, only this one was decked out in a black-and-crimson merry widow strained to the breaking point, net stockings, and spike-heeled pumps, an ivory cameo on a black velvet choker gracing her lovely throat.

"Good evening, gentlemen," she said, in a small, polite, little-girl voice. "Do please come in and make yourselves at home."

After he got his breath back Andrew followed Joey through the door, only to have his breath taken away once more by the sight that greeted him inside. The elegant Georgian facade of the town house was just that, a facade. Inside the place had been redone completely in the most modern Post-Romantic style. The floors were bare black marble, the walls were dark pastels, the furniture was all noveau-medieval, and the decor was Dionysian. Bronze sculptures depicting half-human beasts and demons were placed around the lobby. There were large paintings on the walls done in the style of Dore and Bosch, but even those demented visionaries had never committed such carnal fantasies to canvas. Ingenious flying stairways, apparently suspended in midair, led to the upper floors, and skillfully placed dim, indirect lighting gave the interior a surreal, chiaroscuro atmosphere. Throbbing, driving music came from the ballroom to the right, where costumed figures undulated wildly on the dance floor. Some of those costumes were very spare, indeed. Andrew swallowed hard. This was going to be even better than he'd expected.

"Ah, here is our hostess," Joey said, and Andrew's jaw dropped as he saw Terri Clancy slowly coming down the stairs.

She was wearing a skintight black kidskin leather jumpsuit that was open almost to her navel; high, spike-heeled boots; a studded leather belt; and a spiked, black leather choker. Her jet-black hair hung long and loose, and she wore a small black satin mask that covered just the area around her eyes. She carried a short, silver-handled whip in her left hand.

"Good Lord," said Andrew, swallowing hard as she approached. "Is . . . is that . . . Lady Carfax?"

"What, Terri?" Joey said, chuckling. "Lady Carfax? Heavens, no. Nigel is a confirmed bachelor. Terri is . . . umm, how shall I put it? Nigel's social director?"

"Then she isn't . . . ?"

"No, she isn't, old boy," said Joey with a grin. "Tally-ho, eh?"

"Joey, how nice to see you," Terri said, giving him a light kiss on the cheek. "And this must be Andrew, whom I've heard *so* much about."

She slipped her hand into his and squeezed it softly, then continued to hold on to it.

"What has he been telling you about me, then?" Andrew said, leering at her. "Not the truth, I hope?"

"I've been telling her what an absolutely depraved rascal you are," Joey said. "A shameless pervert. A sexual deviant of the first rank."

"He's an awful liar, you know," Andrew said uneasily.

"Is he?" Terri said, her eyes staring deeply into his. "What a shame! I was *so* hoping it was all true. Most men one meets are so depressingly boring. So... unimaginative. And Joey made you sound so *very* interesting...."

"Did he now?" Andrew gushed, practically drooling. "Well, perhaps we can discuss it further over a small drink, eh?" He winked at her.

"Oh, let's," she said, returning the wink and taking his arm, pressing herself up against him. Andrew was starting to hyperventilate.

"Sh-shouldn't we greet our host first?" he said, stammering.

"Nigel? Oh, why bother? He's bound to be about somewhere," she said. "I've worked ever so hard to bring this party off, I should be entitled to enjoy myself a little, don't you think? I'm sure Nigel will understand. You won't mind if I steal your friend for just a little while, will you, Joey, darling?

"Steal away, love," said Joey with a wink at Andrew. "Good luck, old boy. It's every man for himself, eh, what?"

Andrew grinned salaciously and gave him a thumbs-up as Terri led him away toward the bar. Behind him, the smile suddenly slipped from Joey Lymon's face, and his expression became cold and feral. He turned and went back out the door, down the steps, through the gate, and to his waiting car. He opened up the trunk and took out a black leather roll-up bag, then he slammed the trunk lid shut and got into the backseat. The dark-tinted partition between him and the chauffer slid down soundlessly. The driver removed his chauffeur's cap and ran a graceful, pale hand through his flaming red hair.

"Where to, Your Lordship?" he said, glancing up into the rearview mirror.

"Whitechapel," said Joey softly.

At first he thought it was anxiety. Perhaps it was simply stress from the transatlantic flight, or jet lag, but the headache refused to go away. It kept on growing worse, and now it was a constant, dull, throbbing pain, almost a burning sensation. They went up to their rooms—he and Kira would share Modred's old suite, while Makepeace and Jacqueline each had their own rooms—and the first thing he did was toss his hat onto the bed and head for the bathroom to throw some cold water on his face. As he went through the bathroom door he brought his right hand up to rub his aching forehead and felt the runestone. It was *hot*. He glanced into the bathroom mirror and his eyes widened. The runestone was giving off a soft green glow.

"Kira?" he said, but at the same time she came in behind him, looking down at her hand.

"Hey, warlock, did you notice if—"

She stopped when she saw him. The sapphire runestone set into her palm was giving off a soft blue glow.

"You, too, huh?" she said, staring at his forehead. "Does it hurt?"

"Sort of a burning ache," said Wyrdrune. "I thought it was just a headache from the flight over."

"Yeah, mine aches like hell too," she said, holding her

wrist and flexing her fingers. She bit her lower lip nervously. "What do you think it means?"

He shook his head. "I haven't the faintest idea. Where are the others?"

"The fairy was making noises about having dinner," she said. "Jacqueline only seemed interested in drinking it."

"You don't like her."

Kira shrugged.

"Why?"

"I don't know. Rubs me the wrong way, I guess."

"Couldn't have anything to do with Modred, could it?"

She glanced at him sharply. "What makes you say a thing like that?"

Wyrdrune paused before replying. "She gets a special sort of look when she talks about him," he said.

"Does she? I hadn't noticed."

"Bull. She's in love with him. You can hear it in her voice. It bothers you, doesn't it?"

Kira shrugged again. "Why should it bother me?"

"You tell me."

"Don't be ridiculous," she said. "There was never anything between me and Modred." She snorted. "Besides, he's a little old for me, don't you think?"

"I might think so, if I believed that something like that would make the slightest bit of difference to you, but I know you too well, kiddo. I can hear it in your voice too."

"Maybe it's just the runestones," she said, turning away and going back into the bedroom. "We're all sort of spiritually bonded. Maybe that's all it is."

"Maybe. What do *you* think?"

She spun around. "What do you mean, what do *I* think? I just *told* you what I think. Why don't you just come out and say what's on your mind?"

"I love you."

"Oh, *shit*." She turned around, sighing with exasperation.

"You said to say what's on my mind."

"Yeah, well, you *would* say that! What, have you been taking guilt-trip lessons from your broom?"

"Is that what you think I'm trying to do?"

"Well, what *are* you trying to do?"

"I'm only trying to find out how you feel," said Wyrdrune. "I'll tell you how I feel. I have a feeling that we're getting into something very heavy here, and I don't mean potential problems with our relationship. The last time our runestones started glowing, we became involved in a direct confrontation with the Dark Ones. And if you'll recall what happened, we almost lost our lives because Modred broke the link when Morgana was attacked."

"What are you saying, that he shouldn't have tried to help his own mother, for God's sake?" said Kira.

"This is going to sound terribly cold, and I'm sorry for that," Wyrdrune said gravely, "but it was too late for Morgana, anyway." He gently took her by the shoulders and looked into her eyes. "Because Modred broke the link between us at the crucial moment, we were unable to contain the Dark Ones, and now there's no way of knowing how many of them managed to escape. Now we bear the responsibility for that, all three of us, not just Modred. We can't afford to think of our own priorities any longer. None of us is entirely an individual anymore. On one hand, there's the three of us—you, me, and Modred—and on the other hand, we're each much more than that. The life forces of the Council of the White have been passed on to us through the runestones. And they're changing us. Every day, in some small way, we're changing, becoming much more than what we were before."

He released her, took a deep breath, let it out slowly, and rubbed his aching forehead.

"I don't know," he said, shaking his head. "I don't really understand what's happening to us. Modred always understood more about this than we did; he was always stronger, more intuitive. He was closer to them."

"What do you mean *was*?" she said.

*"Is,"* Wyrdrune said, quickly correcting himself. "I mean *is.*"

"You don't think he's dead!"

"Damn it, Kira, I don't *know*!" he said. He squeezed his right hand into a fist. "I just—don't—*know*. Maybe that's what this is all about," he said, bringing his hand up to his forehead.

Involuntarily Kira stared down at the blue light in her hand, a cold feeling of dread building inside her.

"No," she said, shaking her head. "I can't believe that. He couldn't be dead. I mean . . . we'd know it somehow. We'd know it for a fact. We'd *feel* it."

"I hope you're right," said Wyrdrune. "But even if we were dead, we'd still have to go on somehow. There's far too much at stake for us to think only of ourselves. The important thing is the link that we can forge together, and I don't even know how strong that link can be now. We've never tried it without Modred. Maybe we can't even *do* it without Modred, and if that's the case, God help us. We may not be completely in control of what the runestones can do, Kira, but we can still control ourselves, and the point I'm trying to make here is that we mustn't allow our individual feelings to overcome our greater responsibility. You see that, don't you?"

She nodded. "Yeah, I guess I do. But, damn it, no one ever asked me how *I* felt about it! I never even had the option of a choice!"

"Neither did I," said Wyrdrune. "Neither did Modred, for that matter. But even though we may not always have choices about what happens to us in our lives, we still have choices about how we're going to handle it. I didn't really have a choice about you coming into my life, and maybe I didn't have a choice about loving you, either, but I think that when you love somebody, you shouldn't put conditions on it. I just wanted you to know that. However things turn out."

They stood there looking at each other for a long moment, then she came into his arms and they held each other tightly.

"I'm scared, warlock," she said.

"So am I, kid," he said. "So am I."

Andrew Blood lay on his back, completely naked, staring up at his reflection in the large overhead mirror. He was handcuffed to the brass bedrails behind him, and his legs were spread, ankles held in strong leather restraints. A small rubber ball had been placed into his mouth so that it acted as an effective gag and a leather strap with a hole cut into it that held the rubber ball down was fastened around his neck. He felt absolutely helpless, and in fact he was. He was trembling with anticipation.

Terri stood at the foot of the bed, staring down at him. She licked her lips. Andrew was breathing through his nose like a bellows. Slowly she unzipped one boot and pulled it off, then the other. Then she removed her studded bracelets, then the studded belt. She pursued her lips and held the doubled-up studded belt thoughtfully for a moment, smiled faintly, then very lightly ran it across Andrew's paunchy stomach. His pasty flesh got goose pimples, and he moaned behind the gag.

She dropped the belt down on the floor and provocatively started to remove her leather jumpsuit. Andrew was shivering and making little whimpering noises. Terri slipped out of the one-piece, skintight suit and let it fall to the floor. She stood completely naked at the foot of the bed, wearing only the black mask. Her ample breasts rose and fell heavily as she stared down at him. Her tongue slipped out and licked her lips, but it seemed very long suddenly, and Andrew blinked, staring at her . . . was it *forked*?

Her hair was moving. Something was coming up beneath it . . . he saw the tufted tips of long, pointed ears emerge. Her nose lengthened. Her lips drew back over fangs dripping with saliva. A growl rumbled up from deep down in her throat.

Andrew started thrashing on the bed, making hysterical sounds against the gag.

She raised her hands, fingers now inordinately long and hooked like talons, and razor-sharp claws slowly slid out of her fingertips. She slowly crawled up onto the bed. . . .

# CHAPTER FIVE

It was dark. Somewhere water dripped. Modred could hear the chittering of rats. Hundreds, thousands of them. They were keeping their distance . . . for now. There was a pile of furry corpses beneath him, where he hung chained to the cold, damp wall. The rats had learned the hard way that this was no ordinary morsel they could devour at their leisure. This one could fight back, even when chained. But rats were not easily intimidated, not even by magic. They withdrew and waited. In time they knew that he would weaken. Sooner or later he'd have to go to sleep.

Modred no longer felt the cold, damp stone against his skin. He had passed beyond caring about the burning pain in his arms and shoulders. He had been hanging by his manacled wrists for days, without a wink of sleep, suspended several feet above the floor by thick iron chains embedded in the wall. He had no idea where he was. The last thing he could remember was a whirlwind of crystalline blue fire sucking him into its vortex. When he came to, he was chained and hanging in the cell. He had seen no one. He had not been fed. He had not been given anything to drink. He didn't know what day it was, or even if it was day or night. He had lost all track of time. The only light in the dark, windowless cell came from the faintly glowing

**85**

ruby set into his chest. It was the only thing keeping him alive. The chains that held him had been spellwarded; he could not break free. And something in the cell was slowly sapping all his strength, draining his life force. The stone walls seemed to throb with eldritch emanations.

At first he thought he was hallucinating when a pale blue glow started to fill the cell, but then a figure wreathed in an aura of blue light appeared before him, standing about ten feet away. As the blue glow ebbed, he made a languid gesture with his right hand, little more than a flick of his fingers, and a torch set in an iron wall sconce erupted into flame. Modred stared at the strikingly handsome man with elegantly styled, fiery red hair. He was wearing a soft black cabretta leather suit cut in the noveau medieval style. He looked like an androgynous cross between a dominatrix and Beau Brummel.

"Sorry to have kept you waiting," he said softly, "but I'm afraid I had some business to attend to." He glanced down at the pile of rat corpses beneath Modred's feet. "I see you've managed to keep yourself amused."

"*Water* . . ." Modred said raspily.

"Water? Well . . . why not? Only a little, though. I wouldn't want you to regain your strength."

He made a slight gesture, and it began to rain lightly on Modred. Only on him and nowhere else in the cell. Modred raised his head, turning his face up to the rain-drops, and licked the moisture from his lips. He opened his mouth and tried to catch as many of the droplets as he could, but the cool, light shower lasted for only a moment or two and then stopped, leaving him damp. He groaned and shivered.

"Who . . . who are you?" he asked weakly.

"Your death," the necromancer said. His gaze centered on the faintly glowing runestone over Modred's heart. "Which of you are contained therein, I wonder? Azrael? Moab? Zachariahs? Or have you lost your own identities even as you lost your bodies? Look what has become of you. The mighty Council of the White, reduced to three gaudy little pebbles. Helpless without this common flesh that you have bonded to."

The ruby over Modred's heart suddenly blazed, and his eyes became suffused with blood-red light. Twin crimson beams of pure thaumaturgic energy shot from them, striking the necromancer full in the chest, but the force beams merely passed through his insubstantial form, spending their tremendous force against the far wall of the cell, opening a fissure in the wall as the huge stones cracked, sending chips and dust whirling through the musty air.

"That was foolish," said the shade of the necromancer. "Did you really think that I would risk confronting you in the flesh? No, I have waited far too long to be so careless now. You should have saved your strength. Now you are weaker still. You only hasten the inevitable. Another such blast—assuming you could summon up the strength for it—would only succeed in bringing tons of stone tumbling down upon you."

"Why not kill me and have done with it?" said Modred, his voice a hoarse whisper, his breathing ragged.

"You, halfling, I could kill without a moment's thought. You are nothing to me. But for those whose life force is now joined to yours, I would have long since consumed your energy. But their strength protects you. At least for now. Yet I grow stronger while they weaken. And soon I shall be stronger than they ever were. Still," he added, sounding wistful, "it will be a poor revenge on those who kept me buried alive for eons, because I will not see their faces and I will not hear them scream. But I will take what solace I can find in the agony that you shall suffer, knowing they will share in it. And when I have milked your soul of all its sanity, I will rip that stone out from your chest together with your still beating heart."

The runestone flickered with a feeble glow. Modred's head sagged down upon his chest. He was dizzy with thirst and hunger, exhausted from lack of sleep, and drained by the attack upon the necromancer, which had taken every last ounce of strength he had left. It was all over. He could feel his life force ebbing. Perhaps, he thought, after two thousand years it was only fitting for it all to end in a cold stone dungeon of some ancient castle. A deserving end for one who had committed both patricide and regicide in one fell blow.

"It really is a pity in a way," the necromancer said, his image slowly fading, leaving his voice to echo in the cell. "It is all so easy. Perhaps the other two will provide me with a bit more sport."

They dined at Rumpole's, a chic pub restaurant on Curzon Street, near Shepherd's Market. Kira, characteristically, had ordered hamburger. Jacqueline was having only soup and bread sticks. Wyrdrune was somewhat disappointed. He had wanted to order a steak and kidney pie and some Yorkshire pudding, not that he had the slightest idea what Yorkshire pudding was or how steak and kidney pie was prepared, just that he thought it was the sort of thing that English people ate—only neither was on the menu. In fact, the menu offered nothing very different from the average fare in most American fern bars. The most British-looking thing on it was fish and chips, which was what he chose. Makepeace was gorging on the same, having ordered four portions—all for himself. Wyrdrune watched with disbelief the way the food just kept going in ceaselessly, like coal being fed into a roaring furnace. A liberal spritz of vinegar on the fish, a messy gob of ketchup on the chips, a dinner roll torn in half and slathered with butter, shoveled in and washed down with a hearty slug of ale, all without the slightest pause in conversation.

"So all of his contacts each knew a different man," he said. "To Jacqueline he was a Belgian named Phillipe de Bracy. I knew him first as John Roderick, of New York, and only later learned that he had also established a fully documented identity as an Englishman named Michael

Cornwall. That was after his penthouse in New York was destroyed in a fire and he was forced to abandon the Roderick identity." He turned to Wyrdrune. "And to think that you first knew him only as a nameless professional assassin who had taken a contract on your life! Incredible! But *why*? Who wanted you dead?"

"A fence named Fats," said Wyrdrune. "Kira and I met when we both tried to steal the runestones at the same time. At first we thought it was only a coincidence that we had both independently planned the same job, but the fact is that we were under the influence of the runestones even then. Still, it was a long time before we understood what was happening to us. In the beginning we just wanted to get rid of the runestones *and* each other. So we tried to fence the stones. When they magically returned to us after we had sold them to Fats, he thought we'd pulled a fast one and he hired Modred to track us down, kill us, and get back the stones."

"This is what I do not understand," Makepeace said, frowning. "How would a lowly dealer in stolen goods have access to someone like Morpheus? This Fats person must have been more than just a fence."

"Fats?" said Kira with a snort. "Not in a million years. He was about as low-rent as they come, but he claimed he was connected."

"Ah, connected, yes. That must have been the reason," Jacqueline said. "Someone Morpheus could use as an intermediary. And he doubtless only undertook this contract as a courtesy, *n'est-ce pas*?"

"Something like that, I guess," said Wyrdrune dryly. "You'll excuse me, but somehow I find it a little disconcerting considering my demise as nothing more significant than an exchange of business cards."

Jacqueline chuckled throatily. "The language of business is the same the whole world over," she said. "Only the coin is different. It helps to be flexible, *mon ami,* because sooner or later everyone does business with everyone."

Wyrdrune raised his eyebrows and glanced at Kira. "You know, she reminds me a little of you," he said.

Kira scowled.

"I'd still like to know one thing, though," said Wyrdrune, turning back to Jacqueline. "What makes you so sure Modred is here?"

She shook her head. "I cannot explain it," she said with a sigh. "I just *know* it. You will think me mad when I say that it is no more than a feeling, a powerful intuition that made me bring you here, and yet somehow I am sure that it is much more than that. In my dream I have seen a house. A town house, with a tall, black wrought-iron fence with spikes and black roses—"

"*Black* roses?" Kira said. "Are you sure?"

"It is what I saw," Jacqueline insisted.

"It could be a thaumagenetic hybrid," said Wyrdrune. "The English love their rose gardens."

"They were black, I am certain of it," Jacqueline said emphatically.

"Yes, but a town house with black roses in the garden," Makepeace said, "it really could be anywhere! London, Paris, Rome—"

"It is *here*, I tell you, in London!"

"Yes, but a town house?" Wyrdrune said. "Kira and I saw Modred chained in a dungeon of some sort."

"I saw that as well," said Jacqueline, leaning toward them across the table. "And the town house was not all I saw. In my dream there was also the image of a castle . . ." She frowned, trying to find the words to describe what she saw in her dream. "It was as if I could see the castle *through* the town house once I had passed beyond the gate."

"What did this castle look like?" Makepeace said.

She shrugged. "A castle," she said. "Built of stone, with towers . . . what does a castle look like?" She shook her head. "I am not a student of ancient architecture."

"Would you recognize it if you saw it again?" Make-peace said.

"I think so."

"Then first thing in the morning we'll go to the library and see if we can find a picture of this castle of yours. And in the meantime we can ask around and see if anyone knows of a town house with a garden of black roses."

"Bit of a long shot, isn't it?" said Kira.

"At the moment I can't think of anything else to do," said Makepeace. "Why, have you any other suggestions?"

"Well, not really," she said. "We don't have anything else to go on but these dream messages that we've been getting. But how do we know they're coming from Modred?"

"That's been bothering me all along," said Wyrdrune. "If he can send us these dreams, why hasn't he tried to contact us directly? For all we know, these dream visions we've been getting could be meant to lure us into a trap or to misdirect us."

"I see your point," said Makepeace, "but I repeat my question: "What else have we got to go on?""

"We may not be going about this the right way," said Kira. "All four of us don't need to follow up on what Jacqueline saw in her dream." She glanced from Wyrdrune to Makepeace. "There might be another trail we could follow. Magic always exacts a price, right? Only necromancers like to make sure that somebody else pays it for them. It allows them to accumulate life-force energy to increase their power. If we started looking for a pattern of—"

Wyrdrune smacked himself in the forehead with the palm of his hand. "*Yes*! Of course! The paper!"

"Paper?" said Makepeace. "What paper?"

He smashed his fist down on the table. "*Damn*! I left it back at the hotel! Wait a minute. . . ."

He quickly mumbled a teleportation spell under his breath and disappeared.

"Where has he gone?" Jacqueline said, frowning.

Kira shook her head. "Something in the newspaper? He picked up a copy of the *Times* at the front desk of the hotel. He must have—"

A scream and a crash of dishes announced Wyrdrune's return as he materialized on top of one of the tables next to them. A woman jumped up with a yell, her white wine all over the front of her dress.

*"Albert!"* she wailed.

"Young man, will you kindly keep your bloody hands off my wife's busom?" said the woman's husband, going red in the face.

"I—oh!" Wyrdrune jerked back his hands. "No, wait, you see, I was only wiping..." Without thinking, he wiped her chest again to demonstrate.

*"Albert*! He's doing it *again*!"

"I—what? No! I was only—"

"Right! That does it!" stormed the woman's husband, and he punched Wyrdrune in the jaw.

Wyrdrune staggered backward into a waiter who was carrying a tray with several pitchers of beer on it. The beer went flying, soaking down a tableful of rugby players, one of whom grabbed the hapless waiter and threw him across another table at which a group of tourists from Texas were seated, and they were in a surly mood to begin with. Meanwhile Kira had jumped out of her chair and decked the man who had punched Wyrdrune. He fell back into a table at which some musicians were seated, knocking over their pints and giving them an excellent excuse to start pounding on anyone who was wearing a suit, which happened to include some off-duty policemen. The policemen went after the musicians, the rugby players went after the policemen, and the Texans went after everybody.

Wyrdrune got up off the floor and lurched back to their table, ducking beneath flying furniture and glassware. "You think maybe we should leave?" he said.

"That would seem politic," said Makepeace, turning his

head in time to see a glass pitcher come hurtling at his face. He raised his eyebrows, held up his index finger in an admonitory gesture, and the pitcher froze in midair, about four inches from his face. He pushed himself back from the table, got up, cleared his throat, and said, "Okay." The pitcher resumed its momentum and crashed against the wall.

Wyrdrune gave him a strange look. Kira was busy punching one of the Texans, who couldn't seem to understand that he was supposed to lie down if he was unconscious. Jacqueline flowed gracefully through the donnybrook without so much as losing the ash on her French cigarette. She got only as far as the door, however, before the bobbies came swarming in and turned her around as they swept down upon combatants and innocent bystanders alike, figuring they'd sort the whole mess out after they had saved what little furniture was left. Kira smashed one last hard right into a Texan's face and turned to Wyrdrune, snarling at him through gritted teeth. "Damn it, warlock, when in hell are you ever going to learn?"

She felt a hand on her shoulder, turned quickly, and uncorked one . . . right to the jaw of a sergeant of the Metropolitan Police. He went down like a felled tree.

"Ooops!" she said.

"You were saying?" Wyrdrune said.

Michael Blood turned away from the gory ruin of his brother's body and was sick against the wall. The policemen present averted their eyes. Although the nude body had been savaged abominably, the face had not been touched, and they all knew who it was. One of the plainclothes detectives silently offered the chief inspector his handkerchief.

"Quite all right, Marston," Blood said weakly. "Thank you, I have my own." He wiped his mouth, composing himself with an effort.

It had not been a surprise to him. That would have been

unspeakable. He had been warned that it was his brother, and Marston had tried to dissuade him from looking at the body, though he had known, of course, that it was pointless. Blood was a cop and not just any cop, but chief inspector. Yet nothing, not even seeing five of the Ripper's victims, could have prepared Blood for the sight of his younger brother's corpse.

It looked as if Andrew had been torn apart by a wild animal, but no animal could have carved those . . . *things* into his chest, whatever they were. Macabre designs of some sort, almost like letters in some arcane alphabet. Blood had never seen anything like it. They looked obscene. But they were nothing compared to the hideous manner in which the body had been mutilated. Michael shut his eyes tightly and looked away. He prayed that the *body* had been mutilated, that Andrew still had not been alive when those appalling, horrifying things were done to him. With an effort he made himself glance down at the body once again. A tremor went through him.

"My God," he said softly, his voice barely above a whisper. "Look at his face."

"I know," said Marston. "I can't imagine what he must have seen." He gently took the chief inspector by the arm and turned him away. "Come on, sir, please. *Please.* There's no need for this. We'll take care of it. I'll oversee this personally and give you a complete report, but do please come away now."

He led Blood away, toward the squad cars at the mouth of the alley. Marston reached into his coat pocket and removed a flask. He offered it to Blood.

Blood wiped his mouth and took a slug from it. Good Irish whiskey. He smacked his lips and gasped, then took a deep breath and let it out slowly, handing the flask back to Marston.

"Thanks."

"Have another."

"No, that's all right—"

"Go on now, do you good."

Blood sighed and clapped Marston on the shoulder. "No, it really won't. Here, be a good lad and take it."

Marston took the flask back. Blood took another deep breath and shivered in his coat. "Oh, Andrew," he said. He swallowed hard. "I don't know what I'm going to tell His Lordship."

"You'd best tell your father soon, sir, before the damn reporters get to him," said Marston.

"Hell, you're right. Glad one of us is thinking clearly. Shit. Shit, shit, shit."

"Go on, sir," said Marston. "I'll take care of things here."

"Thanks, Ross," said Blood. He gave Marston a tight-lipped smile and got into his car. "Back to headquarters, McCafferty," he told the driver.

As the police driver levitated the car and pulled away, Blood reached for his notepad and opened it to the sketches he had made of the strange characters carved into his brother's chest. *Andrew's dead, and I'm sketching pictures of what the killer carved into his chest,* he thought bitterly. Sod all. A cop's a cop and a clue's a clue. He wished he had Marston's flask. *Discipline, Michael, discipline,* he told himself. He passed the notepad over the seat to the driver.

"What do you make of these?" he said.

McCafferty was technically a police officer, but actually he was only a graduate student in thaumaturgy who drove for the police while studying for advanced certification. He reached a hand over his shoulder and took the notepad, glancing at it briefly, careful not to lose his concentration on levitation and impulsion spells.

"I don't know," he said, shaking his head. "Runes of some sort, perhaps."

"They mean nothing to you, then?"

"Never seen the like. But then, I'm only a lower-grade adept. You really ought to ask a wizard or a sorcerer."

"Or a mage?" said Blood.

McCafferty gave an abrupt laugh. "Yeah, right. If anyone would know, a mage would. That's if you can find one and if you can manage an appointment. There're only about three of 'em left living."

Blood stared out the car window. "I wonder . . ." he said.

The scene at the Metropolitan Police headquarters at New Scotland Yard on Victoria Street was an absolute madhouse. The police superintendent had assembled a special task force to investigate the Ripper murders (everything the police superintendent did was special, though it was rarely efficient), and though Blood was nominally in charge of this special task force, he did everything in his power to avoid them. Consequently the task of supervising the task force fell by default to Inspector Morris Fitzhugh Harper-Smythe, (or Hyphen-Smythe, as his colleagues in the department habitually referred to him), a man to whom such jobs usually fell because he thrived on them like a rose in horse manure.

Turn Hyphen-Smythe loose with a couple of file clerks and a typist, and before you knew it, the place was awash in confidential memos and eyes-only reports. Give him an entire task force to play with and he could create veritable arabesques of bureaucratic confusion. *Teamwork* was the watchword of the day, as Hyphen-Smythe constantly reminded everyone. There was a team taking calls from psychics who had "seen" the Ripper in various visions and impressions. There was a team searching through the records of every sex offender who had ever opened up a raincoat, and another team searching through past homicide cases to see if any "common threads" could be found. Hyphen-Smythe was obsessed with common threads, as one could see readily by the evidence of his wardrobe. And to help him look for common threads he also had a team of interviewing psychologists and psychiatrists and assorted chat-show experts by the dozens, "assembling a profile" of the killer. Yet another team was actually attempting to draw that profile as everyone who claimed to know someone who knew somebody who had a friend who'd spoken to someone who claimed they "caught a brief glimpse" of the killer was interviewed. Blood's migraine returned the moment he walked in.

The first thing he saw as he came in was a matronly woman in a cloth coat arguing with an Identi-Graph that one of the officers had sat her down with. She was trying to dictate a description of the "suspicious personage" that she had seen, but the Identi-Graph was having none of it. Apparently it had drawn one composite sketch too many and overloaded its thaumaturgically etched circuits, because it seemed intent on drawing whatever it wanted to draw, rather than what the woman told it.

"No, no, *no,* that's not what 'e looked like a-tall!" the woman shrilled nasally. "'E 'ad a mustache!"

"But that's so *passé!*" the Identi-Graph protested. "A mustache with that sort of a hairstyle simply wouldn't do at *all,* luv. Look here, see? It looks *ever* so much better when he's clean-shaven. And look, what say we do a little something with the jawline, hmm? I think it would look absolutely *smashing* if he had one of those lantern jaws with a cleft chin, don't you? I *say,* yes, that's positively Aryan—"

"No, no, no, no, *no!*" shouted the woman, shaking her head vigorously. "That ain't 'im a-tall! That's bloody Lord Nelson!"

"It isn't."

"It *is!*" she insisted.

"Isn't."

"Is!"

"Isn't."

*"Is!"*

"Excuse me," Blood said, picking up the Identi-Graph and tossing it out a nearby open window. It screamed in terror as it fell to shatter on the street below. "We'll get you another one, shall we?" he said, smiling warmly at the woman and desperately hoping that Constable Shavers had some aspirin.

Everywhere he looked, someone was being interviewed either in person or over the phone; reports were being typed up; files were being searched; suspects were being questioned; reporters were being briefed; and computers were angrily upbraiding people for not requesting data properly. The din was incredible. He wondered what the chances were of making it to his office and getting the door closed before somebody spotted him.

Too late. An alert reporter had noticed him coming in and called out his name. Blood winced. Screw this, he thought, and bolted for the door. The woman in the cloth coat grabbed at his sleeve.

"Am I goin' to get another o' them Identi-things?" she whined.

"Yes, immediately! I'm going to get one right now!" Blood said, trying to disengage himself, only who but Hyphen-Smythe himself should come walking in at that very moment, blocking his escape and trailing a small mob behind him.

"Ah, Blood! Just the man I'm looking for!" said Hyphen-Smythe, his square chin lifting, his blue eyes glinting, every hair lying perfectly in place. He was a public-relations dream, handsome, clean-cut, immaculately groomed and impeccably dressed, right down to his old school tie. Everything about him, from his stiff upper lip to his shoot-the-cuffs manner, implied take-charge authority and competence. The fact that it would take another task force just to make any kind of order out of the mountains of paperwork he was generating was entirely incidental. Hyphen-Smythe was going places.

Blood sighed with resignation. "Yes, what is it, Hyph— er, Harper-Smythe?"

"Some witnesses I've brought up for interrogation," Hyphen-Smythe said. "Sent over from Mayfair . . . arrested . . . some sort of row in a pub. . . ."

At that moment the reporters descended upon them.

"Chief Inspector—"

"Any progress on the Ripper case, Chief Inspector?"

"We just heard there's been another victim, is that true?"

"Was this one the same as all the others?"

"We heard you've just come from the crime scene—"

"Who was the latest victim, Chief Inspector?"

"My brother, Andrew," Blood said.

That silenced even the press.

"Good Lord," said Hyphen-Smythe softly.

"For your information, gentlemen, the victim's full name was Andrew Lloyd Blood. He was a twenty-six-year-old stockbroker, son of the eminent merchant banker, Lord Llewellyn Royce Blood. The body was severely mutilated. The direct cause of death was not immediately apparent. An autopsy is pending. At this point we have no evidence—I repeat, *no evidence*—that this latest murder was the work of the Ripper. The modus operandi does not quite appear to match. And that's all the comment I have at this time. You will excuse me. . . ."

He pushed his way past them to his office, passing Danny Shavers on the way.

"I'm so dreadfully sorry, sir," said Shavers, a stricken expression on his face.

"Thank you, Danny," Blood said, clasping him briefly by the shoulder. "No calls for a while, okay? Not unless the bastard's vivisected the P.M. or something. I need some time."

"Certainly, sir."

He opened the door of his office and went in. Billy Slade was seated in his chair, his tatterdemalion leather coat unzipped to reveal a torn black T-shirt, his booted feet up on the desk.

" 'Ey, it's a dam shame about your brother, Mick, but if you want to get the thing what killed 'im, you'll 'ave to do it my way."

Blood gaped at the boy with disbelief, then lashed out

furiously, sweeping his feet off onto the floor. *"Get your damn feet off of my desk! How the hell did you get in here?"*

"Take it easy, Mick. I know you're upset, 'an I don't blame ya, after what's 'appened. . . ."

The door opened and Shavers rushed in. "What's the— *you!"* His eyes widened as he spotted Billy. "How the devil did you get in here? I'm sorry, about this, sir. I can't understand how he could have gotten past me. I'll have him out of here in a—"

Shavers suddenly stumbled forward, shoved from behind as Kira pushed past him into the office. "Look, are you the guy in charge here? Because I'm sick and tired of trying to talk some sense into this asshole Smith—"

*"Smythe,* Harper-Smythe!" said Hyphen-Smythe, hot on her heels. "Really, miss, I must insist that you—"

*"Kira!"* said Billy in a very adult-sounding voice.

"Who the hell are *you*?" she said.

"Kira, for God's sake, you'll get us all locked up," said Wyrdrune, coming up behind her.

"Now see here—" Shavers said.

"Karpinski!" said Billy.

"What?" said Wyrdrune. "Who—"

*"Silence!"* Blood shouted, slamming his fist down on the desk and glaring at them all. "One more sound, and so help me, I'll jail the bloody lot of you and throw away the key!"

"Right," said Hyphen-Smythe. "Now then—"

*"And that includes you, too, Hyphen-Smythe!"* Blood thundered.

The astonished inspector simply gaped at him in disbelief.

"All right," said Blood through gritted teeth, "you"—he pointed at Kira—"sit down!" He pointed to a chair. Kira sat. "You"—he pointed at Wyrdrune—"over there." He indicated another chair. "You, young Slade, stand right over there in the corner where I can see you, and don't you move a muscle, hear me? You"—he pointed at Hyphen-Smythe—"out!"

"But—"

*"Out!"*

With his lips tightly compressed, Hyphen-Smythe drew himself up and stiffly left the office.

"Danny," Blood said, "if *one more person* comes barging into this office—"

"Where the hell *is* everybody?" Makepeace said, sweeping into the room. "What's going on? Are we under arrest or what? This is an outrage! I demand to speak with the American embassy!"

Blood sank down into his chair with a groan and put his head in his hands. "Oh, *sod all*!" he said. He opened the bottom drawer of his desk and took out a bottle of Scotch and a water glass. He filled the glass, kicked back in his chair, put his feet up on the desk, and toasted them all. "Cheers," he said, and tossed back the whole glass.

# CHAPTER SIX

"Very well, let me see if I have all this straight," said Blood, wearily rubbing the bridge of his nose. It was about half an hour later, and the bottle of Scotch was half empty. He glanced at Wyrdrune and consulted his notepad. "Your legal name is Melvin Karpinski, but you go by the magename of Wyrdrune, this despite the fact that you are not certified as an adept."

"There's no law that says I have to be certified as an adept to use a magename," Wyrdrune protested. "I'm free to call myself by any name I choose."

"Indeed you are, but unless you are a certified adept or enrolled in an accredited program of thaumaturgical study, you are *not* free to practice magic. And, according to this arrest report, a number of witnesses saw you use a spell of teleportation. Aside from that, you seem to have no visible means of support, and yet you are staying in the Dorchester, one of the finest hotels in London. And you are wearing what appears to be a rather large emerald, for which I somehow doubt you could produce a purchase receipt. That, coupled with the gem your lady friend with the forged passport is wearing in her hand, leads me to suspect they might be stolen gems."

Wyrdrune gave Kira a painted look. "You *forged* your passport?"

She shrugged. "How the hell was I supposed to get a passport? I don't even have a birth certificate. I didn't figure anyone would check."

"Cosmetic implantation of jewelry is a bit obvious as a smuggling ploy, don't you think?" said Blood dryly. "It's a unique approach, I'll grant you that, but it helps at least to appear to be wealthy if you're going to pull it off. Where did you steal them?"

"Look, Mick, you don't understand," said Billy. "It's not what you think. They didn't—"

"You be quiet, young man, I'll get to you in a moment," Blood said, pointing his index finger at him. Billy fell silent and leaned back against the wall with a sigh, folding his arms petulantly. Blood glanced at Jacqueline. "Mademoiselle Monet."

She smiled at him.

"You, at least, we know something about." He picked up a printout. "From Interpol, no less. It makes for rather interesting reading. Twenty-five arrests for assorted major felonies and not one single conviction. You appear to be a singularly resourceful woman, Miss Monet."

She gave a slight, self-deprecating shrug and lit up another cigarette.

"Which makes me wonder what you're doing in this peculiar company," Blood finished, glancing at the others. He looked at Makepeace.

Makepeace returned his long stare with an amiable smile.

"Dr. Makepeace," said Blood, steepling his fingers, "for a university professor on vacation you seem to have taken up with some rather questionable companions. Aside from having what appears to be a genuine passport and a taste for good whiskey, I don't know a great deal about you, either."

"Allow me to offer you some more of your own excellent Scotch, Chief Inspector," said Makepeace.

"No, I've had quite enough, thank you. My head's muddled enough as it is."

"You don't mind if I . . . ?"

"Oh, help yourself, by all means."

Makepeace refilled his glass.

"Now, I don't know what sort of nonsense you might have told Hyphen—er, Inspector Harper-Smythe—that made him believe you had anything to contribute to this investigation, but I have more than enough to worry about right now without you lot, believe me," Blood said. "I—"

"Can I say somethin' now?" said Billy.

Blood sighed. "Yes, what is it, Slade?"

"Look, what's it gonna take to convince you I'm tellin' you the truth about ol' Merlin?"

"I almost wish you were, Slade," said Blood wearily. "It's going to take a sodding wizard to help me solve this one." He snorted derisively. "I don't suppose you could make yourself disappear? That might convince me."

"There are limits to what I can do with this boy's body," Billy said, his voice suddenly deeper and without a trace of Cockney accent. "He's not fully mature yet, and magic use tires him easily. Just speaking like this is a strain on his vocal cords. I have to allow him to replenish his energies; otherwise I could cause him great harm."

"Well, that's terribly convenient, isn't it?" said Blood with a tight smile. "Honestly, Slade, do you really think that speaking in some sort of comic opera voice is going to—"

"With your permission, Chief Inspector," Wyrdrune said, looking at Billy uneasily. "I studied under Merlin and knew him well. There are things I could ask him that only Merlin Ambrosius would know."

"Oh, why not?" said Blood with an airy gesture of helplessness. "You might as well."

"What were the circumstances of my expulsion from school?" Wyrdrune asked.

"A fire spell you were using as part of a special-effects display for some rock band went out of control and you burned down the concert hall," said Merlin. "You always did overreach yourself, Karpinski."

Wyrdrune's eyes grew wide, and he exchanged shocked glances with Kira. He swallowed hard. "What . . . what was your father's name?" he asked softly.

Billy chuckled. "Gorlois, may he roast, the last surviving member of the Council of the White. I helped Uther kill the bastard."

"My God," said Wyrdrune. "It *is* Merlin!"

Blood sat up in his chair. "*What*? Oh, come *on*! What sort of idiot do you take me for?"

"There's no other way he could have known those things," said Wyrdrune.

"He might have read about them somewhere," Blood said, though he sounded uncertain.

Wyrdrune shook his head. "No. That concert fire made the papers, but I doubt if it would've made the news over here. It might have, but it was five years ago, and in any case, the stories never mentioned my name. And there's no record anywhere of who Merlin's father was. That means he couldn't have read it anywhere."

Blood glanced from Wyrdrune to Billy and back again. "It also means there's no way to check your story. How do I know you haven't cooked this up between you?"

"You know we've never seen each other before," said Wyrdrune.

"On the contrary," said Blood. "I don't know that at all."

"'Ey, I'm gettin' sick an' tired o' this," said Billy, suddenly speaking in his normal voice. "Do somethin' an' show 'em!"

"*I don't want to overtax you, lad,*" said Merlin, though only Billy "heard" him.

"I don't bloody care! 'Ow else can we convince 'im?"

*"I'm sure there are easier ways to—"*

"Look, just do somethin', all right?"

*"Very well,"* said Merlin. *"But don't say I didn't warn you."*

Everything on Blood's desk suddenly floated up into the air.

"What the devil—" Blood snatched at his papers, but they seemed to dance out of his reach. Pens and pencils rose into the air, his wooden in and out trays, his appointment calendar, his paperweight, the bottle of Scotch— Makepeace barely managed to snatch his glass in time— then everything started spinning end over end in midair. Blood's file drawers opened as if of their own accord and Blood yelped in helpless protest as their contents came sailing out, as if all gravity had been leeched out of the room. Then the chairs floated up into the air, turning as they rose, and Blood held on tightly to the sides of his chair as it slowly spun around.

*"Stop it!"* he shouted. "Stop it, I said! Put me *down*!"

The door opened and Shavers came in. "What's the— *good God*!"

The chairs came crashing down, the files floated back into the drawers, the papers went back into the trays, everything quickly and smoothly went right back to where it was supposed to be, as if nothing had ever disturbed it in the first place. Shavers stood in the doorway, staring at them slack-jawed.

"It's all right, Danny," Blood said.

"But—"

"It's all right. Don't worry. I'll explain later."

"If you say so, sir." Shavers backed out uncertainly and gingerly closed the door behind him.

Blood turned to Wyrdrune with a wry grimace. "That was you, wasn't it?"

Wyrdrune shook his head.

"Come on, don't hand me that," said Blood impatiently. "That was all your doing. You've all cooked this up together, haven't you? I don't understand, what are you up to?"

"You just don't want to believe it, do you?" Wyrdrune said. "How were we supposed to know in advance that we'd be brought here for questioning? How would Billy have known where we'd be and when?"

"You could have influenced things somehow," Blood said, as if trying to convince himself. "How difficult would that be for a wizard who studied under Merlin?"

"But I'm not a certified wizard," Wyrdrune protested. "You said so yourself. I didn't even finish school."

"You may not be certified by the Bureau of Thaumaturgy, young man, but you're a wizard, just the same," said Blood. "I'm no expert, but I know enough to know that teleportation isn't exactly the sort of spell your average undergraduate could master. Now, I don't know what sort of game you're all playing here, but frankly I haven't got the time for it."

"It's *not* a game!" said Kira in exasperation. "Will you *listen,* for God's sake?"

"Forget it," Billy said, looking tired. "We're just wastin' our time 'ere."

He spread his arms out in an encompassing gesture and they all vanished from the office.

They reappeared in the penthouse of the abandoned apartment building where Merlin had established his residence. One look around and any remaining doubts that Wyrdrune and Kira might have had were banished instantly.

"Your library!" said Wyrdrune, seeing all the ancient, leather-bound books arranged in meticulous order on the shelves. "You managed to save it from the fire!"

"Most of the thaumaturgic arcana, anyway," said Merlin. "But a lot of the other books were destroyed. All the Simon Brett novels, the P. D. James, the entire Flashman series by Fraser—all gone. An agonizing loss. Absolutely irreplaceable."

He suddenly collapsed with a groan.

"Professor!" Wyrdrune said, running to his side.

"Damn fool kid!" said Merlin weakly. "I warned him about this, but would he listen? What *is* it with you young people? Why don't you ever listen? You think everyone over the age of thirty is senile?"

"Help me with him," Wyrdrune said. Kira took his legs while Wyrdrune took his shoulders. They carried him over to the couch and gently laid him down.

"What the devil?" Blood said, utterly bewildered. "Where am I?" No one paid any attention to him.

"Are you going to be all right?" said Kira. "Is there anything that we can do?"

"Oh, I'm sure I'll be fine," said Merlin, breathing heavily. "Billy simply doesn't understand about the demands that thaumaturgy places on your life energies. He has no patience whatsoever. He reminds me a bit of you, Karpinski. He still thinks there's such a thing as a free lunch." Merlin chuckled. "He thinks magic works like magic."

"Very funny," Wyrdrune said. "You look terrible. Are you sure you're going to be all right?"

"Oh, I'll live," said Merlin. "I'm just worn-out, that's all. It's nothing forty-eight hours of sleep won't cure, but I'm afraid I don't have that luxury. Billy's on the verge of slipping into a coma. My will is the only thing keeping him out of it at the moment. I'm rather tired, but I'm going to have to stay awake; otherwise he may drag me right down with him."

"What do you want us to do?" said Kira with concern.

"Well, some strong black coffee would certainly be welcome," Merlin said, sounding remarkably blasé about it all. "There's some in the kitchen. And keep me talking, to make sure I don't nod off. That could be hazardous at this point, at least until Billy's passed the crisis."

Kira went into the kitchen to make some coffee for them all.

Blood was at the large bay window, looking out. "Are we in Whitechapel?" he said in a bewildered tone. "Where the hell are we?"

"Here, son, have a drink," said Makepeace, handing Blood his own half-empty bottle of Scotch, which he had managed to snatch just before they were teleported from Blood's office.

"How did this happen?" Wyrdrune asked Merlin. "How did you wind up . . . like this? We saw you die!"

"Good question," Merlin said. "I puzzled over that one for quite a while myself, until it occurred to me to search through Billy's unconscious racial memory. Not an easy thing to do, by the way. And there were some truly ugly things in there. Small wonder he turned out the way he did. He's basically a good-hearted kid, but boy, does he have rotten genes." Merlin sighed. "He's descended from me, God help the poor little bastard."

"From *you*?" said Wyrdrune. "But I thought you never had any children!"

"So did I," said Merlin. "However, after that little witch Nimue took advantage of my midlife crisis, it seems she became pregnant with my child. Billy is the last link in a long chain of miscreants that stretches back throughout the ages, featuring such dubious luminaries as Michel de Nostre-Dame, who was better known as Nostradamus, and that old reprobate, Giuseppe Balsamo, alias Count Alessandro di Cagliostro. And there were some other notable offshoots of the family tree that would best go unmentioned. Billy is apparently the last one left, my only living descendant. The lad may not be much, but it seems he's all I've got."

"So you became reincarnated as your own lineal discendant!" Wyrdrune said.

"My spirit still had work to do," said Merlin. "And I suppose it gravitated to the only body whose genetic makeup would provide the necessary compatability. An ordinary human body simply wouldn't do, you see. I needed a body that was extraordinary." He cast a disapproving glance down at Billy's fringed leather patchwork wardrobe. "Although this is rather stretching the point a bit."

"So is calling your resurgence a reincarnation, if you ask me," said Makepeace. "If that's what you believe, then you're just bullshitting yourself."

"What do you mean?" said Merlin. "What the devil are you talking about?"

"I mean that you're just playing at semantics, Ambrosius," Makepeace said. "Reincarnation, properly speaking, means to be reborn in another body. But you were not *born* in this body; Billy Slade was. His is not an old soul that was you in a previous life. He clearly has his own separate identity. Your spirit only recently arrived and settled in his body. That's not reincarnation, my friend. That's possession."

"Now just . . . one . . . moment," Merlin said, sitting up with an effort. "Are you actually implying that I'm a *demon* of some sort?"

"I'm implying nothing of the kind," said Makepeace. "What I'm saying is that you were never reincarnated into Billy's body because, in a manner of speaking, you never really died."

"*What?*" Wyrdrune and Merlin said simultaneously. Kira and Jacqueline listened with fascination. Blood stared at them all, completely out of his depth, then he just sighed, shook his head, and sank down into an armchair with his Scotch.

"Naturally I wasn't there when your so-called 'death' occurred," said Makepeace, "but I can make an educated guess about what must have happened. At the moment when you realized that your death was imminent and that there was absolutely nothing you could do about it, you were still unable to accept it. Your very soul screamed its denial. Now, faced with imminent death, most ordinary men would simply resign themselves to the inevitable, but you were no ordinary man, Ambrosius. You never were. You saw yourself hurtling down to your death, and rather than accept the unacceptable, you *flung* yourself away from your doomed body and your astral self flew out into the ether. And when you found, as you put it so appropriately, a body whose genetic makeup provided the necessary compatability, you simply moved in, like the proverbial cowbird muscling in on a sparrow's nest."

"No," said Merlin. "No, it can't be. If that were true, then that would indeed be . . ." his voice trailed off.

"Admit it, Ambrosius," said Makepeace. "You possessed the boy."

"If what you say is true," said Merlin slowly, "then it would answer many questions, such as why I don't remember dying, or why I have no memory of anything that's happened between my so-called 'death' and my awakening in Billy."

"You must have blanked it out subconsciously," said Makepeace. "Part of you, your physical self, had actually died, though you had removed your spiritual self from that event via an out-of-body experience. So, in one sense, you died . . . and in another sense you didn't. You broke the rules, Ambrosius. In effect, you became a ghost, trapped between this world and the next. Until your astral self was drawn to Billy.

"Anyway," Makepeace continued, "it seems to me that the important thing is how Billy feels about it. If he doesn't want you in there, then ethically you're on pretty shaky ground. In that case, if you want to be really moral about it, I suppose you'll have to vacate. But that doesn't seem like a very practical solution, does it?"

"Not really, no," said Merlin. He blinked rapidly several times. Then he took a deep breath and moaned.

"What is it?" Wyrdrune said.

"The kid's starting to come out of it," said Merlin. "I have to give him credit—he's a tough little lad. A real fighter. It infuriates him, having to relinquish control to me. He keeps resisting."

"Can you blame him?" Makepeace said.

"No, I suppose I can't," said Merlin. "He's a good lad. He doesn't really mind my being along for the ride, he just hates to let me drive. I suppose I'll have to work things out with him as best I can. Anyway, the important thing is that you're all here. I could certainly use your help."

He turned to Wyrdrune. "You were drawn here by the runestones, weren't you? You sensed the Dark Ones' presence?"

"Well, not exactly," Wyrdrune said.

"What do you mean, not exactly? What brought you here?"

"Modred's been taken," Kira said.

*"Taken?"* Merlin started to sit up, but Billy's body was still too weak, and he collapsed back down on the coach. "What do you mean, *taken?* How?"

Briefly Wyrdrune related to him the story of their shared dreams and what they had discovered since they had arrived in London.

"I have a strong feeling that these Ripper killings are related to Modred's disappearance," he finished. "I think the Dark Ones are here, in London. Or at least one of them is."

"I believe you're right," said Merlin. "The Ripper killings are tied into it. What's more, they're only the beginning. Necromancy. The gathering of thaumaturgic energy through death. I can sense it. I've been trying to get Chief Inspector Blood here to work with me, but he simply refuses to believe me, and Billy doesn't make things any easier. He keeps insisting on taking over at the most inopportune moments, addressing Blood in that flippant manner of his. To say that the boy is socially awkward would be the understatement of the year. One simply doesn't refer to an Irish policeman as 'Mick,' even if his first name *is* Michael."

"I give up," said Blood, starting to slur his words. "This is all some sort of alcoholic nightmare."

"Have another drink," said Makepeace.

The bottle of Scotch was almost empty. Looking a little ropy, Blood tipped the bottle back and took a big, hearty slug from it. The level of the amber-colored fluid slowly rose back up until the bottle was completely full again. Blood stared at it, dumbfounded.

Wyrdrune gave Makepeace a strange look. "What are you doing?" he said.

"Oh, the poor guy's had a real hard day," said Makepeace. "He needs to get a little shitfaced. Bottoms up, kiddo," he said to Blood, and the chief inspector obligingly took another long pull at the bottle.

Merlin frowned, watching Blood chug the Scotch down as if it were water. "Does that man realize what he's doing?"

Makepeace grinned. "Not really, no."

Kira passed her hand in front of Blood's face several times. He was oblivious. "Wow," she said.

As if in slow motion, Blood started to lean forward, stiff as a board. As he toppled to the floor Makepeace stretched his arm out and made a grasping motion with his right hand. Blood's momentum stopped, and he froze, floating motionlessly about three inches above the floor.

"Bedroom?" said Makepeace, raising his shaggy eyebrows.

"That one," Merlin said, pointing at a door.

Makepeace wagged his index finger, and Blood, stiff as a carp, rose up until he was about three feet off the floor. Then, as Makepeace slowly moved his arm in a sweeping gesture, guiding him, Blood floated toward the bedroom. Jacqueline opened the door and stood aside to allow the policeman's body to pass through, then slowly settle down onto the bed. The door closed by itself behind him.

Merlin glanced at Wyrdrune and grunted. "Maybe he really *is* a fairy," he said.

"And maybe he's just a neurotic sorcerer who thinks he's Aiken Drum, the Brownie," Wyrdrune mumbled under his breath so that only Merlin could hear. He leaned closer and lowered his voice even more. "There's really no such thing as fairies, is there?"

"'Ow the bloody 'ell should I know?" Billy replied, pushing himself up off the couch with an effort. "Gor', the ole geezer nearly done me in!"

"Billy!" Kira said. "You're all right!"

"'Course I'm all right, luv. 'S that fresh coffee I smell?"

"Yes, but should you be drinking coffee?" she said anxiously. "Merlin said you were almost in a coma!"

"Black, please, wi' three lumps," said Billy. "Lovely bird you got there, mate," he said in an aside to Wyrdrune. "'As she got a younger sister?"

"'Fraid not," said Wyrdrune.

"Ah, well, that's 'ow it goes," said Billy. "'Ere, Sebastian, where's that Scotch ol' Mick was drinkin'? Go well in the coffee."

"It would, indeed," said Makepeace, "but you're not getting any."

*"Why not?"*

"Because you're not old enough to drink, that's why."

"What about Merlin? Don't he count for nothin'? 'E's several thousand years old, or so 'e says."

"That may well be," said Makepeace, "but he's in a body that's only about twelve years old."

"Thirteen," said Billy sourly.

"I stand corrected. In any case, that's entirely too young a liver to handle an aged single malt. You shouldn't even be drinking coffee."

"'Ey now, look, I need a proper pick-me-up after what I've just been through. 'Sides, this is *my* place, you know."

"It isn't, either," Makepeace said. "Ambrosius arranged all this, not you. Still, your point's well taken. I'll allow you a tiny drop in your coffee and no more. What the hell, with Ambrosius stuck inside you, you probably need a good stiff drink."

"That's the ticket," Billy said, holding out his coffee cup while Makepeace poured a small dash of Scotch into it.

Something brushed against Wyrdrune's leg. He looked down and saw a boxy little computer come waddling past, heading toward the couch where Billy sat.

"I beg your pardon," said Archimedes as Wyrdrune scooted back his chair in surprise.

*"Archimedes?"* he said.

The computer halted, turned awkwardly, and leaned back slightly, angling its screen up so it could scan him. "Wyrdrune, isn't it? Karpinski, Melvin. I recall your file."

"Archimedes, it *is* you!" Wyrdrune said.

"Yes. Nice to see you again," said the computer. It turned to Billy. "Look, I don't mean to be a pest, especially with your having guests in, but I've been waiting and waiting. You promised me . . ."

"Yeah, yeah, right," said Billy, still feeling a bit groggy. He reached into the large inside pocket of his leather coat and pulling out a thin, rectangular box. " 'Ere, this what you 'ad in mind?"

"My modem!" The little computer actually jumped with joy. It wasn't much of a jump, only about two inches off the floor, but it was a joyful reaction just the same. "Can I see it, can I have it now, please? Give it to me!"

"Now 'ow the 'ell am I supposed to give it to you?" Billy said. "You ain't got no bloody *'ands,* you silly twit."

"You help me with it," Archimedes said anxiously. "You can hook it up."

" 'Ey, I don't know nothin' 'bout computers, mate," said Billy. "I don't even know what the 'ell that gizmo is. I looked for what you told me to, but I 'ad to nick it quick like, so I just 'ope it's the right one."

"Maybe I can be of some assistance," Jacqueline said.

"Give 'er a go, luv," Billy said, tossing her the box.

She caught it and examined the label. "Ah, yes. This

should do nicely." She knelt down and showed the box to Archimedes. "Come on, *mon petit,* we shall tune your new peripheral for remote broadcast compatability, *oui*?"

The computer waddled over to her with the air of a small child anxious to receive a brand-new toy. Jacqueline picked it up and set it down upon the desk, where it watched anxiously as she unpacked the radio modem and the thaumaturgically charged power pack.

"Well, what happens now?" said Kira. She jerked her head toward the bedroom. "What are we going to do with Sleeping Beauty in there?"

"He'll come around in the morning," Makepeace said. "Then we'll see if we can't convince him to cooperate with us."

"I'd settle for convincing him not to put us in jail and throw away the key," said Wyrdrune. "How do you think he's going to feel about being kidnapped and magically induced to drink himself into a stupor?"

"Yes, well, I think he may listen to reason," Makepeace said. "Nothing like a hangover to make one more receptive. After all, we did try our best to explain things to him, and he simply wasn't listening, so something had to be done."

"Wouldn't we be better off looking for Modred on our own?" said Kira. "If we get the police involved, we're only going to have problems."

"They can probably save us a great deal of work," said Merlin, causing Wyrdrune, sitting right across from him, to do a double take. It was hard to get used to the way that Merlin and Billy kept switching personalities back and forth without any warning.

"Maybe," Kira said. "but assuming that we could even get them to believe us about the Dark Ones, they'd immediately want to notify the B.O.T. and turn it over to their agents. And when you have that many people who know about it, there's no way you'll be able to keep it from the public. They'll panic. They'll suspect every magic user they see of being a necromancer.

"Besides," she continued, "we can't afford to have anyone check us out too closely. After you died, Professor . . ." She paused, shaking her head. "Man, that sounds weird! Well, let's put it this way, since the last time we saw you, Modred got some of his people to cut a deal with the Annendale Corporation and Boston Mutual. He paid them off to drop the charges against us. The United Semitic Republics were so happy to get rid of Al'Hassan that they went along and dropped all charges too. But that simply means that there aren't any outstanding warrants against us. We're no longer wanted for stealing the runestones, but we're not quite home free, not by a long shot.

"The N.Y.P.D. and the Boston Police still have files on us," she explained, "and by now so does the B.O.T. I'll bet the Bureau is just dying to bring us in for questioning. Morgana was one of their agents, remember? And so far as the Bureau knows, she simply disappeared while working on our case. We know she died, and we know how it happened, but we can't explain it to the Bureau without telling them about the Dark Ones, or that Agent Fay Morgan was actually an immortal sorceress named Morgan Le Fay. And that means we can't talk to the Bureau at all, which means we can't talk to the police." She jerked a thumb at the bedroom door. "Chief Inspector Blood has just become a liability. If you want my advice, I'd give him a good case of amnesia and send him home."

"I can see your point," said Merlin, "but I'm not convinced that it would be the wisest choice. I still think we'd be better off having the police working with us rather than against us. Even if they did refer this case to the Bureau of Thaumaturgy—something I was hoping to avoid, though arguments can be made in favor of it—I am not without some influence there, after all—" His voice cracked, just like a young boy's changing voice has a tendency to crack. For a moment he sounded like Billy once again, only without the Cockney accent. He cleared his throat several times and continued. "Anyway, I'm sure I could explain to them about Morgana and how she was killed by Al'Hassan."

"And you could explain about who killed Al'Hassan?" said Kira. "And who clouded the mind of the New York police detective who was in charge of the case? And who paid off Boston Mutual and the Annendale Corporation and arranged for the U.S.R. to drop all charges? And where all that money came from?"

Merlin took a deep breath and slowly let it out. "Yes, I see the problem. The Bureau of Thaumaturgy cannot very well afford to overlook thaumaturgic felonies."

"Or the fact that our partner, the man we're trying to rescue, is otherwise known as Morpheus, possibly the most wanted criminal in the entire world," said Kira.

"Yes," Merlin said with a sigh, "Modred always was difficult. You're quite right. I had hoped to persuade the authorities to help us without actually having to tell them everything, but I see now that that will be impossible. I could probably deceive the police without much trouble, but I could not deceive the Bureau. They are all sorcerers, and I taught every one of them. They might not guess the truth, but they'd know enough to look for it."

"That still leaves us with one more option," Makepeace said. "Sort of a compromise solution."

"What do you mean?" said Wyrdrune.

"We prevail upon our friend Michael to help us without telling anyone else about it. Put him under a spell."

"Could you do that?" Kira said. She glanced from Makepeace to Wyrdrune. "I mean, could you guys compel him?"

"That sort of thing's beyond my level," Wyrdrune told her. "It takes a full-fledged sorcerer, and at best I'm an unofficial lower-level wizard."

"Good Lord, Karpinski," Merlin said, "I never thought I'd live to hear you admit that you had limitations!"

"You didn't," Wyrdrune replied wryly.

"Ha, ha, guess 'e told you, 'ey, old man?" said Billy.

"D-don't call me 'old man'!" said Merlin, his voice cracking once again.

Wyrdrune and Kira exchanged glances. It was unsettling, watching two people in the same body arguing among themselves.

"The point is, Merlin could do it, and I could too," said Makepeace. "I would prefer having Blood's voluntary cooperation, but if he refuses, well, he can be persuaded, so to speak."

"I don't like it," Wyrdrune said. "It's wrong."

"I agree," said Merlin. "And there is also the fact that a man under a spell of compulsion, especially a spell that compels him to act in a manner radically opposed to his basic nature, is not functioning at one hundred percent capacity. His reasoning becomes impaired, his reactions are slowed down, he tends to hesitate. In a policeman such a state would render him physically vulnerable. It's not quite the same as making a man who already likes to drink get drunk. A spell of compulsion could easily get him killed. I couldn't justify it."

"Yeah, it would make us no different from the necromancers," Wyrdrune said.

"Okay, forget I mentioned it," said Makepeace. "We'll just have to use reason to persuade him. And if that doesn't work, we'll cloud his mind about what happened during the past few hours, teleport him out of here, and do our best to keep out of his way. In the meantime, as soon as Jacqueline gets Archimedes all set up with that modem, we can try a little creative hacking. We can locate the appropriate public records office, break into their files, and see if can find out anything about recent real-estate transactions."

"Real-estate transactions?" Wyrdrune said, puzzled.

"You did say you dreamed that Modred was being held prisoner in a dungeon?" Makepeace said. "Maybe somebody bought a castle lately."

* * *

Every day after work, Roger Harris hit the pubs, prowling for secretaries or salesgirls, always approaching them aggressively on the theory that it would be more difficult to say no to a man who came on strong and forcefully. He also came on strong and forcefully in the office, at the watercooler, in the company cafeteria, in the corridors of the building where he worked, and even in the supermarket, where he was not above crashing his cart into a likely prospect, just so he could apologize and "break the ice." He believed in occasionally varying his approach and in working volume on the principle that if you got turned down nine times out of ten, the tenth time made it all worthwhile.

He had it all down to a science. He had an entire library of books on how to pick up girls, how to talk to single women, how to find a woman's G-spot, how to conduct affairs with married women, how to make love to the modern woman, and how to make your shyness work for you. (This last area was not really a problem for Roger, but the book was rather more Machiavellian than its title indicated, concentrating on the right way to act shy in order to arouse women's maternal instincts). He also made it a habit to read women's magazines, which always had articles in them telling their readers how to find the right sort of man. Roger studied these articles carefully and tried to act like that sort of man. Besides, he thought that being able to converse on topics written about in women's magazines made him seem quite progressive and free.

He spent tons of money on clothes, hairstyling, jewelry, and after-shave, worked out hard to keep himself in shape, and often answered personal advertisements in the papers, as well as placing them, usually beginning with the line, "Attractive, successful single male, uncomfortable in pubs . . ." The fact that Roger often achieved success in his endeavors with young women said less about him or the validity of his approach than it did about the desperate loneliness of many young women living in a crowded city.

Still, there was one type of woman Roger had yet to "make it with," as he would put it, and that was the sort of woman who appeared on the covers of the women's magazines (and sometimes the same models would appear in the centerfolds of male magazines as well.) She was the drop-dead-gorgeous sort of women, like young television actresses or the models in the shampoo and makeup ads. Occasionally Roger would encounter such women in his forays through the pubs, but women who looked like that encountered lots of Rogers, and as a result they had no difficulty saying no.

Except for this one.

This one had been alone, sitting in the corner of the bar, drinking by herself. She was the most beautiful women he had ever seen. She had met his gaze for just a second when he had made eye contact with her, then she shyly dropped her gaze, raising it again a moment later to see if he was still looking at her, then immediately dropping it again with a shy smile. Roger's heart had skipped a beat.

He had sauntered over to her casually and said hello, asked if the seat next to hers was taken. No, it wasn't. Was she waiting for someone? She was, but it appeared that she had been stood up. No! What sort of madman would stand up a woman like her? She smiled shyly and thanked him for the compliment. He asked if he could buy her a drink. She nodded, and it had progressed rapidly from there, with Roger boldly taking the initiative. They had gone back to his apartment "for a nightcap," and it wasn't long before they were in a tight clinch on the couch, tearing at each other's clothes. Moments later they were in the bedroom.

Roger lay upon his back, looking up with awe at the sheer perfection of her naked body, at the jet-black hair cascading down her shoulders, framing that astonishingly lovely face, at the dusky look in her eyes and the lightly

parted lips, at the way her chest rose and fell as she
breathed heavily, and he could not believe his luck.

"God, this is the greatest night of my life," he said.

Terri smiled. "It's also the last night of your life," she
said, and then she growled and started sprouting fangs.

Roger screamed.

# CHAPTER SEVEN

It was a door that she was never meant to open. He had forbidden it expressly. And so, of course, she opened it the very first chance she had. It opened onto what appeared to be a perfectly ordinary basement staircase. She tried the light switch. A torch set in an iron wall sconce erupted into flame.

Terri pulled back, startled. The flaming torch illuminated a stone stairway that only a moment ago she could have sworn was wood. The wall was not plaster or brick but huge stone blocks, cold and damp. She reached out for the torch, and as her hand passed through the doorway she felt a strange sensation, almost as if she had plunged it into ice-cold water. She jerked her hand back and looked at it, but aside from a brief tingling sensation, it seemed fine. She reached out again, farther this time, and the eerie sensation returned. It felt like bracing cold water going up her arm. She swallowed nervously, took a deep breath, and stepped through the doorway, down onto the first stone step.

It was just like diving into a deep mountain lake, except without the splash or any sensation of wetness. The feeling was there only for a brief instant, and she gasped, then just as suddenly, it was gone and she stood on the top step of the basement stairs, feeling no different than she had a moment earlier, only it was slightly cooler... and she wasn't on the top step of the basement.

She stood on a landing, with stone stairs leading down directly before her and up directly to her left. Behind her, where the door to the basement should have been, was a solid wall of huge, rough-hewn stone blocks. She reached out to the wall on her right and took the torch down out of its iron sconce, shaped like a gargoyle's head. Below it hung a large ring of iron keys. She took those also. She hesitated, then started down.

The torchlight threw her shadow on the wall as she descended. It was the shadow of a wolf. There were rats down there—she could hear hundreds of them—but as aggressive as they were, they fled at her approach, almost as if they sensed something different about her. She got down to the bottom of the stairs and found herself in a narrow stone corridor with a low ceiling. The top of her head just brushed it. The air was damp and musty. The dust lay thick upon the floor, but to the right it had been disturbed. She could see a trail of footprints and long streaks, as if something heavy had been dragged along the floor.

As she walked slowly down the corridor, ducking under cobwebs, she passed a number of low, heavy wooden doors reinforced with iron. There was a small wooden shutter in the upper portion of each door that could be drawn back, revealing a barred window looking through into a cell. So she was in a dungeon! The thought excited her. She was discovering new things about her lover.

She knew he was a powerful sorcerer, perhaps even a mage, and because of what he'd done to her, she knew he practiced necromancy. That made him even more exciting. Terri didn't know a great deal about thaumaturgy, and she knew even less about its history. For that matter, there was no historical record of the existence of the Dark Ones, necromancers belonging to a race separate from humans. All Terri knew was that necromancy was black magic and that black magic was forbidden, a felony punishable by death. And that was the most exciting thing of all.

Terri had never killed a man before she had been changed. Andrew Blood had been her first. Roger Harris was the second. And she was eagerly looking forward to her third. She never would have believed that of herself, that she was capable of murder. Capable of destroying men, yes, but certainly not in the literal sense. Yet she had found it thrilling, more thrilling than anything she had ever done before. It was as if she had discovered some long-buried predatory instinct that made her long to kill. Had he done that to her? Or had he simply recognized it in her and brought it out into the open?

She couldn't remember much of what she had done to Andrew Blood. She perceived it all through a haze, a thick, red mist of gore. She remembered everything up to the moment she'd attacked him with an astonishing, hard-edged clarity, and then it was all a fog. She remembered the surge of anticipation, the sexual thrill unlike anything she'd ever experienced before. She had never, ever, found satisfaction with a man until the night he changed her, but this was different . . . even better. This was the slaking of a thirst she'd never known she had, though now she realized that it had always been there, hidden deep beneath the surface, driving her. Later she had experienced a sated, languid, dreamy aftermath, and she knew that she had finally found herself. She had been born to be a werewolf.

And now, like the creature of the night she had become, she stalked through the musty corridors of the dungeon, following the trail in the dust, anxious to learn the secret that he kept from her. She wondered if this was the secret that would give her power over him. The thought made the hairs on the back of her neck rise. He would be the ultimate challenge. But she could never let him guess what she was thinking, never, until the time came when she was ready for him. And that time would come. Sooner or later she would find his weakness. After all, she always did. He was only a man. Wasn't he?"

She came to a heavy door at the end of the corridor. The trail in the dust stopped here. She set the torch into a wall sconce beside the door and tried the keys in the ancient lock. One of them finally turned the bolt, and she swung open the door, leaning against it with her shoulder. It opened with a loud, protracted creaking sound. She took down the torch and went through into the cell on the other side.

It was larger than she had expected. It looked as if it had been built to hold a large number of prisoners. Where she stood, just inside the door, was a sort of elevated platform, like a landing, with stairs leading down to the floor of the cell off to her right. The floor was about twenty feet below her. She imagined that prisoners had once been brought here in chains and thrown down off the landing to the floor below. She held the torch up higher, and it was with a thrill that she noticed a body hanging manacled to the far wall. When that body moaned, she almost dropped her torch.

She hurried down the stairs to the floor of the cell and ran over to where the man hung manacled to the wall. She held the torch up, so that she could see him better.

His unkempt hair was a dusty blond, as was his beard. He had handsome, classically Saxon features, and he appeared to be in his late thirties or early forties. His chest was bare and well muscled. He couldn't have been hanging there for very long, she thought, or he would have been dead by now. At the very least, the ravages would have shown on his emaciated body. As it was, he appeared severely dehydrated. His eyes were deeply sunken and his breathing was shallow. He smelled terrible. And there was a jewel set into his chest, directly over his heart. A dark blood-red ruby. Her eyes gleamed at the sight of it.

"Wa . . . ter . . ." he said in a voice barely above a whisper.

She shook her head. She had none to give him. And then

she heard the dripping sound. She went over to where a trickle of water was seeping down through a fissure in the wall, and pressed her scarf into it, dabbing at the damp wall until the scarf was wet. Then she went back to his side, stood up on tiptoe, and stretched out the wet scarf. She could just barely reach his mouth. She pressed the scarf against his lips, and he nuzzled at it weakly. She couldn't take her eyes off the jewel in his chest.

"Who are you?" she said.

He did not respond. He was having a hard time swallowing. His eyelids twitched, as if they were too heavy for him to open. His tongue came out to lick the drops of moisture off his lips. She repeated the process with the wet scarf.

"Easy, take it easy," she said, dabbing at his lips with the scarf. "Why are you chained up down here?"

"Help . . . me . . ."

"Why is he hiding you down here?" she persisted. "Who are you? What's this all about?"

"Help . . ."

"Yes, that's right, I'll help you. But first you've got to tell me who you are and why he's done this. What's this? With her forefinger she lightly traced an outline on the skin of his chest around the ruby. "That's a real ruby, isn't it? It must be worth a fortune. Why didn't he take this off you?"

She touched it lightly and stiffened with a jerk. It felt as if a small charge of electricity had passed through her, up her finger and into her arm, through her chest and . . . no, *down* her arm and through her finger, into . . . She recoiled and backed away from him, feeling alarmed and slightly light-headed. The jewel set into his chest started to emit a soft glow.

"You're just like him, aren't you?" she said softly. "You've got the power too."

As she watched, his breathing became more regular. His skin tone improved. He was becoming stronger, recovering right before her eyes. She put her hand up to her chest. She felt weak and dizzy. And suddenly she realized what he had done. He had drawn off some of her strength, absorbed a portion of her life energy. And he was feeding on it, using it to revitalize himself.

As she watched, stunned, he inhaled deeply, exhaled in a sigh, then opened his eyes and looked directly at her.

"Who are you?" he said in a strong, clear voice.

She shook her head and backed away toward the stairs leading to the door of the cell.

"No, wait, come back!"

She turned and fled the dungeon.

Stephie Baker shivered in her short, unbuttoned coat as she slowly sashayed down the street in what she hoped was an irresistibly provocative manner. She was wearing an extremely short dress and high heels, showing off more of her attractive legs than she had ever done before, except at the health club. She was cold, and for the past two hours she'd been thinking that this had been a truly stupid idea.

She had never done any sort of undercover work before, and when she was approached about acting as a police decoy to trap the Ripper, she had thought that it would be an exciting assignment and possibly an opportunity to advance in the force. She was a lower-grade police administrator, which essentially translated as clerk-typist, and this assignment held forth the promise of real investigative police work out on the streets, where it was all happening.

The decoy squad had been the brainchild of Inspector Harper-Smythe, who was directing the special task force. Each police decoy would be dressed up to look like a prostitute and sent out to work the streets of Whitechapel with a backup team of two armed police officers dressed in civilian clothing who would watch the decoy at all times and move in at the least sign of trouble. The decoy would be equipped with a tiny wireless transmitter, so that she could keep in constant touch with her backup team. It all seemed fairly safe to Stephie. She would be in sight of her backup at all times, and if she perceived the slightest threat, she could call for help and they would respond immediately. If the Ripper was to attack her, they could shoot him down at once. She realized there was some risk, but it seemed reasonable in light of the way that the setup was explained to her. However, now that she was actually out on the streets of Whitechapel, she wasn't all that certain anymore.

It was dark, and a heavy mist had descended on the streets. Visibility was very poor. The thought that somewhere out there, at that very moment, fifteen other female officers were in exactly the same straits did little to dispel her gloom and apprehension.

At first, dressing up in her "hooker rig," as Officers Stuart Canfield and Bill Turner called it, seemed like a bit of silly fun. They had been assigned as her backup team, and she knew them both quite well, professionally if not socially. They had all gone shopping for the clothes together, and Canfield and Turner had helped her assemble the outfit. At first they had all pretended to take it very seriously, but it hadn't lasted. As each man suggested sexier attire for her to try on, it became more and more of a game, and she found herself enjoying their reactions.

"I never knew you had such nice legs, Steph!"

"Ooh, be still my heart! Stephie, love, you busy Friday night?"

All delivered in a playful mood, yet with an underlying seriousness that told her it wasn't all entirely in jest. And she enjoyed it. She had never really seen herself as "that sort" of woman, but it was fun to play at it, and she had to admit that although she never would have actually considered purchasing such clothes for herself, she did look rather sexy in them.

But it had stopped being a game several hours ago, when it grew dark and started getting cold. She felt self-conscious parading down the street in such a trashy outfit, and she felt humiliated when the inevitable propositions came. She treated each one as if he might have been the Ripper, and it was more frightening than she had thought it would be, even with Canfield and Turner staying very close and moving in to flash their badges before things got out of hand. They had stopped their joking too. It was no longer a game. It was police work, and tawdry work at that—to say nothing of the danger.

He came out of the mist, sauntering slowly down the street, wearing a black Inverness and carrying a soft black leather bag. The sound of his boot heels on the sidewalk seemed very loud.

"Hard night for a working girl, eh?" he said with a smile.

She was surprised. He was well dressed and very handsome. Obviously slumming in this wretched neighborhood. She wondered why such a man would want a whore. Perhaps for something he couldn't get at home, she thought. She wondered just how many seemingly respectable men went in for this sort of thing.

"'Evenin' to ya, guv," she said, putting on the Cockney. "Lookin' for a good time, are ya?" She gave him a hip shot and a sultry look, then pursed her lips and pantomimed a kiss.

"What did you have in mind?" the man said, staring directly into her eyes. There was something unsettling about that look, and she just barely resisted the temptation to look around for Canfield and Turner.

"I know what ya need, luv," she said, inclining her head coquettishly and giving him a wink. "'Ow's about we step right into this alleyway, where it's nice an' dark, like?"

As he followed her into the alley he reached into the leather bag. There was the sound of running footsteps and a cry of, "Hold it right there! Freeze! Police!"

As they had instructed her, she quickly moved away as the man turned, putting as much distance between them as possible and getting over to the side against the wall, so that she'd be out of the line of fire.

"Don't make a move," said Turner, his gun held out

before him in a two-handed combat stance. "Not even a twitch."

"Let's see what's in the bag," said Canfield.

With one smooth, breathtakingly swift motion, the man drew a long, gleaming knife out of the black leather bag, and the two-foot steel blade whistled through the air faster than the eye could follow.

*Whooooosh!*

The razor-sharp blade swept down, severing both of Turner's hands cleanly at the wrists, then, in the same smooth motion, the Ripper's arm swept up and he released the blade, hurling it underhanded with incredible force. Turner screamed with agony, and Canfield fired as the blade struck home, embedding itself deeply in his chest. His shot went wild and he pitched forward, dead before he hit the ground. Turner stood there, screaming hoarsely and staring with disbelief at his hands, one of them lying at his feet, still holding the gun. His wrists spouted blood. The Ripper reached into the bag and withdrew another long-bladed knife, similar to the first. It whistled through the air, and blood spattered on the alley wall with a sound like rain pattering down. Turner stopped screaming. As if in slow motion, his head rolled off his neck and tumbled to the ground with a soft thud. His body collapsed like a marionette with its strings cut.

Stephie's mouth was open in a silent scream. She stood petrified, absolutely frozen with terror, unable to believe the horror she'd just witnessed. Two men, both armed with guns, and only one had time to get off a shot . . . and even then it had been too late. She had no chance. None whatsoever. The Ripper slowly turned back to her. Something snapped. She turned and ran screaming down the alleyway.

Joey slowly walked after her, his pace unhurried. The alley ended in a cul-de-sac.

She reached the end and stopped, staring at the brick wall with an agonized expression. She spun around and saw him coming toward her purposefully. Her eyes were drawn to the gleaming steel blade he held at his side. She started to cry. Then she noticed the long black limousine pull up and stop at the mouth of the alley. The door opened and someone got out.

*"Help!"* she screamed. *"Help me! Please, help me!"*

The Ripper turned and looked over his shoulder, but the dark figure just stood there by the car, motionless, silhouetted in the light from the lamppost at the mouth of the alley.

Sobbing, Stephie shook her head, unable to believe that no one was going to help her. The Ripper seemed to nod at the figure standing at the mouth of the alley, then he turned back to face her.

"You said you knew what I needed," he said with a smile.

And then he started coming toward her.

Blood awoke to the insistent beeping of his pocket pager. It felt like sonic needles going through his brain. He slapped at it repeatedly until he managed to shut it off, then he grabbed his head and groaned. It felt as if someone had pumped up his brain until it threatened to explode his skull.

"God," he said, moaning, "if you make this go away, I'm never going to take another drink as long as I live."

But God was apparently not feeling very sympathetic. The pain of the hangover persisted. Against his better judgment, Blood opened his eyes. And immediately closed them once again.

"All right," he said to himself, pressing his fingers up against his temples, "it seems you didn't spend the night at home. Now think. Where the hell *were* you last night? What happened?"

Through the fog of pain the memory came back to him, and he sat up quickly. Much too quickly. The room started spinning.

"Ohhh, dear God..." He moaned, closing his eyes and grabbing his head again. He slowly counted ten and risked opening his eyes once more. Then, with deliberate care, he put his feet down on the floor and got up off the bed. He swayed slightly, then staggered toward the door.

"Ah, *bonjour,* Chief Inspector," Jacqueline said, padding past him barefoot, wearing nothing except a very sheer black bra and panties. It was indicative of the degree of Blood's condition that he was unable to appreciate the sight. "Would you care for some coffee?"

Blood groaned.

"I will take that as a yes," she said. "Sebastian, black coffee for the chief inspector!"

Blood winced as Makepeace's booming voice came from the kitchen. "Black coffee coming right up!"

A moment later a steaming mug of coffee came floating across the room toward him. Blood blinked, then plucked it out of the air before it could bump into his chest. He could smell breakfast cooking.

A door at the other end of the living room opened, and Kira came shambling out, barefoot, in panties and a sheer, sleeveless black tunic. Her hair was uncombed, hanging down over her face.

"Someone making breakfast?" she mumbled.

"Sebastian is making eggs and bacon," Jacqueline said, stretching out on the couch and lighting up a cigarette, completely unconcerned about being *en déshabillé.* It was like the morning after a fraternity party, Blood thought. It all seemed somehow surreal.

He staggered toward the kitchen.

"How do you like your eggs?" Makepeace asked Kira.

"Over light," she said, taking a beer from the refrigerator.

"Over light it is," said Makepeace, standing in the center of the kitchen, dressed in his habitual beret, as well as embroidered Turkish slippers with turned-up toes and an outrageous, full-length robe in orange-and-red brocade. Makepeace held his hand out, palm up, then quickly turned it palm down. The eggs neatly flipped themselves over.

"Good morning," Makepeace boomed jovially. "Sleep well?"

Blood moaned again. "I . . . I have to make a call. . . ."

"Certainly, but it can wait," said Makepeace. "You're in no shape to go anywhere right now, in any case. Might as well sit down and drink your coffee. I don't imagine you have much of an appetite."

Blood started to shake his head and quickly stopped, realizing that even that motion was upsetting his equilibrium. He took a sip of his coffee.

"There's whiskey in here," he said.

"Hair of the dog," said Makepeace. "Do you good. Drink up."

"Please," said Blood. "Don't say 'drink up.'" He sipped his coffee and slowly lowered himself into a chair at the table. "I seem to remember trying to empty a bottle that kept refusing to stay empty," he said.

"Mmm, I've had nights like that," said Makepeace, making motions toward the range as if he were conducting an orchestra. Flapjacks did elaborate somersaults in the air, turning themselves over, and strips of bacon crawled out onto the range like inchworms committing suttee.

"You people are in a great deal of trouble, you know," said Blood, trying unsuccessfully to ignore his splitting head. "You've not only kidnapped a police officer, but you're also guilty of several counts of thaumaturgical malpractice and—"

"Look, Blood," Kira said, "before you read us our rights or whatever it is you English policemen do, I think you'd better listen to what we have to say. Otherwise I'll be forced to raise my voice and shout, and you wouldn't want that to happen, would you?"

Blood put his hands up to his temples. "Oh, good God, no. Whatever you do, *please* don't shout."

"Right," said Kira, moving to sit next to him at the table. She held out her hand to him, palm up. The sapphire set into her palm was glowing softly.

Blood frowned and glanced up at her.

"You're not seeing things," she said. "It's been glowing off and on ever since we arrived in London. It's very weak now. Look at it closer."

He leaned over her hand, staring intently at the stone.

"What do you see?"

"There're . . . some sort of carvings on it," he said.

"Runes," said Kira. "This is an enchanted runestone, one of three that were found in an excavation in the Euphrates Valley, Wyrdrune and I stole them."

"So I was right, they are stolen," Blood said. "You'd do best to tell me all about it. If you were to cooperate—"

"Look, will you stop being a cop for just a little while and listen?" she said.

"All right, yes, anything," said Blood, wincing. "Jut don't raise your voice. Please."

"They're keys to an ancient spell," she explained. "One of the oldest and most powerful incantations in the world, a spell that goes back to the dawn of time.

"Three stones, three keys to lock the spell.
Three jewels to guard the Gates of Hell.
Three to bind them, three in one,
Three to hide them from the sun.
Three to hold them, three to keep,
Three to watch the sleepless sleep."

As she spoke the incantation the sapphire in the palm of her hand glowed brighter, giving off sparkling rays of light as if it were a star. Blood listened as she told him the story of the Old Ones, of the war between the white mages and the necromancers, and of how the Council of the White had given up their lives to infuse their powers and life energies into the enchanted runestones, all except for Gorlois, who had sealed up the tomb of the Dark Ones and gone out into the world to marry a girl from the De Dannan tribe and become Merlin's father, and later, with another wife, to father the three halfling girls—Elaine, Morgause, and Morgana—whose descendants they were, chosen by the runestones as their avatars to seek out and destroy the Dark Ones.

"You mean yourself and Wyrdrune," Blood said. "You're telling me that you're descended from these three witch sisters or whatever?"

She nodded.

"Aha. I see. And who's the third descendant, the one who carries the third runestone? Would that be the good doctor, here?" He looked at Makepeace.

"Oh, no, not me," said Makepeace, wolfing down his flapjacks and bacon. "She means the one we came here to find. His real name is Modred, though you may be more familiar with his alias. It's Morpheus."

"Wait a moment," Blood said, frowning. "Surely you don't mean the mercenary, the international hit man, not *that* Morpheus?"

"One and the same," said Makepeace, his mouth full.

Blood put his head in his hands and groaned. "I truly wish you hadn't told me that. My headache just got immeasurably worse." He sighed heavily. "It's one thing to put up with a couple of brash, young American jewel theives, a potty sorcerer academician who thinks he's a damn fairy, a French femme fatale who's been arrested more times than a bloody gangster, and a deluded Cockney street urchin who thinks he's Merlin the Magician. That's all bad enough, but when you go dragging a professional assassin like Morpheus into it—"

At that moment Wyrdrune and Billy came back, carrying several bags of groceries and a number of different newspapers.

"Well, the bloody bastard's gone an' done it again," said Billy, tossing the newspapers down on the table.

"This time he's killed three cops," said Wyrdrune.

"*What?*"

Blood lunged for the papers, his hangover suddenly forgotten. The headlines said it all: RIPPER BUTCHERS POLICE DECOY TEAM! THREE OFFICERS SLAIN! WHITECHAPEL SLAUGHTER CONTINUES! POLICE HELPLESS!

He felt the blood rushing to his face as he quickly scanned the stories. That damned idiot, Hyphen-Smythe! What the hell was he thinking, taking an inexperienced officer, an untrained file clerk, for God's sake, and sending her out as a decoy . . . ? Blood suddenly remembered his pager going off and waking him. And he had turned it off. Of course. They were trying to locate him. Three officers slain, and the man who was supposedly in charge of the investigation was nowhere to be found. The superintendent would be in a frothing rage, and who could blame him?

Because he had not wanted to get trapped running a paper chase at headquarters, he had delegated that job to Hyphen-Smythe while he went out into the streets to work in the only way he knew how. But who would have expected Hyphen-Smythe to pick up the ball and run with it, to actually display initiative and pick out his own decoy teams and send them out to . . . ! He threw the paper down onto the table in a fury.

"This is what comes of your meddlesome nonsense!" he shouted at them in furious frustration, ignoring his headache as he leapt to his feet and shoved the chair back violently. "If I'd've been there, I could have prevented this! So help me, I'll have you all in jail for obstructing a police investigation! I'll have you all charged with—"

The emerald in Wyrdrune's forehead blazed, and a bright green beam of thaumaturgic energy suddenly shot forth from the runestone, striking the policeman in the chest, not hard enough to injure him, but with enough force to knock him off his feet and send him flying backward into his chair, which tipped over as he struck it, dumping him on the floor.

"All right, I've had about enough!" said Wyrdrune.

"Take it easy, kid," said Makepeace.

"Damn it, we haven't got *time* to take it easy!" Wyrdrune shouted in reply. "And we haven't got the time to waste trying to convince a stupid cop who can't see his own damn nose in front of his face! *People are dying!*"

"'E's got a point, y'know," said Billy. He went over to where the astonished Blood sat on the floor, holding his chest and staring at them. "Look, Mick, what's it gonna be, 'ey? You in or out?"

Blood looked at them, shifting his gaze quickly from one face to another. They were all watching him intently. At first they had seemed like some sort of thaumaturgical bohemians, a gang of colorful dropouts who had banded together like magic-using Gypsies, not above bending the truth or breaking the law. Who could take such an assemblage seriously? He looked down at his chest again. It was if he had been shot at close range, only without having a bullet actually penetrate. The fabric of his shirt was smoking slightly, and he realized that Wyrdrune just as easily could have killed him.

"You don't understand, Michael," Kira said gently. "I've been trying to explain it to you. What you're up against is something more powerful than you could possibly imagine. Something that isn't even human. It's a nightmare. You haven't seen anything yet. It's only getting started. Believe me, without us, you haven't got a prayer."

# CHAPTER EIGHT

"You really ought to come, old boy," Hastings had told him. "A night out would do you a world of good. Take your mind off your troubles."

"I don't know, Jeremy," he'd said, "but I'm not really up to it, especially after what's happened. Besides, I've never really gone in for these society things. Word is this Carfax chap is rather on the young and energetic side. Wild parties, loud music, young girls, all that sort of thing. Not really my cup of tea, you know. A bit too old for that. I don't think I'd quite fit in."

"Too old? Good Lord, Royce, you're the same age as I am! Anyway, it's all in the attitude, old boy! All in the attitude! What's the matter, don't you like young girls?" Hastings had said half jokingly.

"Oh, Jeremy, honestly..."

"You make it sound as if I'm inviting you to some damn orgy, for God's sake. You know, you might be surprised to learn what sort of people show up at Nigel's parties. Alderdyce is quite a regular, for one...."

"What, not the minister?"

"One and the same. And then there's Lord Willoughby, Bob Paddington, Q. C., Judge Featherstone, and—"

"Old Featherstone? You're joking! And Willoughby must be nearly seventy!"

"Oh, it's usually quite a varied group," said Hastings. "Don't let his youth fool you, Nigel likes too assemble all sorts of interesting people and allow them to mingle in their own way. One finds one's own depth, so to speak. Do come, Royce. You really ought to get away for a while, get out of town. Look, you haven't got anything on for tonight, anyway, have you? You said there isn't any family coming by, so you don't really have any plans, do you?"

No, in light of his son Andrew's death, Llewellyn Royce Blood had to admit that he certainly hadn't made plans. He had thought that perhaps he and his two remaining sons might have a quiet family evening together, talk about what happened, find a way to live with it, but Ian had called up to commiserate briefly and then begged off, and he hadn't even heard from Michael, who, of all people, should have been the first to call. But nothing. Not a word.

Not even his own coworkers knew where Michael was. There had been a call from some policeman named Shavers, who thought Michael might have been at home, consoling his father in his grief, and it was with a great deal of awkwardness that Royce admitted that since Andrew's murder he hadn't even heard from Michael. That had produced a long silence on the other end, and then a painfully uncomfortable, "Oh. Well, sorry to bother you, Your Lordship."

Damn them to hell, then, Royce had thought. It was the final straw. Ever since his wife, Emily, had died, they had all been drifting farther and farther apart. His sons had made no secret of their dislike for one another. He was tired of being the only one who had any sense of family, heartbroken over Andrew's death and embittered by what he perceived as the failure of his children to get on with life and with each other.

Ian was forty-two and had yet to present him with any grandchildren. All he seemed to care about was politics, and if he occasionally showed up at some function or another with a woman on his arm, she was usually as dull as dishwater, more often than not one of those university feminist intellectual types, too old to act like the spoiled brats they were, and not old enough to be taken seriously. Yet Ian seemed to find them mildly amusing. Royce had a hard time believing that his son actually could be interested in any of them. Andrew, at least, had shown some promise. He had always thought of Andrew as the runt of the litter, the one who'd have the most trouble getting on, but despite his weakness of character, Andrew finally seemed to have made a start, and now...

Royce Blood was completely ignorant of the fact that Ian was a closet drag queen, and Andrew had always been very careful not to let his father find out about all his debauched excesses. Michael alone had never hidden anything from him, not even his growing drinking problem; consequently Michael was the biggest disappointment to him. Royce simply couldn't understand what on earth had possessed him to become a policeman, of all things. Every young boy thinks of being a policeman or a fireman at one time or another, but Michael apparently had never outgrown it. What sort of a career was being a policeman? What could one accomplish? You always saw people at their worst, day in and day out, and no matter how many of them you arrested, you couldn't even make a dent in the evils of society. All it did was make you callous and bitter. Small wonder that policemen had such a high divorce rate. Who could live like that? It was like pissing into the wind.

So, rather than be alone with his grief and his bottle, something Royce considered the ultimate sign of weakness, he had allowed Jeremy Hastings to talk him into this affair at Carfax Castle, a medieval keep just outside of London that had been rebuilt during the reign of Henry VIII and then restored again during the nineteenth century by some wealthy peer, to be sold eventually—along with the peerage—to an Australian multimillionaire. Since the collapse it had stood vacant and decaying until the young Lord Carfax had bought it and performed extensive renovations that had to have been ruinously expensive.

The castle stood upon a hill overlooking a gently sloping valley. The keep itself had thick stone walls, with four round, crenelated corner turrets complete with embrasures and cruciform loopholes. All very authentic, if not original architecture. The original outer wall had long since crumbled into ruin, but Carfax had reconstructed it after a fashion. He had the wall rebuilt a bit closer to the keep and a great deal lower than the original one must have been. An average jumper with a decent rider could have cleared it. Carfax had incorporated miniature sally ports and a cosmetic wall walk that ran through the towers placed along the wall at all four corners. The bailey, or courtyard, was a beautifully landscaped garden with slate walkways curving through it and a number of small fountains. On seeing it for the first time, Royce thought wryly that the only thing that Castle Carfax lacked was a scaled-down barbican in the narrow moat. Carfax apparently had his main residence in London, somewhere in Mayfair. The castle was a lovely and fabulously expensive toy.

Upon arriving, Royce discovered that the evening was to be devoted to a "neo-medieval festival," complete with costumes supplied to all the guests. It turned out that Jeremy had known about it all along and hadn't mentioned it because he had been afraid that Royce would find it frivolous and refuse to come. In point of fact, he would have, but since he had come down with Jeremy, it seemed that there was no retreat now, and no choice but to put on a good face and go along with all the nonsense.

It seemed grotesquely inappropriate to Royce to be playing at such glorified schoolboy games the day after his youngest son had been found murdered, and he regretted his decision to come. He wanted to leave immediately, but as if Jeremy had expected just such a reaction, he had promptly disappeared the moment they'd entered the great hall.

The spacious, two-story-high great hall of the castle bore only a superficial resemblance to what the interior of an actual medieval castle must have looked like, with huge, beamed wooden ceilings—graced with large, very unmedieval chandeliers—and an arched cross wall dividing the room. Colorful tapestries hung upon the stone walls, as well as emblazoned shields with broadswords, spears, and battle-axes crossed behind them. Torches set in iron sconces shaped like gargoyle heads with crystalline eyes blazed upon the walls.

There was a raised dais at the end of the hall, where the lord was meant to hold court, but instead of a lord and his retinue seated at a table, there was a five-man band wailing away, complete with a thaumaturgic light show orchestrated by the band's effects adept. Multicolored explosions blossomed in midair like orchids, flowing into graphically sexual Rorschach images that shifted in time to the driving tempo of the bass line and then burst apart into flurries of strobing moths and butterflies or multicolored insects with prism-glass wings and carapaces.

Elaborate stained-glass windows set high up in the walls depicted Dionysian scenes of a shockingly blasphemous nature, and hidden diffraction laser lighting augmented the illumination from the torches, making it appear as if a heat storm had erupted within the hall. Shadowy figures dressed in a cacophony of neo-medieval and renaissance punk styles gyrated on the floor, and other groups congregated around the several bars that had been set up at the sides of the hall. Royce groaned inwardly. It was just the sort of thing he'd been afraid of. He felt about as out of place as an archbishop at a Black Mass.

He fled back out through the heavy iron-studded wooden doors to the entrance hall and out into the garden, where he took a deep breath of the cool night air.

"Excuse me," said a low, feminine voice behind him, "I

don't mean to intrude, but you looked as though you could use one of these."

Royce turned to see a stunning-looking young woman standing just behind him, holding a goblet in each hand. She had raven-black hair held back by a thin, hammered-gold circlet, and a lush figure draped in a long, clinging white gown with a thin gold cord worn loosely as a girdle around her waist. She looked like a medieval fairy princess.

"Brandy?" she said, offering him one of the goblets.

"Thank you," he said, accepting it.

"A bit close in there, isn't it?" she said.

"Yes, rather," Royce said. "I'm afraid it's not really my sort of thing. Bit on the frantic side."

"Isn't it just?" she said. "I don't know what I'm doing here. I feel so out of place."

"Really?" Royce said, sipping his drink. "Funny, I was about to say exactly the same thing."

"Great minds think alike," she said with a lovely smile.

Royce found himself strongly attracted to her. *Get hold of yourself, old boy,* he told himself, *she's young enough to be your daughter. Granddaughter, even. She would hardly be interested in an old duffer like you.*

"I'm afraid I made a mistake in coming," Royce said. "I was . . . well, I was having some personal troubles, and a friend convinced me that a night out would be just the thing, but I fear he misled me somewhat as to the nature of the company. I thought I'd be seeing some old friends here. I rather expected . . . well, I don't know what I expected, to be perfectly honest. I just sort of went along with it, and now it appears I'm stuck."

"It sounds as if we have the same sort of friends," she said wryly. "Two of my girlfriends talked me into coming and promptly disappeared within moments after we arrived. I don't know a soul here, and I'm afraid I'm not much for dancing and cocktail-party levity. I've only been here about half an hour, and already four men have tried to pick me up."

"Can't say that I blame them," Royce said, wincing inwardly even as he said it.

She raised her eyebrows in pleased surprise. "Well, aren't you nice? Thank you. You know, I don't even know your name."

"Oh. Sorry. Royce Blood," he said. "First name is Llewellyn, actually, but my friends all call me Royce."

She took his hand and held on to it just a bit longer than necessary. "Hello, Royce. I'm Terri Clancy."

"Black roses," said Chief Inspector Blood. "Black roses and a dungeon? That's all you have?"

"I know it isn't much," Wyrdrune said.

"No, it damn well isn't," Blood said. "And you say the black roses are associated with a town house in London, yet town houses do not ordinarily have dungeons, do they?"

"I know it doesn't seem to make any sense—" said Kira.

"None of this makes any sense," said Blood, shaking his head. "For one thing, why wouldn't these necromancers, these Dark Ones as you call them, all get together and concentrate their efforts on disposing of you if you're such a threat to them? Why split up and go off in all different directions?"

"Because magic has its price," said Wyrdrune. "The Dark Ones would have been severely weakened after their escape. The Council of the White defeated them before, and they're not likely to forget that. Together, especially in their weakened state, they'd be an easy target. Well, no, on second thought it would hardly be easy, but it would be a hell of a lot easier than if they split up the way they've done. We can't be everywhere at once. This way they can send the strongest ones among them up against us, while the others establish strongholds for themselves and start building up their strength. Before long, individuals among them will be stronger than all of them together would have been right after their escape. And they can recover their powers much more quickly than we can, because we won't take our strength from killing, and necromancers don't have any reservations on that count."

"So what you're telling me is that eventually you're bound to lose," said Blood.

"Maybe not," said Kira. "See, a few things have changed since the days of the Old Ones. For one thing, thanks to Merlin, humans can use magic now. Maybe not as well as the Old Ones can, but put enough human wizards and sorcerers together and the Dark Ones would have a hell of a fight on their hands."

"Only then you'd have a full-scale mage war," Wyrdrune said, "and the world almost did not survive the last one."

"So where does that leave us?" Blood said.

"Exactly where we are," said Kira. "We have to try to track them down one at a time and take them out. If we can."

"And to do that," added Wyrdrune, "we have to conserve our strength as much as possible, because we can't recover anywhere near as quickly as a necromancer, who doesn't rely on his own life energy."

"Those symbols you saw carved into your brother's body were part of a necromancer's spell," said Merlin. His voice was now the same as Billy's, only without the Cockney accent. "Certain ancient druidic cults, those that practiced human sacrifice, used to paint such symbols on the bodies of their victims. Similar rites could be found among other primitive tribes, from the blue body-painting of the Picts to the war paint of the Native Americans. They believe it was a way of increasing their power. What you saw on the body of your brother was the original version, only necromancers don't use paint."

"Does that mean his"—Blood hesitated—"his soul was destroyed?"

"It was eaten," Merlin said.

Blood closed his eyes tightly. "My God," he whispered.

"Perhaps now you can appreciate what it is you're faced with," Merlin continued. "The police are not equipped to deal with an immortal necromancer. If you send more police officers against him, more police officers will die, and their deaths will only make him stonger."

"What can I do?" said Blood.

"What we need now most of all is information," Wyrdrune said. "We need to tap into Scotland Yard's data banks."

"With your help," said Jacqueline, "we could network Archimedes with your police computers. Archimedes could download whatever information your special task force has managed to come up with so far, and then we could request data through Scotland Yard that would be fed through your computers directly to Archimedes."

Blood stared at her with astonishment. "You can't be serious! Do you realize what you're asking? I can't give you that kind of access! You're asking me to help you set up a security feed from the police data banks directly to Archimedes. That would be criminal, to say nothing of using counterfeit police authority to call up information!"

"But it wouldn't be counterfeit police authority," said Jacqueline. "The request for data would be coming from Scotland Yard's computers, and they would be receiving it directly."

"And feeding it straight to you," said Blood, "through a security link, bypassing the police entirely! No, absolutely not. I can't allow it." He rolled his eyes in exasperation. "I don't even know what I'm doing here talking to you people! I'm supposed to be running an investigation! By rights, I ought to be running you all in!" He shook his head and sighed. "I can't believe I'm doing this.'

"Believe it or not, Mick, you're doin' the right thing," said Billy. "After this is done, they'll prob'ly go an' 'ang a medal on you."

"They'll be hanging something, I have no doubt of that," said Blood sarcastically. "Oh, what the hell. My father never wanted me to be a policeman, anyway." He got up and went over to where Jacqueline sat at the computer. "Let's get on with it."

Royce hesitated as she opened the arched door to the bedroom. They had climbed the spiral staircase up to the top floor of the keep because Terri had said that she wanted to go out on the parapets and take in the view in the moonlight. But now she had gone into one of the bedrooms with a coy "I wonder what's in here?"

He remained by the door.

"Come on in and close the door," she said, looking directly into his eyes. There was no mistaking the invitation.

"I don't think this is a very good idea, Terri," Royce said, not coming in and leaving the door wide open.

"Why not? You don't like me?" she said, looking stricken. "I've done something to offend you, haven't I?"

"No, no, it isn't that at all. I think you're a very lovely girl."

"So what is it, then? I'm being too forward, is that it? I'm sorry, perhaps I misunderstood, but I thought you were attracted to me."

"I *am* attracted to you, Terri, any man would be, but my dear girl, I've got boots older than you are!"

"What does that have to do with anything?"

"Everything," said Royce. "There's nothing more pathetic than an old fool making an ass of himself over a girl young enough to be his daughter. I am far too old and a bit too old-fashioned for a brief romantic fling, however tempting it might be, and you are far too young for a serious relationship with someone of my age."

"That's a lot of nonsense," she said.

"It is not a lot of nonsense," Royce protested, determined to be strong about it. "I'm very flattered, truly I am, but I have absolutely no intention of catering to a young girl's father fixation. It wouldn't be healthy, not for either one of us. It couldn't possibly last, and as I've already said, I have no interest in settling for anything less. Besides, I have my position to think of. If I suddenly took up with a beautiful young girl and started acting like a randy young swain at my age, my partners would think that I'd gone off my nut, and I wouldn't blame them. So please, let's just forget about this and pretend it never happened."

"No," she said in a low voice, and with a deft motion she shrugged out of her dress and let it fall to the floor. She was stark naked underneath, save for a thin gold chain around her hips.

Royce caught his breath. He tried to swallow, but there suddenly seemed to be an obstruction in his throat. His heart started to hammer away inside his chest like a wild thing trying to claw its way out. He had never in his life seen anyone so lovely, so carnally sensual, so incredibly desirable. . . .

"Royce," she said, her voice sultry, "I want you."

He bit his lower lip and shut his eyes. A little voice within him seemed to say, "Go *on*! Are you *insane*? My God, man, she *wants* you! *Look* at her, for Christ's sake! When will you ever have a chance like this again? Go on, for one last shining moment, be *young* again!" But with a supreme effort of will, the same strength of will that had made him the success he was, he ignored that voice and backed out through the doorway, shaking his head, keeping his eyes shut, not daring to open them for fear of losing what little self-control he had remaining.

"*Royce!*"

He turned and ran back down the spiral stairs.

Terri stood there, stunned, unable to believe what had just happened. There was the sound of a soft chuckle behind her, and she spun around to see him lying on the canopied bed, one black-leather-clad leg stretched out straight, the other bent at the knee. He wore high-heeled black boots and a loose-fitting black silk shirt open at the neck to reveal a gold, upside down crucifix on a thin gold chain. His hands were clasped behind his head, and a thick shock of flame-red hair hung down in his face.

"And lo, how the mighty hath fallen," he quoted, laughing. "Well, I suppose this is what I get for sending out a girl to do a woman's job."

She stood there, not bothering to cover herself, her face flushed with fury.

"*Don't*! Don't you dare laugh at me! Don't *ever* laugh at me or—"

He stopped laughing and gave her a look that sent shivers down her spine.

"Or what?" he said softly.

She swallowed hard and moistened her lips nervously. "Nothing." She lowered her head slightly and looked at him with a faint smile. "As long as you're here..." she said, moving toward the bed.

He smiled and pulled her down next to him, taking her into his arms and rolling over on top of her, kissing her deeply, holding her tightly, so incredibly tightly. . . . She gasped and broke the kiss. His eyes stared down at her, and suddenly they were golden eyes, eyes with black, vertical-slit pupils. His long, forked tongue flicked out at her. His skin gleamed with an iridescent sheen; scales started to form. She felt the large, powerful coils squeezing her, and she shook her head, gasping for breath.

"*No! No, please, don't. . . .*"

And then she screamed.

"Lord Carfax?" Blood said.

"You know him?" asked Kira.

"Only by reputation," Blood replied. "He's the latest social darling, young and fabulously wealthy. Must have inherited it all, because it seems no one knows exactly what it is he does, assuming he does anything at all. Hasn't been in England long. Arrived recently from Hong Kong or Japan or Sri Lanka or some damn exotic place—there seems to be some question about where. There's always something about him in the papers. Apparently he keeps to himself a great deal and avoids the press, won't be photographed, yet on the other hand he throws all these lavish parties, which are supposed to be quite exclusive and rather on the wild side. As a matter of fact, only the other day I was speaking to my brother, Andrew, about . . ." His voice trailed off.

"Go on," said Wyrdrune. "What is it?"

"Interesting coincidence," said Blood. "He called me to pick my brain about the Ripper case. He wanted to have some inside dope that he could use for party chat. My younger brother was something of a social butterfly. We didn't have very much in common, I'm afraid. I recall he was quite excited over having secured an invitation to one of Lord Carfax's celebrated parties, and he went on about it a great deal. I'm afraid I didn't pay very much attention. I was rather anxious to be rid of him," he added with a grimace that underscored the irony. "And the very next morning he was found dead."

"I'm sorry," Kira said.

Blood shrugged. "We were never really close. I feel a bit guilty about that now. To be honest, Andrew didn't have a lot of character, but to go like that . . ." He sighed. "Hard to believe it was only yesterday. Time doesn't pass, you know, it stretches. Especially when you're drunk. The newspapers will doubtless make him out to be another of the Ripper's victims, but I don't believe he was. The M.O. didn't match, and serial killers generally stick to the same pattern. Poor Andrew looked as if he'd been torn apart by some wild animal. Won't know for certain till I see the lab results."

"Is there any way you can get hold of them right now?" asked Wyrdrune.

"Yes, I expect so," Blood said. "Danny Shavers is a good man, he'll cover for me. Why? What are you thinking? You suspect Carfax?"

"You're a cop," said Wyrdrune, "you tell me."

"There's absolutely no evidence against him," Blood said. "Not even circumstantial."

"But what does your instinct tell you?" Wyrdrune said.

"My instinct is telling me to be very leery of your lot," said Blood. "If I antagonize a man in Carfax's position—"

"Just what exactly *is* his position?" Wyrdrune asked. "Is he actually a lord?"

"Well, difficult to say," said Blood. "Since the Collapse there's been nothing like *Burke's* or *Debrett's*. Records have been lost and no one really pays very close attention to that sort of thing these days. The House of Lords is more a gentleman's political debating society than anything else, and only a handful of the so-called 'old aristocracy' go in for it. And even they probably couldn't stand very careful scrutiny. I suppose, to anticipate your next question, that given enough imagination, money, social contacts, and the right sort of manners, one could easily phony up a title. Or simply buy one outright."

"And Carfax has plenty of money, and his parties undoubtedly provide him with all the social contacts he needs," said Wyrdrune. "Seems interesting that no one knows exactly what he does or where he came from, doesn't it? I wonder if anyone's ever seen his passport. For that matter, I wonder if there's even a record of his entry into this country."

"You're an extremely suspicious young man," said Blood. "Ever think about becoming a policeman?"

"Not even once."

Blood smiled. "It's like that, is it? Still, I should think if he'd gotten into the country illegally, the press would have ferreted it out by now. They all dearly love to unearth any sort of scandal."

"And they also love to get pictures of people who don't like being photographed," said Wyrdrune. "They usually manage somehow, don't they? Has Carfax ever been photographed?"

"Damned if I know," Blood said. "I don't really read the society pages." He got up and walked over to the computer. "Jacqueline, can I cadge one of your cigarettes?"

She offered him the pack.

"Doctor, have you any more of that inexhaustible fairy Scotch of yours?"

"Coming right up, Michael."

"Right, then," said Blood, sitting down. "Archimedes, if I might avail myself of your keyboard and modem for a moment?"

"At your service, Chief Inspector," said the computer.

"My sergeant's got a computer terminal with a secure line on his desk," said Blood, looking at the others. "I'll see if I can't get him to find out a thing or two for us. . . ." He started typing. Moments later words appeared on the screen.

"Chief Inspector? Is that you?"

"It's me, Danny," Blood typed. "How are things over there?"

"How are things? Don't you know? Where have you been, for God's sake? Everyone's screaming for you, from the superintendent on down to the press! Haven't you heard what's happened? Where are you? Why didn't you call? Why are you contacting me via my terminal?"

"I can't explain now. I've heard all about what's happened, Danny. Don't ask any questions. I'm Blood hesitated slightly, then typed, ". . . undercover. I think I may be on to something, but I'll need your help, no questions asked. Understood?"

"Understood."

"Good man. First: Hyphen-Smythe must immediately stop sending out his decoy squads. I don't care what he says. Tell him it's a direct order from me. Tell him I called and told you to tell him that. I have good reason to believe that we may be up against a powerful adept, and I'll not lose any more police officers, is that clear?"

"Yes, sir."

"Good old Shavers," Blood said, watching the screen and smiling. "Right down to business, no wasting time with silly questions." He resumed typing.

"Second: Get the lab report on Andrew's death and enter the details into your terminal, in a secure file. Without telling anyone about it."

"I understand. Anything else?"

"Assemble a dossier on Lord Nigel Carfax. Everything we have. In particular, passport records. Date of entry, point of origin, etc. Photographs, if any are available. Got that?"

"Got it. Is there any way that I can get in touch with you?"

Blood glanced at the others.

"We could have Archimedes check his terminal for messages every fifteen minutes or half hour or whatever," Jacqueline said.

Blood nodded and typed, "Leave a message for me on your terminal. Secure file, got it? Our password key will be Archimedes."

"Understood. Archimedes. Good luck, sir."

"Thanks, Danny. Over and out."

"Well, that's that," said Blood, looking at the others. "We'll know soon enough."

"Yeah," said Wyrdrune, "I just hope that it *is* soon enough."

He stood at the bottom of the stairs, watching Royce Blood at the bar across the room drinking whiskey to steady his nerves. He smiled. It must have taken all the nerve the poor man had to resist Terri. And that had to be considerable. Still, it would be good for her. Take some of the wind out of her sails. She'd been getting a bit too full of herself and starting to forget her place. She had needed a little reminder.

A change came over him as he watched Royce Blood. His clothing seemed to shimmer and blur, like waves of heat dancing on the desert, and when he stepped off the stairs, his black leather pants and black open-necked silk shirt had changed to an elegant dark suit, impeccably tailored in the height of conservative fashion, the sort of thing a successful executive would wear. He approached Royce Blood at the bar.

"A bit too much for you, was she?" he said casually as he signaled the bartender for a drink.

Royce started. "I beg your pardon?"

"I happened to notice you going upstairs with one of Lord Carfax's young ladies a few moments ago, and now here you are, having a good stiff drink."

"Sorry, I'm afraid I don't know what you're talking about," said Royce stiffly.

"Ah, well, perhaps I misunderstood you. You see, I recognized you from your photographs in the financial pages, and I was about to warn you. I didn't know if you knew about the sort of things that went on here. Perhaps I assumed too much and spoke out of turn."

"No, wait," said Royce. "Warn me about what? What did you mean about the sort of things that went on here? Who are you?"

"Agent Damon, B.O.T.," he said, reaching into his jacket pocket and producing an ID that hadn't existed a second earlier. He flashed it covertly, glanced around, and put it back into his pocket. "I've had occasion to work with your son, Chief Inspector Blood. Good man. I take it this is your first time at one of Lord Carfax's little soirees?"

"Yes. I'm not really much of a party goer, but a friend of mine talked me into coming. Why?"

He nodded knowingly. "I thought as much. You had that sort of overdosed look of someone who's encountered rather more than he expected." He leaned closer. "I gather you didn't know that Lord Nigel Carfax is one of those people known as an 'information broker,' if you get my meaning. Works very much behind the scenes, but he makes it his business to find out what people's weaknesses are, and then he exploits them for personal gain."

Royce frowned. "Are you telling me that he's an extortionist, a blackmailer?"

"One of the very best. His methods are often quite ingenious. Sometimes they're even legal." He glanced toward the stairs. "You've just met one of them."

"You don't mean Terri? Miss Clancy?"

"Oh, yes. I know it must be very gratifying, having a beautiful woman like that seem attracted to you, but at the risk of wounding your ego, the truth is that Terri Clancy is a calculating nymphomaniac—and a felon, to boot. We have quite a dossier on her, and we're very familiar with her modus operandi. First she will make her attraction to you seem self-evident by subtle means, then she will start a coy flirtation. After that, if you still have any reservations —which most men don't, I might add—she'll try to convince you that the difference in your ages means nothing, that she prefers older men with more experience and wisdom. Younger men act as if they have so much to prove, after all, and they can be such beasts. And if that doesn't work, she'll—"

"Stop, please," said Royce. He looked down at the floor, embarrassed. "I owe you a debt of gratitude, Mr. Damon. The fact is, she did attempt to seduce me. To be quite truthful, I was sorely tempted, but I knew that it would be unwise. I didn't want to act the fool, and I had no confidence in my willpower, so I fled like a nervous schoolboy. However, I've had a few drinks in the interim and was starting to wonder if I hadn't been too hasty, if it wasn't terribly unkind of me to run out on her like that, and if perhaps I shouldn't go back and apologize. . . ." He grimaced and shook his head. "I'm afraid I might have made a very bad mistake if not for you. There's no fool like an old fool, eh?"

"I wouldn't be too hard on yourself, sir. She's made a lot of young fools as well, if you'll excuse the pun. That's one woman who comes loaded for bear."

"Yes, indeed," said Royce. "She let me have both barrels."

"It's a wonder you're still standing."

Royce chuckled. "I wouldn't be, if not for your timely intervention. I gather you're collecting evidence against this Carfax chap? Must be quite serious for the Bureau of Thaumaturgy to be involved."

"We've been investigating him for quite some time now. We're convinced he makes felonious use of sorcery, but we haven't been able to prove it yet. He's quite clever. We know he uses sexual entrapment, through women such as Miss Clancy, but unfortunately that does not come under our jurisdiction."

"But surely the police could help you there," said Royce.

"I'm sure they could, if we wanted to convict him of a lesser offense. However, we're after him on the charge of illegal use of thaumaturgy, and if we're very lucky"—he looked around and dropped his voice lower still—"we might even be able to get him on necromancy."

Royce stared at him with disbelief. "Necromancy!" he whispered, deeply shocked. "Dear God! You don't actually mean he *kills* people?"

"We don't know that for certain, but we've heard some very disturbing rumors. It seems that Carfax uses these gala affairs of his to recruit people into his inner circle of initiates. As the party wears on and inhibitions start to fall away, he allows certain people admission into a private sanctum of his here at the castle somewhere. A sort of party within a party. And he's highly selective. Only goes after those who are extremely rich and influential."

"Which would make me a logical candidate, I suppose," said Royce.

"Exactly. And I, of course, wouldn't have a hope of getting in without—"

"Without someone in my position to vouch for you," Royce finished for him.

"It's a great deal to ask, I know. I wouldn't blame you one bit if you were to refuse."

"Think nothing of it, old chap," said Royce. "You've done me a good turn, so I'd be only too glad to help. But I'm afraid that I don't really know this Carfax fellow. I don't even have any idea what he looks like."

"I think we can fix that. Care to go and meet him?"

# CHAPTER NINE

"I wish there was something more that we could do," said Kira, pacing back and forth across the room. "This waiting is driving me crazy."

"Now you know how a police detective feels," Blood said, "especially when he's pursuing a serial killer. When you've exhausted everything else, you're left with waiting. Waiting for the killer to strike again so that you can see if he's left any clues for you to work on. On the one hand, you're hoping for something more to go on, but on the other, someone must die before that happens. And there you are, caught squarely in the middle and unable to do anything about it, one way or the other."

"There's nothing else we can do at the moment," Merlin said.

Wyrdrune noticed that he was now speaking almost entirely in Billy's voice, the main difference being Billy's Cockney accent. There was also the difference in their mannerisms, the most obvious one being that Billy smoked cigarettes and Merlin still had a fondness for his pipe. At the moment he was stretched out on the couch, a large bowled briar with a deep curve to it clamped between his teeth. He had packed it with his usual blend, a magical concoction that smelled different with every puff. He was always experimenting with it, never quite able to get it just right. He took the pipe out of his mouth and blew a succession of smoke rings that smelled like fresh-baked cinnamon-raisin buns.

"You're going to stunt his growth, you know," said Wyrdrune.

Billy's face scowled at him, though it was Merlin behind the scowl.

Makepeace chuckled, then frowned. "Phew! What a stench! How can you smoke that stuff?"

The tobacco had mutated its aroma once again, changing to something that smelled remarkably like tires burning.

"I don't mean to ask an obvious question," said Jacqueline, "but couldn't you use your magic to try to track him down?"

"Not really," Wyrdrune replied. "For the same reason Modred couldn't contact us to tell us where he is. Something is interfering. A spell, obviously, a very strong one. And Modred is also probably in a severely weakened condition."

"And you could not get through to him somehow?" she said.

"Perhaps we could," said Wyrdrune, "but then we'd have to overcome the spell that's warding him, wherever he is, and that would deplete our energies. And the moment we tried it, we'd give ourselves away. It's just what the Dark Ones want us to do. They'd realize what we were doing and strike back. Hard. When the time comes for that confrontation, and it's coming soon, we'd better be at full capacity."

"Meanwhile . . . what if he dies?" Jacqueline asked softly.

"That's a risk we're going to have to take," said Wyrdrune.

Jacqueline's voice took on an edge. "A risk *you* are going to have to take? What risk is there to you?"

"Now you just hold it right there, Frenchy," Kira said.

"Kira—" Wyrdrune said.

"No, screw that! Who the hell does she think she is? I'm not going to let her get away with that!"

"Come on, Kira, she didn't mean anything. She's just worried, that's all. We're all pretty tense."

"Forgive me," Jacqueline said with a sigh. "I apologize. But I still think there is something more we should be doing."

"Perhaps there *is* something we can do," said Blood, looking up from the newspaper he was reading. "Here we are, waiting for Shavers to come up with information on Lord Carfax, and there's something about him right here in the *Daily Mail*."

"What's it say?" asked Billy. Or was it Merlin? No, Billy, Wyrdrune realized as the boy put aside the pipe with a grimace of distaste. "Gor', what's that old fart been smokin' in 'ere? Smells like a bloody blancmange!"

"'Lord Carfax hosts neo-medieval ball,'" read Blood. "'The realm's chicest and sleekest will be turning out in force this weekend for a gala neo-medieval festival at Carfax Castle. Hosted by that reclusive raver'—dear God, reclusive raver? They really wrote that, didn't they? Anyway, it gushes on in that vein for another six or seven paragraphs before we get to anything substantive, but the gist of it seems to be that Carfax is hosting some sort of costume ball tonight, and there's some sort of tournament on for tomorrow, with actual jousting, God save us, and a melee, whatever that is."

"A lot of aggro with swords an' things," said Billy. "You get these two teams together, see, an' then someone blows a trumpet or whatnot, an' they all 'ave a go smashin' away at one another till only one team's left standin'."

"How the devil did you know that?" said Blood.

"I *din't* know it," Billy said, "old Merlin did."

"I'm getting really tired of your referring to me as 'old Merlin'!" Merlin said.

"Well, you're two thousand bleedin' years old, for chrissake!" Billy replied, his facial expression and body language undergoing dramatic, rapid changes as he switched from one personality to the other.

"That's not the point. You might still show some respect," said Merlin.

"Stuff it!"

"*Stuff it*? Did you say *stuff it*?"

"You bloody well 'eard me! Stuff it!"

"You miserable little delinquent, I've turned people into toadstools for less!"

"Yeah? Let's see you turn me into a toadstool. You'll be a mushie, too, then, won't you? Fat lot o' good that'll do you, won't it?"

"*Aarrrgh*!"

"Aarrgh, yer bloomers! Get out of it!"

"You believe these guys?" said Makepeace. "It's like putting two alley cats in the same sack."

"I think it couldn't hurt to check out that party," Wyrdrune said.

"But it's a real toff sort of affair," said Blood. "You have no invitations. How will you get in?"

"Same way we used to get into parties like that back home," said Kira. "We'll crash."

"Crash?" said Blood, frowning.

"Excuse me for interrupting," said Archimedes, walking to the edge of the desk, "but I've just picked up a message from Constable Shavers."

They all crowded around the computer.

"Put it up on the screen, Archimedes," said Blood. A second later the message from Danny Shavers appeared.

"Shavers to Chief. Don't know exactly what you're on to, but you're on to something, that's certain. Re: Lord Nigel Carfax—I've assembled a file of what little information I could find, along with some relevant newspaper clippings (enter Command LNC for download), but the gist of it is that he's independently wealthy, reclusive, and averse to the press, yet entertains lavishly at his recently renovated castle outside London and his Mayfair townhouse."

"That's it! The townhouse!" Jacqueline said. "Where is it?"

"Must be in the file for downloading," Blood said. "Let's see the rest of it, first."

"Carfax appears to be extremely well connected, but I have no idea what he's into. My inquiries, discreet though they were, have met with considerable resistance. Carfax apparently carries lots of weight. The superintendent himself, no less, had me on the carpet for looking into his affairs. Demanded to know what I was doing and on whose authority. Demanded to know where you were and what you thought you were doing. I explained that you were undercover, following up a lead. The superintendent was not pleased. Perhaps I'm being paranoid, but I suspect something very peculiar's going on."

"Christ, he's even got the damn superintendent in his pocket!" Blood said.

"Or someone who can pull his string," said Kira.

"Couldn't discover anything about Carfax's background. The moment I started looking into it, steel shutters started slamming down. Access denied... access denied... all across the board. What is he, a bloody secret agent? S.I.S.? B.O.T.? I have no idea. No records available. No photographs known to exist, though Carfax is described as tall, dark, very handsome, mid-twenties, about twelve stone. Not much help.

"Interesting sidelight: I called Geoff Chalmers, at the *Gazette*, who owes me a few. Had him check with their society page reporter. Apparently there's some social cachet in knowing 'Nigel' and being able to drop his name, but it seems that many of those who have been to 'Nigel's' parties break under cross-questioning and admit that they had never actually *seen* Nigel. Word is that only the right sort of people are actually admitted into the presence, rather like being let into the back room of an ultra-exclusive private club. And, in fact, there apparently is just such a club, which his lordship calls 'The Inner Sanctum.' The society reporter claims that the beautiful people would gladly disembowel each other to get in. Rumor has it that some very highly placed VIPs can be found in attendance—which I can believe, based on the interference I've encountered—and that the entertainment there makes Roman orgies look like tea with the Queen Mum.

If you're thinking what I think you're thinking, for God's sake, tread softly and be careful. Over and out."

"Well, that's cheerful news," Blood said. "Looks like our friend's got his hooks well and truly into the Home Office, and God only knows where else. Let's see what's on this file Danny has for us."

He called it up, and seconds later Archimedes displayed it on the screen.

"There it is!" Jacqueline said excitedly. "The townhouse is in Charles Street! I *knew* it was a townhouse here in London!"

"That's in Mayfair," Blood said. "Coincidentally, not very far from where you were arrested. But you also mentioned a dungeon of some sort, and I can't imagine any townhouses in Mayfair that have dungeons, unless someone's converted a basement flat into a prison cell or something."

"No, my money's on Carfax Castle," Wyrdrune said.

"And black roses," Blood continued, scanning the screen. "I have no idea what that means. Where do they fit in? Are you quite certain the meaning was literal? You actually saw black roses in your dream vision or whatever it was?"

Jacqueline nodded. "I saw them growing around the door."

"Well, if that's the case, it won't be hard to check it out," said Makepeace. "We have Carfax's address in Charles Street. Let's go take a look."

"We might be better off splitting up," said Kira. "Half of us can go check out the townhouse while the rest of us can crash the party at the castle."

"All right," said Wyrdrune. "Sebastian, you and Jacqueline go check out the townhouse. Take the chief inspector with you, just in case you run into any trouble trying to get inside."

Jacqueline gave him a wry look. "The day I cannot break into a house without getting caught is the day that I retire, *mon cher*. But come along, Chief Inspector, it will be amusing to have a policeman along on a housebreaking."

She looked up at the mirror mounted beneath the canopy of the bed and saw that her entire body was covered with massive purple bruises that curled around her like a serpent's coils. She moaned and crawled weakly from the bed. She fell onto the floor as she tried to stand. Gasping and squeezing her eyes shut against the pain, she struggled to her feet, steadying herself by holding on to one of the canopy uprights on the bed frame. She waited until the wave of nausea had passed, and then she walked unsteadily to where she had let her white dress fall to the floor when she'd tried to seduce Royce Blood. With an effort she bent down to pick it up, each little movement causing her intense pain. It felt as if her entire body had been squeezed in a vise. She thought some of her ribs must have been fractured.

She draped the dress around her neck like a shawl, then pushed her tousled black hair back away from her face, took a deep breath, and walked unsteadily over to the fireplace on the other side of the room. Just a simple act like that took an incredible effort. She leaned against the carved stone mantelpiece a moment to catch her breath, then pressed down hard on one of the stone gargoyle heads adorning it. The head pivoted downward, and with a heavy, scraping sound the back wall of the fireplace opened inward, reveling a secret passageway. She ducked down, stepped into the fireplace, and went through the concealed doorway into the darkness of the secret passage.

Once inside, she pulled down on a lever set into the wall, and the fireplace wall slid back into position, leaving her in total darkness. For a moment she simply stood there in the silent darkness of the stone passageway, breathing heavily, wanting nothing so much as simply to lie down, shut her eyes, and wait for the pain to go away. But she would not allow herself to do that. She would not give in. She would get even.

Her breathing slowed and grew deeper, with a low, guttural rasp to it. She groaned with pain as her chest rose and fell heavily, the rib cage bulging outward and lengthening as her system suddenly started manufacturing adrenaline peptides and growth hormones at an impossible rate, altering her body chemistry and causing her temperature to soar. Saliva mingled with blood dribbled down her chin as her incisors grew longer and larger. Her swollen gums bled as her teeth reshaped themselves, layers of new calcium reforming them with incredible speed, making them longer and sharper. She felt a tingling sensation as hair started to sprout from her forehead and cheeks, the sensation spreading downward as hair growth occurred on her throat and chest and stomach, on her thighs and calves and on the tops of her feet, which throbbed with agony as the complex bone structure was altered and thick pads formed on her souls, at the balls of her feet. Her entire body trembled fiercely as her jawbone lengthened, forming into a snout, and her fingers dripped blood as sharp claws took the place of her fingernails. A low growl rumbled from deep down in her throat.

She could see clearly in the darkness now. The pain was gone. The accelerated growth caused by her transformation had healed her physical injuries, but it did nothing to heal the harm that had been inflicted on her mind. It only intensified it. She had a sharp, feral focus for her burning hatred now.

She moved quickly down the dark stone corridor, walking lightly on the balls of her feet. Then she dropped down to all fours and began to lope quickly along the corridor. She reached the end, where it curved around and became a long, spiral stair leading down to the lower floors of the castle, down to the underground chambers, to the cold, damp, rat-infested dungeons.

There were two liveried guards standing at the doors of the library. They were both armed with long halbreds and nasty-looking daggers. Royce wondered how they managed to stand there in those feathered, floppy velvet hats and silly medieval costumes and keep their faces straight, but apparently they took their roles quite seriously. As they approached the library doors the guards slammed into a sort of parade-rest position, crossing their halbreds before the doors to bar their way, all the while continuing to look straight ahead, expressionlessly.

Royce turned to his companion with a grin. "I say, Damon, you think these chaps would actually use those weapons if we tried to force our way past them?"

"Shouldn't wonder. They look quite serious to me. Let's not push our luck, eh?" He spoke to one of the guards. "Lord Llewellyn Royce Blood would like to pay his respects to Lord Carfax."

Without acknowledging their presence in any way, but continuing to stare straight ahead, the guard knocked loudly on the door three times with the back of the hand holding the halbred. A moment later it was opened from inside by a ravishing blonde in a thin gown very similar to the one that Terri had been wearing, only it was black with a silver girdle, to offset her flaxen hair.

"Lord Llewellyn Royce Blood to see Lord Carfax," intoned the guard, looking dead ahead.

"One moment, my lord," the blonde said in a whispery voice. She gave a slight curtsy and turned to go back into the library, leaving the doors open, though the guards still stood with their halbreds crossed, barring the way.

Royce glanced into the room and saw that the richly paneled walls were mostly obscured by built-in mahogany bookshelves all containing handsome, leather-bound editions. Illumination came from crystal chandeliers, and thick Persian carpets covered the parquet floor. One wall held an emblazoned shield with crossed broadswords behind it, a crossbow underneath it, and mounted above, what appeared to be a facsimile of a human skull with a stuffed raven perched on it. The shield was emblazoned with a curious device, an eye within a pyramid, with the number six in each corner of the triangle formed by the pyramid.

The guests mingling in the library were all men, some dressed formally, as Royce was, others already in medieval costume. Most held drinks in their hands, which were continually replenished by young, gorgeous women moving sinuously among them carrying silver trays on which sat fresh drinks. Royce spotted a number of faces he knew, some of which he was surprised to encounter at such an affair. One of them looked in his direction and recognized him.

"Good Lord, Royce, is that you?"

"Good evening, Judge Featherstone."

"Hah! Good to see you! What the devil are you standing there for? Come on in and have a drink."

"I'm afraid these, uh, gentlemen have not received instructions to admit us yet," said Royce, glancing at the guards.

At that moment the young blonde returned and, with the

courtly instruction "Let them pass" directed the guards to uncross their halbreds, which they did with another smart slam-bang-clash worthy of a couple of regimental color sergeants practicing their drill. Royce looked for Judge Featherstone, but he had already been swept aside into another conversation and apparently had forgotten them.

"Please, follow me, gentlemen," said the blonde, dimpling prettily and giving them another curtsy. Royce couldn't keep from smiling as he followed the girl toward a clutch of people standing by the giant fireplace.

"Carfax really has his people do it up right and proper, doesn't he?" he said, looking to his companion, but suddenly there was no sign of him. It was as if he simply had vanished into thin air. He frowned, but before he had a chance to wonder where the man had disappeared to, he was being introduced to his host.

"Lord Carfax," said the pretty blonde, "May I have the honor to present Lord Llewellyn Royce Blood?"

The handsome young man who turned to face him was dressed all in black—black hose with black velvet slippers embroidered with silver, black loose-skirted tunic with a large embroidered silver dagger over the heart, and a long black hooded cloak. He had a large, jeweled silver dagger in a gem-encrusted scabbard at his waist, and except for his black hair, which was worn short, he looked for all the world like the Black Knight had stepped out of the stories of Sir Walter Scott.

"Ah, good evening, Lord Blood," he said, smiling charmingly and offering his hand. "So good of you to come. I don't believe I've ever had the pleasure."

"No, we haven't met. And please call me Royce."

"Then you must call me Nigel," Joey Lymon said. "Everybody does. Tragic news about your son. My deepest sympathies. It was a terrible shock."

"Yes, it was," said Royce. "Did you know Andrew?"

"Only slightly, I'm afraid. We'd only just met socially."

"Ah," said Royce awkwardly.

"Yes, terrible thing. Still, one must go on. May I offer you a drink?"

A redheaded young woman of incomparable beauty had suddenly appeared at his side with a tray.

"Yes, thank you," Royce said, suddenly feeling the need of one. *How did she know to bring me Scotch?* he wondered. "I came with someone..." he began, but was uncertain of how to finish. He looked around for Damon, thinking perhaps that he should perform an introduction. "Can't seem to find him now."

"No matter. If he's a friend of yours, I'm quite sure he's all right. He's bound to be about somewhere, mingling. We have our own rather exclusive little club here, you know."

"No, actually, I didn't."

"Yes, we call it the Inner Sanctum." A self-deprecating smile. "Sounds rather foolish, doesn't it? Schoolboy sort of thing."

Which was precisely what Royce had been thinking, only Carfax coming out and admitting it like that made it seem somehow less pompous and self-indulgent.

"Still, I find that's part of its charm, in a way. Brings back that whole boyhood secret society sort of thing. A refreshing bit of foolishness in a depressingly serious commercial world. You know, it's often been said that the more complex the life one leads, the greater the need for simple play. Men are just big boys, after all, only with more sophisticated playthings."

"Yes, I'd noticed," Royce said wryly, looking around at the "serving wenches."

Their hip-rolling gait, coy smiles, and come-hither glances seemed to be as much a part of their function as their medieval costumes, which managed to cover them chastely while at the same time leaving precious little to the imagination. He had to admit that he had never before seen such a stunning group of women. He had a suspicion that they might be professionals, but if they were, they had to be the crème de la crème of their profession. He was getting altogether too strong an exposure to beautiful women for one night, Royce thought. He made a note to moderate his drinking for the remainder of the evening. In such surroundings it would be all too easy for a man to make a fool of himself.

But then Royce noticed that it didn't seem as if that consideration was affecting any of the other club members, all of them powerful and influential men in government and industry. The normally staid and terribly proper judge Featherstone was slamming down drinks like a paratrooper on leave, and the conservative, respectable Queen's Counsel, Robert Paddington IV, had his arm around one of the girls and seemed to be nibbling playfully on her ear. And that staunch septuagenarian, Lord Willoughby, actually had one of the young women in his lap and was openly fondling her. None of this seemed particularly remarkable to anyone, least of all Lord Carfax, who went on as if nothing out of the ordinary was happening.

"Anyway, it's good to have you with us, Royce. I've actually been anticipating the pleasure of this meeting. I think you'll find that our little club has some unique attractions. And I don't mean only the ladies," he added with a lecherous smile. "Our meeting hall, for example, is something I'm particularly proud of."

"Yes, I see there's quite a collection of books on hand," said Royce, thinking that Carfax was fishing for a compliment.

Carfax smiled. "Oh, I didn't mean the library," he said. "This is only the antechamber, so to speak. " He glanced around. "Are we all assembled then?"

The lovely blonde had appeared unbidden at his elbow once again, as if he had given her some sort of signal, though Royce hadn't noticed it if he had.

"Everyone is here, my lord," she said in her whispery voice. "The doors to the library were closed.

"Good." He clapped his hands together loudly. "Gentlemen, your attention, please! Now that we all seem to be present and accounted for, let the meeting come to order!"

From somewhere came the sound of a huge gong, and all the lights went out. The gong rang once again, a deafening sound, and Royce covered his ears. Suddenly he felt the floor moving underneath him. The entire floor of the library was sinking, slowly descending down a huge shaft with walls of solid rock. If there was any sound of machinery, it was completely drowned out by the repeated ringing of that giant gong. The sound grew louder and louder the farther they descended. Soon they reached the bottom, and Royce saw an arched cavern opening appear where the entrance to the library had been. The opening was like the mouth of a cave. It led straight back, down a corridor carved from solid rock. The walls were thickly veined with crystals. Torches set into iron sconces in the walls made a dazzling display as the firelight was reflected and refracted in the crystalline formations.

At the end of the corridor stood a giant brass gong, fully twenty feet across. A large figure in a hooded black robe was ringing it with a massive striker. Conversation was impossible in all the din that it created, but no one tried to speak. They all filed out of the library, two by two, and headed down the corridor dressed in long black robes that they must have donned during their descent. Royce felt someone come up behind him, holding a robe for him, and without thinking, he slipped into it as if he were being helped on with a coat. The blond girl came around in front of him, smiled and stood up on tiptoe to kiss him lightly and lingeringly on the lips. He was so taken aback, he couldn't even speak. Then she took his hand and led him down the corridor after the others. Behind them, a rock wall slid into place across the entrance to the corridor.

It was getting late when the cab pulled up to the gates of Carfax Castle.

"I'm tellin' you, I really don't think they're goin'ta let

us in here," the cabbie said. His name was Liam McMurphy, and he was an experienced transportational adept, which meant that over the years he'd learned how to maintain his levitation and impulsion spells while carrying on a conversation at the same time. Being Irish helped. "They don't just go lettin' anyone through, you know. This here's *Lord Carfax's* place."

"Yes, we know," said Wyrdrune patiently. "It's where we asked you to take us, if you'll recall."

"Right, an' if *you'll* recall, I said I'd take you anyblood-where you wanted to go, but I didn't think you'd be gettin' into Carfax Castle, 'specially not on the night of the big bash they're havin'. How'd you expect ta get past the guard on the gate in a bloody taxi?"

"You just don't believe we were invited, do you, Liam?" Wyrdrune said.

"Now, would you be drivin' down in a bloody taxicab if you were the likes ta get yourselves invited to a bash at Carfax Castle?" Liam asked sarcastically.

"No, you've got a point. We'd probably be coming in a chauffeured limo," Wyrdrune said as they pulled up to the gate. "Which is exactly what the guard on the gate will see."

"Eh? How's that again?" said Liam, but the guard on the gate was already approaching what appeared to him as a long, midnight-blue stretch limo with a uniformed chauffeur.

Wyrdrune rolled down the window and held up his hand. There was nothing in it, but the guard saw an engraved invitation. He said, "Thank you, sir," the gates opened, and he waved them through.

"Didja *see* that, now?" said the astonished cabbie, to whom the whole thing had appeared as an inexplicable mystery, since he had not seen what the guard had seen. And then Liam recalled Wyrdrune's words and glanced up in the rearview mirror. "Wait a bit! You did somethin' back there, didn't you?"

"Sssh!" said Wyrdrune, holding a finger up to his lips. "You'll give it all away, Liam."

"Holy Mary Mother o' God," said Liam, comprehension finally dawning as he took them up the long drive to the castle. "And why would a reputable adept be sneakin' into this high-class party? I'm askin' myself. Sure, an' a reputable adept wouldn't. Whatever it is you're up ta, you've done dropped me in it as well now, haven't you?"

"Don't worry, Liam," Wyrdrune said. "That guard didn't even look at you. He only saw a chauffeur driving a long, dark limousine. You know how many chauffeured limos have gone by tonight? Anybody looking at this cab tonight will see a limo. And anyone looking at you in it will see a uniformed chauffeur. So you can turn around and leave as soon as you drop us off. No one will ever know that you were here tonight, and by the time you get back to London, you won't remember either."

"So that's how it is, is it?" Liam said.

"That's how it is," Wyrdrune said. "I'm sorry."

The cabbie sighed. "I see. You're goin' ta toss this place, aren't you?"

"In a way. You might say we have a very old debt to settle with Lord Nigel Carfax."

"Ah, it's like that, is it? An' how do you know I won't give you away?"

"We don't know that, mate," said Billy, leaning forward over the seat. "But we could fix it so you couldn't, see? Or we could fix it even worse, if you get me drift', 'ey?"

The cabbie glanced at Billy with alarm, then he looked at Wyrdrune. "Hell, is he one as well?" he asked.

Wyrdrune nodded "And he's real short-tempered too."

Liam sighed. "Must be a bloody prodigy to be an adept at his age. Ah, well. So there's nothin' for it, then, is there?"

"I'm afraid not, Liam. Sorry."

"Well, in that case I suppose you'll be needin' a ride back to London when you're finished, won't you?"

Wyrdrune glanced at Kira and raised his eyebrows. She shrugged.

"I mean, if I won't be rememberin' anythin', anyway," said Liam, "I may as well stick around an' see what it is I'm goin' ta forget."

"All right, Liam," Wyrdrune said with a grin. "But you remember what I said. We don't want any trouble, do we?"

"I don't know. You sure about this, warlock?" Kira said.

"Oh, I think he'll be all right," said Wyrdrune. "Hell, if we get caught, he's an accessory, isn't he? And he'll be all right so long as he stays with the cab."

They pulled up in front of the entrance and got out. With many of the guests in costume, their appearance did not draw any comment, and though there were a few puzzled looks in Billy's direction, the general consensus seemed to be that they'd gotten in, so they probably belonged there.

"Well, so far so good," said Kira. "What happens now?"

"Now we see if we can find a stairway leading down," said Wyrdrune. He stepped up close to her and lifted his headband slightly. "Is it glowing?"

Kira nodded. She pulled off her fingerless black glove. The sapphire set into her palm was strobing brightly. She quickly pulled the glove back on.

"Modred's here," she said "I can feel it."

Wyrdrune nodded and moistened his lips. His mouth suddenly felt very dry. "Yeah, I can feel it too," he said. "Billy, stay close."

"I can take care of myself, Karpinski," Merlin said. "Or perhaps I should say *we* can take care of ourselves. You just worry about finding Modred. Remember, he was taken prisoner for the express purpose of drawing the two of you here. And now that he's served that purpose, there's no longer any reason for Modred to be kept alive."

"The coast is clear," said Blood, returning to their vantage point across the street from Lord Carfax's townhouse, which they'd been watching carefully for the past half hour or so. "It doesn't look as if anyone is home."

"What coast?" said Jacqueline. "I don't even see any water."

"Never mind," said Blood wryly. "I suppose I was being a bit melodramatic. It just feels very odd to be on the other side of the law for a change."

"You never know, you might get used to it," she said, smiling. "Come on, Sebastian. Let's go quickly while the coast remains clear."

Makepeace chuckled, and Blood gave him a disgusted look. They crossed the street, and Blood tried the gate. "It's locked," he said, frowning.

Jacqueline rolled her eyes. "I hope, *mon ami,* that you are a far better policeman than you are a burglar," she said. "Stand aside and keep a lookout."

She reached into her jacket pocket and brought out a cased set of lock picks. She was about to select one when Makepeace taped her on the shoulder and shook his head.

"Don't bother," he said. He waggled his fingers at the gate, and with a click it unlocked and quietly swung open.

"Sebastian, my love, you are wasting your talents in that university," she said. "When this is over, you and I really must have a long talk."

"Please, do you mind?" said Blood. "I'd appreciate it if you would discuss your impending criminal partnership some other time. I *am* a policeman, after all, remember?"

*"Oui, mon cher,"* Jacqueline said. "One who is about to commit his first offense of breaking and entering." She pushed open the black wrought-iron gate and beckoned him in with a grin. "After you, Chief Inspector."

They closed the gate behind them and went up the short walk to the front door.

"Well, it looks like a rather ordinary garden to me," said Blood, glancing around. "And not much of one, at that. A few shrubs, some creeping ivy, but no black roses."

"Are you sure?" Jacqueline said. She pointed at the front door. "Look."

On either side of the carved front door were decorative stained-glass window panels with a black floral design on a bright red-and-violet background.

"I'll be damned," Makepeace said. "Black roses."

"I knew it!" Jacqueline said excitedly.

She ran up the steps to the front door.

"You mean, we're simply going to walk right in the front door?" said Blood.

"Why not?" said Jacqueline. "I think it will arouse less suspicion than if someone were to see us trying to force open a widow in the back. Besides, having Sebastian with us makes it easy." She gestured toward the lock. "If you would be so kind, Doctor?"

"My pleasure," Makepeace said. He waggled his fingers at the door lock, then blew on the door. It swung open. *"Voilà!"*

Blood glanced at him and shook his head. "Someone like you could make life exceedingly unpleasant for me," he said. He looked around guiltily. "It's hard to believe that I'm actually doing this."

He pushed open the door and went inside, drawing his pistol from his belt holster as he entered. Jacqueline pulled a small, lightweight, polymer-framed 10-mm semiautomatic from her purse.

"Where the devil did you get that?" said Blood.

"Surely you do not expect me to reveal all of my professional secrets, do you, Chief Inspector?" she said with a smile. She was tempted to tell him that it was a present from Modred, one of Morpheus's special pistols that were spellwarded against detection so that it could ride in the hidden compartment of her purse and never be picked up by scanning devices.

They paused briefly in the entryway.

"Do you think guns will do any good against one of these Dark Ones?" Blood whispered.

"I don't know," whispered Makepeace. "I've never met a Dark One. For that matter, I've never fired a gun, either, so I suppose your guess is as good as mine."

"Why are you two whispering?" said Jacqueline.

"In case someone can hear us," Blood whispered.

"I thought you said nobody was home."

"Ah, yes. Well . . ." Blood's voice trailed off lamely. He felt like a complete fool. Of course, he knew better, but the very idea of breaking into a house had him feeling so preposterously nervous and guilty that he seemed unable to think straight. And the prospect of encountering an immortal necromancer did nothing to placate his nerves, either.

"Look, no one is home," Jacqueline said, "and I could discover no alarm system, which means that if there *is* an alarm system, it is a very clever one and we have already set it off, so whispering will not help us, *n'est-ce pas*? Besides, if Lord Carfax is what we think he is, then he has no need of alarm systems, believe me. In that case we can expect to encounter something a great deal more formidable than the police, eh? No offense, Chief Inspector."

"None taken," Blood replied uneasily, wondering just what it was they *could* expect.

The spacious entry hall had a black marble floor and a crystal chandelier. A wide mahogany staircase led to the upper floors. There was a formal dining room to their right and a large sitting room to their left, through a set of French doors. It was richly carpeted and filled with valuable collectibles and paintings, and there were some antique firearms mounted on the wall, to either side of what must have been the Carfax crest.

"I must admit that I am puzzled, though," Jacqueline said, frowning as they went through the house "Look at all this. It must be worth a fortune. If Carfax is not a necromancer, then why *doesn't* he have an alarm system? And if he *is* one of the Dark Ones, then why have we been able to get inside so easily?"

"Perhaps because he wanted us to," said Makepeace.

"What do you mean?" said Blood, glancing at him sharply.

"Well, maybe not us, specifically," Makepeace said, "but think about it. He captured Modred, and having taken him by surprise, he might just as easily have killed him. Only he didn't. Why?"

"So that Wyrdrune and Kira would come after him," said Blood.

"Precisely. The three of them together constitute the single greatest threat to the Dark Ones. They can form the living triangle and call upon the full power of the spell. It would be like facing the Council of the White all over again, embodied in the three of them."

"But with one of them in his hands, he can hold something over the other two," said Blood. "He knows they'd come after him, but it's a risk. He's got to get them where they'd be vulnerable, but he can't allow them to get close to Modred; otherwise they can activate the spell and call upon the full power of the runestones. So he's got to set a trap of some sort.'"

"And the moment Wyrdrune and Kira walk into it, Modred dies," said Jacqueline. "Only what if *we* are the ones who have walked into it?"

# CHAPTER TEN

She reached the end of the stone passageway and stood, panting, on all fours, willing the transformation to begin again. She trembled as it started, and a doglike whimper escaped her throat, then she collapsed upon the ground, jerking as she began to revert back to human form again. Moments later she lay curled up on her side, naked, breathing hard. The changes always took a lot out of her, and she knew she'd have no choice but to feed again soon, but there was something else she had to accomplish first. She stretched slowly. There was no longer any sign of the injuries the necromancer had inflicted upon her. The accelerated, spell-mutated growth she'd experienced during her transformations had healed her supernaturally, but the strain on her body was tremendous.

She got to her feet slowly and waited for her breathing to become steady, for her heartbeat to slow down. Her dark hair fell to her shoulders in disarray. She was burning with fever, covered with a sheen of sweat. She picked up her white dress and put it on, then she pulled the lever in the wall that opened the concealed door. She slipped out into the corridor, then ran down the steps leading to the dungeons.

\* \* \*

It didn't take long for Liam McMurphy to grow bored with sitting in his cab. The meter was still running, but he had long since given up on getting paid. He grimaced at it with disgust and turned it off. A short distance away, he could see some of the other chauffeurs gathered together, having a smoke and drinking coffee that had been sent out to them. Being a cabbie, he didn't much feel like hobnobbing with the chauffeurs—they were paid more than cabdrivers and tended to be snobbish about it—but he could use a cup of coffee, so he opened the door and got out of the cab.

A couple passing by, arm in arm, out for a moonlight stroll, stared at him strangely as he got out of the cab. He glanced down at himself, wondering if perhaps he'd left his fly open, but everything seemed to be in order, and he set out toward the knot of chauffeurs standing perhaps twenty or thirty yards away.

"Hello, lads," he said, coming up to them. "Any more of that good coffee, then?"

They all fell silent and stared at him, giving him a once-over. "Who the devil are you?" one of them said.

"Oh, I'm one o' your lot," Liam said. "Drove a party over in that limo over there." He pointed back toward his cab.

"What, dressed like *that*?" said one of the other chauffeurs with obvious disbelief.

"Here, how did you get in here?" another said.

Liam glanced down at himself, and then it dawned on him that he obviously appeared to these chauffeurs the way he really looked. The spell that gave him the appearance of a chauffeur must have been placed around the cab! The moment he had left it, everyone saw him exactly as he really was.

"Ah, never mind," he said, backing away. "I wasn't really thirsty, anyway."

He turned and plunged into the garden shrubbery. Damn it all, he thought, that wizard might've told me it only worked while I was in the bloody cab! Then he heard a moan coming from close by. He stepped out of the bushes onto a garden path and saw a man dressed in neo-medieval costume sitting doubled over on a stone bench.

"Here, are you all right?" said Liam.

The man turned an unfocused gaze up to him and moaned. His eyes and his breath told the complete story.

"Too much to drink, eh?" Liam said. "Some fellas just can't hold it."

As if in agreement, the drunk moaned again, then pitched forward off the bench and onto his face. Liam prodded him gently with his toe. There was no response. Liam turned him over on his back. The drunk had passed out.

"Well, I guess you've had your partyin' for this night," Liam said. "Too bad. Looks like things are just warmin' up in there." He glanced back toward the castle, then looked down at the unconscious man, who was just about his size. "An' I'll bet they serve a good drink too," he said thoughtfully.

He glanced down at the unconscious drunk again. "Ah, well, my dear ol' Dad always told me, 'Liam, never waste an opportunity to advance yourself'. An' if this here isn't an opportunity starin' me straight in the face, I just don't know what is."

He bent down and started to remove the drunken man's clothes.

Royce had never seen anything like it. The corridor they passed through opened out into an underground chamber designed to resemble a small cavern. The floor was gleaming black veined marble, but the ceiling looked like the rock roof of a cave, complete with small stalactites hanging down. There was a carved stone dais at the back, flanked by huge stone idols that looked like ancient Egyptian deities, human figures with the heads of beasts. In the center of the floor was a round, gold-inlaid circle with a golden pentagram inside it. Placed around the perimeter of the circular room were Roman-style couches and floor cushions. Bronze braziers stood evenly interspersed around the room, with two large ones on either side of the stone dais. Behind the dais, carved in relief on the wall, was a pyramid with an eye inside it. The entire surface of the carving appeared to be covered in hammered gold.

My God, thought Royce as the blond girl led him to a couch, Carfax was being absolutely literal when he was talking about men being nothing more than boys with more sophisticated toys. He was so overwhelmed with how elaborate the whole thing was that he couldn't even speak. What on earth was there to say? Before he had seen this, if anyone had told him that some of the richest and most powerful men in England, peers, heads of corporations, respected jurists, even ministers, dressed up in black robes and gathered in a secret underground grotto hidden beneath a rebuilt medieval castle, where they participated in elaborate orgies with lissome young girls, he would have said it was preposterous.

All right, perhaps not totally preposterous. A few among them easily could have had some secret vices along such lines, but for so many of them to actually join together and openly participate in such a thing as if they were debauched Roman senators and Carfax a reincarnation of Caligula, it was simply mind-boggling! He had known some of these men for years. They were all men of position with families; he never would have believed this. He wanted to go over to Bob Paddington and ask him what in hell was going on, but Paddington was ensconced upon one of the couches with a brunette, and Royce could only gape at what was going on.

Then the next thing he knew, the blonde was pushing him back down onto the couch and fastening her mouth on his. He felt her warm tongue probing between his lips, and it was with an effort that he gently pushed her away. His heart was pounding, and he felt the blood rushing to his face.

In spite of himself, he wanted her. The male animal within him was asserting its brutish nature. His willpower already had been subjected to a fierce assault from Terri, and now this girl, who couldn't have been a day over eighteen and whose name he didn't even know, was pressing up against him and rubbing her leg up and down alongside his. She was young and beautiful and ever so much more than willing as she gazed deep into his eyes, her lips slightly parted, her tongue moistening them seductively. She seemed to have little sparks dancing in her pupils, tiny little fireworks that burst apart, and he felt himself drawn deep down into her gaze, unable to tear his eyes away.

He opened the door and looked down a flight of wooden steps leading to the dark basement. His hand felt strangely cold as he reached out to flick on the light switch, and he blinked, startled, when he saw a torch set in an iron wall sconce suddenly erupt into flame. Then he noticed that the wall was no longer brick but mortared stone, and that the stairs leading down were no longer wooden but stone.

"Hey, have a look at this!" he said.

Jacqueline and Makepeace came up behind him.

"I turned on the light switch, and this damn torch suddenly blazed up!" said Blood. "What's more, I swear those stairs were wood only a moment ago. There's something else too. There's a strange sort of coldness just past this door, a sort of . . . icy watery feeling. . . ."

Makepeace extended his arm past the doorframe. "Aha, what have we here?"

"What is it?" said Jacqueline.

"I believe we've hit the jackpot, my dear," said Makepeace. "I think our friend has just discovered a dimensional portal."

"A what?" said Blood.

"A magical doorway through space and time," explained

Makepeace. "You go through there and you wind up some-place else. It could be somewhere nearby, or on the other side of the world. Something like this takes a great deal of skill and an incredible amount of power to maintain. I don't think there can be any question about Lord Carfax now. Looks like we've found our necromancer."

"And something else as well," Jacqueline said, holding up a soft black leather roll-up case. "I found this upstairs." She opened it, displaying a lethal collection of gleaming knives.

"Perhaps we've found our trap as well," said Blood swallowing nervously.

"Either way the answer is through there," Jacqueline said. She shivered as she stepped through the coldness of the portal, and to Blood it appeared as if she had stepped through some sort of clear, semipermeable membrane. There was a visible disturbance in the air, an effect not unlike that of water rippling as she passed through, took down the torch, and started down the steps.

"After you," said Makepeace.

Blood hesitated.

"You don't have to come if you don't want to, Michael," Makepeace told him. "No one will blame you."

"That's where you're wrong, Sebastian," Blood said. "I'd blame myself." And he stepped through the portal.

Terri opened the door to the cell and ran down the steps with the keys in her hand. She only hoped she wasn't too late. The man chained to wall was motionless. How long had he been down here without food or water? Surely no ordinary man could have lasted this long, but she knew that this was no ordinary man. She lifted up his head and saw that he was breathing but only barely. His eyes were closed.

"Wake up!" she said, slapping his cheek. "Come on, *wake up!*"

Modred groaned faintly.

"Alive!" she said. "You're still alive! You can make it! Come on!"

She unlocked the manacles, and he collapsed to the floor like a sack. She went down with him. Grunting with effort, she extricated herself and rolled him over onto his back. She tore a strip from her dress and dampened it in the water dripping down the wall, then applied it gently to his lips.

"Come on, snap out of it! Use your jewel, like you did before! Go on, take strength from me! Go on, it's your only chance!"

He showed no sign of hearing her, but the ruby set into his chest began to glow faintly. Terri suddenly felt afraid. What if he took too much? What if he drained her of everything she had—what would happen then?

She started to feel dizzy. She was suddenly overwhelmed by a vertiginous, falling sensation. The runestone was glowing brighter. Terri's breathing became more labored, and her chest began to hurt. She started to see colored spots before her eyes. She slumped forward on her hands and knees, gasping for breath. Too much! He was taking too much!

"Stop!" she pleaded. "Stop, *please*!"

And suddenly the terrifying, falling sensation went away, and she felt the pressure on her chest ease off. She sat back, taking deep breaths, feeing weak and dizzy. She looked down at him and saw his chest rising and falling steadily. His eyes opened.

"You," he said, his croaking voice barely audible. "Who—"

"Don't try to talk," she said. "Save your strength. I've come to help you. We've got to get you out of here. Try to stand up."

He started to sit up but immediately fell back again.

"Come on, try! I'll help you!"

She put an arm around him, but he had weakened her by draining off her energy, and it was all she could do just to raise him up several inches before she had to let him back down. She simply didn't have the strength.

"I can't," she said, breathing hard from the exertion. "I can't do it. You've got to make it on your own. You've *got* to. Come on, get up, you can do it. Come on. . . ."

He tried and fell back once again, shutting his eyes and shaking his head.

"No, don't give up!" she said. "Come on! Come on, get up! Get *up*!"

"Need some help, Terri?" came a voice from behind her.

She turned and saw five hooded figures standing on the landing at the top of the steps, just inside the cell door. Four of them were robed in black, the fifth was dressed in a dark red robe. He pulled back his hood and smiled at her.

"*Joey!*"

"The name's Nigel, you cheap slut," he said. "Lord Nigel Carfax. Joey Lymon's dead. And so are you."

"Nigel, listen—"

"Listen, nothing!" He pulled a gun out from under his robe and leveled it at her. "And don't you go trying to change on me, either! This isn't loaded with silver bullets, but I understand that plain, ordinary lead ones will do just as well. Now get away from him! Move!"

He gestured with the gun, and she got up unsteadily and moved away from Modred.

"Joey . . . Nigel . . . you don't understand. You've got the wrong idea. I was only—"

"*Shut your cakehole, bitch!*" he shouted. In his fury he started slipping back into his Cockney accent. "You take me for a bloody fool? You're just like them other slags I done carved up. Oh, I've been waitin' for a crack at you! He promised me! He promised me that I could 'ave you. Oh, I've wanted you so bad! I've got a nice, long *sharp* one especially for you!" He stood there, glaring at her wildly, the gun shaking in his hand. Then he managed to compose himself again and gestured to the robed figures behind him. "Bring them!"

The hooded figures started down the steps to the floor of the cell. Terri glanced at Modred with desperation. He was lying motionless on his back, his eyes closed. He was barely breathing. Her heart sank. She'd been too late, after all. But she couldn't give up now. She knew only too well what would happen to her if Joey had his way. She could expect about as much mercy from him as her victims had received from her. She made up her mind that she'd make him shoot her before she would submit to his savage ministrations.

Two of the robed men took hold of her while the other two picked up Modred. The men carrying Modred preceded them back up the steps and out the cell door. Joey followed them, his pistol aimed at her back. And suddenly she realized exactly what he planned to do, what he'd been ordered to do, and she knew that she'd been meant to be a part of it right from the start. She went with them meekly, as if resigned to her fate, and when they reached a bend in the corridor, she summoned up all her remaining strength and shoved herself hard into the robed figure on her right, slamming him into the corridor wall, twisting out his grasp as the impact stunned him, and immediately whipping the other man around and sending him staggering into Joey. The gun went off as both men fell, but she was already leaping over the two men and running back down the corridor as fast as she could, stumbling and gasping for breath.

Behind her, Joey shoved aside the body of the hooded man who'd taken his bullet and got up, furious. She already had gone around a bend in the corridor, so there was no opportunity to take a shot. The man who'd been slammed against the wall started to give chase, but Joey stopped him.

"Never mind her," he said. "I'll settle with her later." He put away his gun and gestured at Modred. "She'll have to wait. We have to take care of him first. Go on."

\* \* \*

The Great Hall of the castle throbbed with deafening music, and illusory bolts of jagged lightning stabbed down from the roiling thunderheads conjured up by the band's effects adept. A synthesizer with thaumaturgically etched chips did a waddling sort of dance across the stage, emitting a mixture of rising power chords and screams that sounded like a chorus of the damned as the lead singer flailed at it with a long black whip. Bodies dressed in all sorts of outlandish renaissance punk and neo-medieval costumes collided and rebounded on the dance floor. Wyrdrune had young women press themselves up against him on several occasions, and Kira had angrily shoved away at least half a dozen men who had tried to paw her. The air was filled with the heady fumes of opium and hashish, as well as some of the newer, far more potent, thaumagenetic hybrids.

*"This is crazy!"* Kira shouted into Wyrdrune's ear. *"We're not going to find anything here!"*

*"There's got to be an entrance to the lower levels somewhere,"* Wyrdrune shouted back into her ear over the deafening music.

*"Awwright"* shouted Billy, his head banging in time to the music and moshing his way into the crowd, slamming into bodies and rebounding off them to spin crazily off in another direction.

They followed him, pushing their way through the crowd, going through one of the arches in the cross wall to a small corridor with a flight of stone steps leading upward to the next floor. Wyrdrune started toward it.

"Hey, warlock," Kira said. "We want to go *down*, not up, don't we?"

"The only other way is to try getting through that crowd again," said Wyrdrune. "Let's try upstairs and see if we can't come down on the other side. There's got to be another stairway somewhere. And grab *him,* for God's sake!"

Kira's arm lashed out, and she caught Billy by the coat as he was about to go back into the Great Hall.

"Don't worry about me," said Merlin. "You go on ahead. Find Modred. Carfax is expecting you, but he doesn't know about me yet."

"You sure?" said Kira.

"'Course I'm bloody sure!" said Billy. "G'wan, now! Git!"

Kira shrugged and followed Wyrdrune. "Man, that's a spooky kid," she said. "I hope he knows what the hell he's doing."

"Do we?" said Wyrdrune.

"Hmm, you've got a point there, warlock. Hell, let's go."

They went up the stairs, past a couple locked in a passionate embrace on the landing, and through an archway into the corridor on the second floor. The corridor ran straught along the cross wall for the full width of the building. As they headed toward the opposite end Kira hesitated and grabbed Wyrdrune's arm.

"Hey, warlock. Check this out."

She was looking through an open archway into the castle chapel. In the dim light of the candles they could see several couples huddled together in the dark corners. It didn't look like they were praying. But then, it wasn't that kind of chapel. Above the altar, which was covered with a black velvet cloth emblazoned with a golden circle with a pentagram inside it, was a huge, gleaming sliver cross hung upside down. The stained-glass windows showed grisly scenes of human sacrifice, on top of Mayan temples, in Druidic torchlight rituals, in ancient Egyptian rites and secret ceremonies in Restoration England. The very walls seemed to throb with malevolence.

Wyrdrune simply stared at it with astonishment.

"You believe this?" Kira said. "Right out in the open, as if he didn't care who knew."

"He doesn't," Wyrdrune said, shaking his head. "There's a level of arrogance here that's frankly terrifying.

What does it matter what we know or what we think? We're only humans, after all."

"Are we?" Kira said.

"What?"

"Are we still human?" she said. She glanced down at her palm, covered by the fingerless black leather glove. "I mean, what the hell are you when you've got an enchanted runestone that's become a part of you, a stone that's animated by the souls of immortal archmages from the dawn of time?"

"Christ, at a time like this you start getting metaphysical on me?" Wyrdrune said.

She looked up at him and grimaced. "Yeah, sounds more like something you'd do, huh? Come on, let's get the hell out of here and go find Modred. I think I see another stairway down at the end of the hall."

They went down the spiral stairs, passing some drunken party goers on their way, and came out in a small room at the side of the Great Hall. There was a bar set up in the corner, and a huge fireplace with a carved stone mantelpiece against the opposite wall. There was a large blond man in an ill-fitting leather doublet leaning on the mantelpiece, having a drink and talking to a pretty young woman.

"Hey, isn't that—" Kira asked.

"Our cabbie, Liam!" Wyrdrune said. "What the hell is he doing here?"

"Crashing the party, obviously," Kira said.

Wyrdrune rushed over to him. "Excuse me," he said to the young woman, "do you mind if I have a word in private with my friend? It's about his wife and kids."

She gave Liam a disgusted look and walked away.

"Well, now, what the hell didja do *that* for?" said Liam. "And how in blazes didja know I had a wife an' kids?"

"Liam, what the hell are you *doing* here?"

"Oh, havin' a drink or two or three, takin' in the atmosphere—"

"Get out of here right now!" said Wyrdrune. "Get back to the cab at once!"

"Well, is that the way it is, now?" Liam said. "A fine thing. You can go sneakin' into this fine party, and I have to be sittin' in the bloody cab all night, without even a drink to keep me warm? And here I was nice enough to stick around an' give you a ride back—after you went an' burgled the place too."

"Liam, you idiot, don't you realize that you're in danger here?"

"No, maybe you'd better explain it to him,'" Kira said wryly.

"Yes, maybe you'd better explain it to me," Liam said, leaning on one of the stone gargoyles. It swiveled down suddenly and dumped him on the floor as the back wall of the fireplace opened inward with a low, scraping sound "What in bloody hell?" he said.

"A secret passage!" Kira said.

"No wonder we couldn't find a way down to the lower levels," Wyrdrune said. "The entrances must all be camouflaged like this. Come on."

He ducked down under the mantelpiece and stepped over the hearth, batting at his clothing as the sparks shot up. Kira followed him, bending down and lightly hopping over the blaze. Once on the other side, Wyrdrune felt around on the wall, and his fingers found the lever that closed the secret door. He pulled it down, and the door slid to once again, leaving them in darkness. Kira slipped off her leather glove, and the glow coming from her runestone seemed much brighter now, illuminating the secret passage with a soft blue light.

"Now we're getting somewhere," she said as Wyrdrune stood there furiously slapping at his smoldering coat. "Come on, put yourself out and let's get going."

Liam got back up to his feet and stared at the fireplace. The door had closed, and there was no sign of Wyrdrune and Kira. The gargoyle had pivoted back up again. He frowned and pulled it down once more. It swiveled, and with a scraping sound the back of the fireplace opened inward once again.

"Faith, an' you're gonna regret this, Liam McMurphy," he said to himself as he stopped down low and, shielding his face, stepped over the flaming hearth.

A woman standing by the bar poked her companion in the side with her elbow and slurred, "George . . ."

George turned around and fixed her with a bleary stare. "Yes, darling?"

"George, that man there just went into the fireplace and he didn't come back *out*!"

George glanced at the fireplace. The back wall had swung closed. He looked from the fireplace to her, then he beckoned to the bartender. "I say, old boy, give me whatever it is *she's* having."

Terri collapsed on the stairway, unable to run any farther. She sobbed for breath, trying desperately to fill her burning lungs. She had passed the limit of her endurance, and she almost wept with relief when she realized that she wasn't being pursued. She put her head down on the step before her, feeling the damp coolness of the stone, swallowing hard and trying to regulate her breathing. She was on the verge of passing out. She had to make the change. It was the only chance she had. Once the transformation was complete, she would get her strength back.

And then what? Escape into the night? Could there ever be any escape from *him*? Her one chance had been that mage he had imprisoned, the one with that strange gem embedded in his chest, but now that chance was gone. She understood now that he had been chained up in the dungeon in order to weaken him, bring him to the very point of death, where he could no longer offer any resistance, and then . . .

She trembled violently and groaned with pain as the change began. Perhaps escape would be impossible, after all, she thought. Perhaps she'd never get away. Perhaps she'd finally met the one man who would be her master, the one man she had never thought she'd meet, the one man she'd always sought with a perverse and desperate longing, hating all other men because she found them wanting. Weak. Contemptible.

She had always taken a grim satisfaction in destroying them, telling herself that she had brought them to their just desserts. The bastards deserved it for seeing her as nothing but the object of their desires, a possession to be fought for and won, then displayed as a badge of their own worth. They deserved it for trying to manipulate and use her, and then, through their own weakness, allowing her to turn it all around on them. And so she had grown bitter and cynical and hard. And maybe it was only fitting that she had ended up like this, she thought, because it was only now that she realized why she hated Joey Lymon with a loathing greater than she had ever felt before for anyone or anything except, perhaps, at that very moment, for herself. For Joey Lyman, with his sick hatred of all women, was her mirror image. To look at him was to see a reverse reflection of herself. And for showing her that, she wanted to kill him.

She suddenly heard voices.

*"Aha, what have we here?"*

*"What is it?"*

*"I believe we've hit the jackpot, my dear. I think our friend has just discovered a dimensional portal."*

The voices seemed to be coming from behind the wall. They were talking about a doorway, a magical doorway through space and time . . . and suddenly she realized where she was. She had collapsed on the stairs leading down to the dungeons, just below the landing where the magical doorway connected the castle with the house in Mayfair.

*"Either way, the answer is through here,"* she heard a female voice with a French accent say, and a moment later

an arm came through the wall and took the torch down from the iron sconce. An attractive, dark-haired woman in a maroon velvet suit stepped through the wall and onto the landing. She took a couple of steps down, and then she noticed Terri sprawled upon the stairs. At the same moment Terri noticed the gun that the woman was holding in her other hand.

For a moment Jacqueline was frozen with shock at the sight of Terri, halfway through the change. She looked down and saw a grotesque vision, a raven-haired woman with fangs protruding from her bloody gums, saliva dripping, fur sprouting from her arched back, her fingers hooked like talons, long claws scrabbling at the stone, and in the same moment that Jacqueline brought her gun up and fired, Terri launched herself backward off the steps and onto the floor of the corridor below. She rolled and came up on all fours as Blood fired his pistol, too, and then she fled, half running, half loping down the dark corridor.

"Did you hit it?" Blood asked.

"I don't know," said Jacqueline, still stunned by what she'd seen. "Did you?"

"I think I winged it. What in God's name *was* that creature?"

"A werewolf," Makepeace said from behind them.

"A *werewolf*!" Blood said. "I always thought such creatures didn't exist!"

"They don't occur in nature, if that's what you mean," said Makepeace. "They have to be created. They're among the foulest examples of the necromancer's art. He seizes upon some weakness in the soul and plants his will there like a cancer, working his perverted spell, bringing the beast forth out of the subconscious in a transformation such as you've just seen. Their victims become the necromancer's victims too. The flesh feeds the werewolf; the necromancer takes the soul."

"My brother..." Blood said.

"Yes, I'm afraid so," said Makepeace.

"Will bullets kill it?"

"Oh, yes," said Makepeace. "And they don't need to be silver. She may not look it, but she's still human. You would have done that poor creature a favor if you'd killed her."

"Then let's go finish the damn job," he said, starting down the stairs.

"That isn't why we came," said Jacqueline. "We must find Modred first."

"Go and look for him, then. I'm not going to let that creature get away."

"Michael, wait!"

"We'd better go after him," said Makepeace. "That stubborn cop's going to get himself killed.

"I'm worried about Billy," Kira said, holding her hand up and lighting the way as they went through the narrow passageway.

"He can take care of himself," said Wyrdrune, following her.

"Hell, he's' just a kid."

"Kira, he's two thousand years old."

"You're talking about Merlin. I'm talking about Billy."

"What's the difference?"

"You're talking as if they're the same person," Kira said.

"They *are* the same person!"

"Look, warlock, I'm not stupid, all right? I know they're both sharing the same body, but the fact is that it's *Billy's* body and Merlin just sort of moved in and took control."

"Looks to me more like Billy takes control most of the time," said Wyrdrune.

"You don't think he's entitled to?" she said. "Look, I know how you feel about Merlin; he was your teacher. In a way he was the father that you never had, but the point is that he's *dead*."

"He isn't dead. You heard Sebastian explain how—"

"He might as well be dead," said Kira, interrupting him.

"His body is. All that's left of him is his personality, his soul, his ego, whatever the hell you want to call it. The fact is, he's a *ghost*. And if he gets himself in over his head again, he can always flee his body, just like he did the last time. Only where does that leave Billy?"

"No," said Wyrdrune, shaking his head. "I can't believe he'd do that. He wouldn't needlessly expose Billy to a risk like that."

"Oh, no? What do you call coming here? A grade-school field trip?"

"Well, for one thing, Billy's not exactly a grade-school kid. He's more mature and he's got better survival instincts than most adults I know. What he didn't have until Merlin came along was a future. What kind of life did he have to look forward to? Living in the streets, sleeping in garbage, stealing, getting arrested . . ."

His voice trailed off as he realized what he was saying. He might just as well have been describing Kira's childhood.

"Yeah," she said, looking back at him over her shoulder. "I know something about that sort of life, remember?"

He suddenly understood where her concern was coming from. It wasn't just maternal instincts. She identified with Billy. And Billy identified with her as well. They recognized each other, two different people cut from the same mold. Street people. Hustlers. Survivors. People nobody else ever game a damn about.

"I see," said Wyrdrune. "He would've been happier the way he was, is that it? The way you were?"

"Maybe," she said.

He reached out and took her by the arm, stopping her for a moment. "Listen," he said, "I don't know about you, but all my life I've wanted to do something that *mattered*. Not necessarily something that would make me famous or rich, but something that would make a difference. The man we came here looking for, the one you've got all these feelings for that you don't want to talk about, he understands. And he's willing to die for it."

"And that's supposed to be noble?" Kira said. "Look where it got him."

"Hey, I don't know what's noble and what isn't, and frankly I couldn't care less, all right?" he said. "It isn't about nobility. It's about what matters. It's about what you believe. It's about making your life count for something."

"What does it count for if you're dead?" she said.

"I guess that depends on what you did with it while you were alive," said Wyrdrune. "And if you didn't do anything, than I guess that's what it counts for. Don't worry about Billy, Kira. He's a lot more than just a tough kid from the streets now. And for that matter, so are you."

He took her hand, the one with the runestone in it, and held it in both of his, the soft blue glow illuminating their faces.

"This doesn't mean that you were taken over or forced into doing anything you really didn't want to do, just as Merlin becoming part of Billy doesn't mean that Billy is possessed. Not really."

"No? What does it mean, then?"

"It means he's not alone anymore," said Wyrdrune. "And neither are you."

From somewhere far away they heard the deep sound of a large gong being struck.

"What the hell was that?'" said Kira.

The gong sounded again.

"It came from somewhere below us," Wyrdrune said "And somehow I have a feeling that's not a bell calling folks to church. Come on, let's move."

# CHAPTER ELEVEN

With an effort Royce Blood wrenched himself out of the dreamy fugue induced by the dancing lights in the blond girl's eyes. He tried to push her away gently, but she continued to press down against him, her lips seeking his, and he finally took her by the upper arms in a firm grip and forcefully rolled her over onto the couch so he could get out from under her. He started to get up off the couch, but she pulled him back down beside her again, putting her arms around him and pulling him close.

"Stop it!" Royce shouted. "For God's sake, stop it, please!"

But his voice was lost in the booming reverberations of the giant gong as several hooded figures came into the chamber, carrying the body of a bearded, bare-chested man on their shoulders. Carfax came out on the dais, dressed in his crimson robe and flanked by two hooded acolytes. He slowly raised his arms, bent at the elbows, palms up, and the golden circle and pentagram set into the floor began to rise, revealing that it was a round black marble column about three feet high. As Royce watched in stunned silence the hooded figures placed the unconscious, bare-chested man down upon the altar, flat on his back. Royce noticed that there was a red stone over the man's heart.

The man looked dirty and emaciated, his beard and hair were unkempt, and there were the cruel red marks of shackles on his wrists. Carfax beckoned to one of the hooded figures, and the man came forward. Carfax reached into his robe and took out a long, gleaming ceremonial dagger and handed it to the man he had beckoned forth. Comprehension suddenly dawned on Royce, and he looked around in astonishment at all the eminent men around him, lying on the couches in various stages of undress beneath their hooded cloaks, each with a beautiful young woman in his arms, each with a sort of glazed, drugged look about him, and he shook his head, muttering, "No, it isn't possible. They can't actually mean to . . ."

He looked up at the hooded figure stepping up to the altar where the unconscious man lay, raising the dagger high overhead in both hands. . . .

"*No!*" screamed Royce.

The hooded figure hesitated, looked up, and his hood fell back.

"My God!" said Royce. "Ian?"

His oldest son stared at him, and Royce saw the recognition in his eyes. Ian smiled and raised the knife once more.

"*Ian, no!*" shouted Royce, and suddenly there was a low, throaty growl behind him and he felt sharp claws sink into his shoulders.

Terri gasped with pain as she loped down the dark corridor. She was bleeding from the side, where Blood's bullet had struck her. If she had been in human form, the wound would have incapacitated her, but the transformation was complete now, and raw, animalistic rage surged through her. Even so, with the strength Modred had taken from her, and with Blood's bullet lodged in her side, she was in severe pain and pushing herself to the limits of her endurance. She didn't know who those people with the guns were, but she knew she was leaving a trail of blood, and she could hear at least one of them not too far behind, pursuing her. And she knew just where she was going to lead them. Perhaps she hadn't lost yet.

Liam McMurphy couldn't see a thing. He slowly felt his way along the secret passageway, running his hand along the cool, damp stone. He was beginning to think that this had been a very bad idea. The darkness was starting to get to him, and he kept up a steady monologue to steady his nerves.

"All right, Liam, old son," he said softly, "you saw those two come in here, an' you haven't tripped over them yet, so they must be up ahead somewhere. This bloody tunnel must go somewhere, mustn't it? Christ, I wonder if there're any rats in here?"

He froze and squeezed his eyes shut as he felt something slither over his shoes.

"Ach, McMurphy, you stupid git, you had to go an' say that, didn't you?"

With a convulsive movement he shook the creature off his foot, swallowed hard, and pressed on through the darkness.

Billy sat on the stone balcony wall in a large arched opening overlooking the Great Hall, nodding his head in time to the music. He leaned back against the side of the stone archway, one leg bent at the knee, the other dangling over the side. Directly below him was the band, playing loud enough to make the stones groan, and the dancers on the floor had become even more frenzied as the night progressed. From where he was sitting, roughly at eye level with the huge chandeliers, Billy could see the entire Great Hall, most of the upper balcony, and the outer entry hall.

There were other people on the balcony, mostly couples, but two pretty young women who were on their own, standing at the balcony across from him, spotted him and waved. One of them blew him a kiss and beckoned him over. Billy laughed and shook his head.

"Gor', d'you see that?" Billy said, inhaling sharply. "Best offer I've 'ad all year, an' I'm sittin' 'ere shakin' my 'ead like a bleedin' loony."

*"You can get yourself into a great deal of trouble if you go running every time a pretty girl beckons,"* Merlin said inside his mind. *"Believe me, I know."*

"Yeah, well I wouldn't mind 'avin the chance to find out for myself, y'know."

*"I can appreciate that,"* said Merlin, *"but the timing is rather unfortunate at the moment. We need to stay alert and on our guard."*

Billy reached into his pocket and brought out a pack of cigarettes. He stuck one in his mouth and started rummaging in the pockets of his coat for matches.

*"Here,"* said Merlin. Billy's right hand came up and he snapped his fingers. A flame appeared at the tip of his thumb.

"Thanks," said Billy, lighting the cigarette, inhaling deeply and then blowing out his thumb.

*"Don't mention it."*

"Y'think anything's 'appened yet?"

*"Not yet,"* said Merlin, and Billy felt butterflies in his stomach. *"Not yet, but very soon. Very, very soon."*

Royce cried out with pain and twisted away, turning as he did so, and he gasped at what he saw. The beautiful blond girl had become transformed. Her ears had become long and pointed; her teeth had lengthened into fangs, and her eyes were yellow, without irises or pupils. She had changed into something inhuman, demonic. Saliva dribbled from her lips as she bared her teeth at him and growled, reaching for him with fingers twice their normal length, with long, hooked talons at the ends.

"Is that your dream girl, Father?" Ian asked, laughing at him.

And as the creature grabbed him Royce saw that all the other women were turning into hideous monsters as well.

*"Kill him!"* Carfax shouted. *"Kill him now!"*

And as Ian raised his knife once more, Royce struggled to break free of the creature's grasp and screamed, *"Ian, for God's sake—"*

And then the man lying on the altar opened his eyes, and the jewel embedded in his chest blazed suddenly, sending out an intense beam of crimson light that bathed Ian in a glowing red aura.

As Carfax stood motionless, stunned by the sight, one of his acolytes screamed, *"No! No, it can't be! Stop him! Kill him, you fool! Kill him! Kill him!"*

As if suddenly awakened, the other men slowly started coming to their senses, but when they saw what horrors their beautiful companions were turning into, they started to scream in mindless terror. Carfax suddenly leapt off the dais, reaching into his robe and pulling out a gun as he ran toward the altar in the center of the chamber. In desperation Royce tried to wrench himself away from the creature that held him, and only his twisting action saved his throat from being torn out. He felt the fangs sink into his shoulder, and he screamed in agony—

And then a dark shape came hurtling across the chamber, meeting Carfax as he came running across the floor toward the altar, where Ian stood motionless, swaying unsteadily as his life energy was drained away.

In a growling, bestial voice, Terri cried out, "Joey!" and launched herself at him.

A shot cracked out.

But it didn't come from Joey's gun.

Terri howled with pain as the bullet took her in mid-leap and her momentum carried her into Joey. They both fell to the floor, and Joey scrambled away from her as she dragged herself across the floor, trying to crawl away.

Michael Blood stood motionless in a combat crouch on the stone steps that led into the chamber, his pistol in his hands. He had fired at the werewolf as she leapt, but only now did the scene that confronted him fully register, and he stood as if rooted to the spot, staring with slack-jawed shock at the macabre tableau before him.

"Ian . . ." he said.

*"Michael!"* Royce screamed in agony

"Father!" Galvanized into action, Michael shifted his aim and fired. His shot struck the creature that had been the blond girl in the head, and it fell back, lifeless, but in that same moment Joey came up with his gun and fired twice.

The first bullet missed him, but the second one struck Blood in the upper chest and sent him flying backward, to land hard on the steps. Then Joey turned quickly and leveled his gun at Modred.

With a scream of rage Royce charged as Joey fired.

They came out of the passageway into the dungeons at a point where three corridors intersected. They stood uncertainly in the open area lit by torches on the walls, but there was nothing to tell them which way to go. And then they heard the sharp cracking of gunfire off to their left.

"Shots!" said Kira. And then she grunted with pain and doubled over, clutching at her side.

*"Unnnh!"* Wyrdrune staggered, also grabbing his side. "Come on," he said, grimacing with pain. "Modred's been shot! Run!"

*"Carfax!"*

Bellowing with rage, Royce slammed into Joey, his fingers going for his throat, but Joey brought the gun up sharply and smashed it into the side of Royce's head. Royce went down with a grunt, and Joey kicked him savagely, then turned to aim the gun at Modred once again, but another shot cracked out and he felt the bullet whistle past his ear. Jacqueline stood on the stairs holding her semiautomatic in both hands and firing rapidly. Joey scrambled across the floor to get out of the line of fire.

"Get them!" he shouted. "Kill them!"

With a chorus of howls the beast-women surged toward the stairs. Jacqueline picked up Blood's gun and started firing with both pistols at the attacking creatures, dropping five of them as they charged her, but there were far too many for her to shoot. And then Makepeace came up beside her, took a deep breath, and exhaled. The floor beneath the attacking creatures' feet suddenly turned to ice, and they fell, snarling and spitting, as they piled up at the foot of the stairs.

Joey scrambled up the steps of the dais, turned, and fired his gun at Modred once again, but in that same instant Ian collapsed to the floor as Modred sat up, blood pouring from the flesh wound in his side, his eyes burning with red fire, and twin beams shot out from them, converging on the bullet that was hurtling toward him at thirteen hundred feet per second and incinerating it in midair.

Joey fired three more times in rapid succession, and each bullet was incinerated the same way. He hurled the empty gun at Modred, and it, too, went up in puff of smoke. Then he ran as several of the creatures launched themselves at Modred.

A pencil-thin beam of brilliant green light bisected the chamber and struck the jewel in Modred's chest. He hurled the beasts off effortlessly, and a bright red beam shot out from his runestone, striking Kira's upraised palm where she stood on the opposite side of the chamber, at the end of the dais. As Wyrdrune moved toward the stairs a bright blue beam shot out from Kira's hand and struck the blazing green emerald in his forehead.

The triangle was formed.

The three of them were linked by beams of thaumaturgic energy as they drew upon the full strength of the ancient spell, the most powerful incantation ever devised by the archmages of the Council of the White, who now lived on through them. They raised their arms over their heads, and the glowing borders of the triangle extended upward, forming a pyramid of light that spread out from them to encompass the entire chamber.

The howling beasts created by the necromancer clutched at their throats and fell thrashing to the floor, then, with a sound like air rushing in to fill a vacuum, the pyramid of light collapsed back into itself and they all lay still upon the floor, set free, reverted back to human form.

"Carfax!" Jacqueline shouted, pointing toward the passageway where Joey had gone. "He's getting away! Stop him! He's the necromancer!"

"No," said Modred. "Forget him. He's not the one."

"He's not?" said Wyrdrune. "Then who . . . ?"

"One of the others," said Modred, looking around. "The red-haired one . . . he's gone."

"It *wasn't* Carfax?" Wyrdrune said.

Kira looked at Wyrdrune with alarm.

"Oh, God!" she said. *"Billy!"*

It had all gone wrong. Terribly, terribly wrong. He couldn't believe it. Modred had been on the very edge of death, past the point where even the power of the Old Ones could have kept him alive. How was it possible that he could have recovered? And to drain a human's life energy to fortify himself? That was against everything the Council of the White believed!

He cursed himself as he ran up the steps to the Great Hall. He had felt the other two drawing closer; he had sensed their presence and had timed it all to exquisite perfection. And it had all gone wrong. Now, instead of them being caught in a trap, he would be caught himself if he could not escape. But there was still one advantage that he held over his old enemies, whose spirits lived on within the runestone.

The fools cared about the humans.

*"It's happening,"* said Merlin. "It's happening right now."

"What do we do?" said Billy.

*"Wait,"* said Merlin.

"But what if they need us?"

*"It's something I learned from Arthur, lad—you re-member, I told you about him—and it's the only damn thing I ever learned from him, because the thickheaded bastard really didn't know that much, in spite of everything I tried to teach him. But fighting, that he knew about. He taught me that in a battle with a powerful enemy, where the outcome is uncertain, always hold some of your strength back in reserve. And if things start to turn against your main force, wait until your enemy thinks he has you beaten . . . and then bring in your reserves and hit him with everything you've got."*

"You mean so 'e'll be tired o' fightin', and you'll be comin' in fresh with more o' your boys when 'e least ex-pects it?"

*"Precisely,"* Merlin said. *"You learn quickly."*

"Nothin' quick about it," Billy said. "Street gangs been mixin' it up that way for years. Gor', wish I knew what was goin' on down there. Makin' me bloody nervous, wai-tin' like this."

*"There!"* said Merlin.

"What? Where?"

*"An incredible surge of thaumaturgic emanations. They've formed the triangle! That must be it! That means Modred is all right! Either that or . . ."*

"Or what?"

*"We'll know soon enough."*

Billy flicked the cigarette over the side of the balcony and stood up, clenching and unclenching his fists. He reached into the pocket of his leather jacket and brought out a flick knife. He hit the button and it snikked open.

*"Billy, I told you, there really wasn't any point in bring-ing that thing. Do you seriously think something like that can—"*

"Ey, look, you use what works for you, old man, an' I'll use what works for me, all right?"

Joey ran up the stone steps toward the landing where the dimensional portal connected the dungeons of Carfax Castle to the basement entrance of the house on Charles Street. He stumbled up the steps, staggered, regained his balance . . . and ran right into the stone wall.

He rebounded off the wall and fell to the landing, stunned by the impact. He felt warm blood trickling down his face. He had almost knocked himself out. He brought his hand up and discovered that his nose was broken. And as he felt his face he also discovered that Lord Carfax had reverted back to Joey Lymon.

"Too bad, Joey," said a familiar voice "It just closed. Another moment sooner and you might've made it."

He looked up and saw Terri standing just above him on the flight of steps leading down to the landing where he lay. She had reverted back to human form, but her nude body was covered with blood. She coughed, and blood bubbled up from between her lips and ran down her chin. Her breath came in wheezing gasps. Then he noticed that she was holding the ceremonial dagger that Ian Blood had dropped back at the altar.

"I'm dead, Joey," she said, smiling through the blood, "but I haven't lost."

He screamed as she raised the knife and fell down on top of him.

He came running out into the Great Hall, glancing over his shoulder to see if he was being pursued. Perhaps they wouldn't come that way, he thought. Perhaps they'd teleport and appear directly in his path. They were at full strength now, while he had used up almost all the power he had left. He needed all of it for the spell that would help him to escape. He'd bring the entire castle down around their heads.

He held out his arms and concentrated on the central load-bearing pillar of the cross-wall. The volume of the music drowned out the sounds of the stone cracking and breaking apart, but up on the balcony, Billy felt the vibrations as he leaned upon the stone balustrade.

A shudder went through the cross wall, and chips of stone and mortar started to rain down upon the dancers. They looked up and started to scream as they saw the fissures spreading through the stone above them.

*"Billy—"*

"Right, I see 'im." Billy put the blade of the flick knife between his teeth and stood up on the wall.

*"Billy, what are you . . . Billy!"*

Billy leapt off the balcony, jumping up and out, his arms stretched out for the massive chandelier. For a moment he seemed to glide like a flying squirrel, his leather coat flapping like wings, and then his fingers just barely reached the lower rim of the chandelier, and he grabbed hold, swinging down and out . . .

. . . and then he let go.

He came down at a steep angle, feet first, and plowed right into the necromancer, who never expected an attack from the air. They both went down hard. Billy rolled in an attempt to take some of the force out of the impact. The cross wall above them was crumbling, and people were milling around in a panic, yelling and streaming for the doors. Billy swore as he felt pain shoot through his leg, and he started to push himself up, but his left leg buckled underneath him. He looked up.

"Merlin, the wall!"

A huge block of stone was plummeting down directly above him. Merlin threw out his arms, the little finger and forefinger of his left hand extended, blue sparks crackling between them. A bolt of pure thaumaturgic energy shot forth from his hand, and the huge block of stone disintegrated in midair. Then Merlin quickly turned his attention to the Dark One—

—and saw the necromancer on his knees, an expression of utter amazement on his face as he looked down at the flick knife protruding from his chest. He looked up with disbelief and shook his head.

"A boy," he said. "A mere *boy!*"

And then he pitched forward onto his face.

"Interestin', ain't it?" Billy said, grimacing with pain. "Didn't know we could do two things at the same time."

*"Billy!"* Kira shouted, running up to him with Wyrdrune and Modred close behind her.

"Better do something about that roof, love," Billy said, "or before you know it, we'll 'ave the rain comin' in."

Liam McMurphy came out of the corridor and stopped in his tracks, staring wide-eyed at the spectacle before him. He gave a low whistle and shook his head. There were half-naked women lying all over the place, on the floor, on couches, moaning softly, many of them apparently unconscious or asleep. There were also men in various states of undress, many of whom he recognized. Some of them were sitting on their couches, staring straight ahead. Others were curled up and snuffling softly to themselves; many of them had been bloodied, and some were simply wandering around the room in a daze.

One of them approached him, moving with a disoriented shuffle, a torn black robe thrown over his tattered clothing, bright red scratch marks on his face and chest. He had a dazed, lost look in his eyes as he came up to Liam and held out his right hand in supplication.

Liam took his hand and shook it with a grin. "Well, good evenin' to you, Minister. Sure, an' it must've been one hell of a party, eh?"

# EPILOGUE

"I still have no idea what in God's name went on out there, Michael," said the superintendent. "It looked like a damned war zone. The press are in an absolute furor over the whole thing; captains of industry and M.P.'s running around, all scratched up and with their clothes torn, naked women, dead bodies, people hurt in some sort of a stampede because the roof was falling in. My God! What the hell happened?"

Blood shifted uneasily in the hospital bed and grimaced with pain. "It's a long story, sir, terribly complicated and rather difficult to explain." He groaned and smiled bravely.

"Well . . . I realize you're in some discomfort, Michael, but . . . damn it all, can't you tell me *something*? I saw your father, and he absolutely refused to discuss it. Ian's in critical condition and under doctor's orders to receive no visitors, and no one else will talk about its. Lord Carfax has disappeared somewhere, and all I've got is some bloody Irish cabdriver who keeps grinning like an idiot and talking about what a hell of a party it was!"

"Yes, I can appreciate your position, sir," said Blood, shifting slightly and grimacing elaborately, throwing in a couple of soft groans for good measure.

"Are you all right? You want me to get the doctor?"

"No, no, shouldn't bother. Perfectly fine, sir. Just a bit of pain—it's nothing, really."

"Well . . . if you're quite sure . . ."

"Oh, quite . . . *unhhh*! Oh, Lord . . ." He managed a brave smile. "Quite sure, sir. I'll manage. All will be in my report, sir, after I've had a chance to . . . *unnnh*!Ohhhh . . . get all the details down . . . *aaah*! . . . straight away, after a bit of rest . . ."

The door opened, and Wyrdrune, Kira, Billy, and Makepeace came in. Kira was carrying some flowers.

"Michael, how are you feeling?" Kira said. She glanced at the superintendent. "Sorry, I didn't realize you had company. Should we wait outside?"

"No, no, quite all right, I was just leaving," said the superintendent. He glanced at the four of them with slight distaste, then glanced at Blood with puzzlement.

"Friends of mine," explained Blood.

"Ah," said the superintendent, frowning faintly. He bent down close to Blood and whispered, *"Really?"*

Blood nodded conspiratorially. "Street contacts," he said softly. "Informants, you know. One has to develop close relationships."

"Ah," said the superintendent. "Pity." He straightened up and cleared his throat, "Well, I'll be off. All hell breaking loose, you know. Suppose I'll have to tell them something. Statement forthcoming, pending full investigation, all that sort of rot. Do try to get that report to me as soon as possible, will you? I'll have a records officer standing by so you can dictate it. Should be a bit easier, what?"

"Thank you, sir. I'll . . . ohhh, *aaah*! Sorry. Slight twinge. Nothing serious. I'll . . . *unnnh*! . . . get to it directly, sir."

"Right, then. Get some rest. I'll be checking back." He glanced at the others "Uh . . . pleasure. Don't overtire him, right? Um. Right." He nodded curtly and departed.

"If that man was any stiffer, he'd be in the morgue," said Makepeace with a grimace.

"'Ey, Mick, if you're in a lot o' pain, we can come back, y'know," said Billy, leaning on his cane.

"No, I'm not so bad, really. I was only exaggerating a bit to get rid of the superintendent because I had no idea what to tell him. What in God's name *can* I tell him? He's expecting a complete report!"

"I see your problem," Wyrdrune said. "You obviously can't tell him the whole story, can you?"

"I don't even *know* the whole story," Blood said.

"Oh, it's simple enough, really," Wyrdrune said. "The necromancer caught Modred off-guard and kidnapped him, taking him prisoner and chaining him up in the dungeon of Carfax Castle, leaving him there without food or water with the intention of weakening him so severely that he couldn't be a threat to him anymore. An ordinary man would have died, but the runestone kept Modred alive. Still, there is a limit to what even magic can do. It uses up energy, and if that energy is not replenished, well, it's obvious what happens. Anyway," Wyrdrune continued, "after taking Modred prisoner, the necromancer sent us those visions to draw us in, knowing we would think they were from Modred. And, in fact, that's exactly what we thought, even though I suspected at first that they might not be. Either way we had nothing else to go on, and he made it especially convincing by giving Jacqueline more information that we had, because we knew that Jacqueline had a longer relationship with Modred than we'd had, and she was in closer physical proximity.

"He meant to lure us to the castle on the night of the party. He arranged for us to suspect Carfax—or whoever he really was—thereby providing himself with a convenient Judas goat. He left us enough clues to lead us there, and in case we were spectacularly stupid, he would've dropped some more hints, maybe in another dream vision."

"But he got all those people there to go along with him," said Blood. "Those unfortunate young women and some of the most respected men in the country. I know how my father was duped into being there, but my brother Ian . . ." He looked away. "I still can't believe it, that Ian would have actually committed murder. . . ."

"He didn't really mean to," Kira said. "He didn't know what he was doing."

"Your father is a very strong-willed man, Michael," Makepeace said "and he almost fell under the necromancer's influence. Ian probably never stood a chance."

"Yes," said Blood. "They look for weakness in the soul, you said."

"Most people have a weakness somewhere," Makepeace said. "Some simply conceal it better than others."

"And other people are simply evil at heart," Wyrdrune said. "Those are the easiest for the necromancer to control."

"Like Carfax," Blood said.

"Yes, like Carfax. He was meant to die, you know. They were all meant to die. Every one of them. The idea was to use Modred to draw us in where we were too close to be able to escape, then kill him just before we could get to him. At the same time those women he'd turned into werewolves and demons were meant to kill those men, so that he could absorb all of that released life energy at peak levels, along with Modred's life energy as well. That would have made it impossible for us to stand against him. And in case anything went wrong, he had it all set up so that we'd attack Carfax, think-ing that he was the Dark One. Only he never counted on Terri offering some of her life energy to Modred, so that he could be strong enough to act when the time came and draw life energy from the very man who had been meant to kill him."

"Ian," Blood said softly.

"Yes," said Wyrdrune. "That was another thing that took the necromancer by surprise, that one of us would resort to the same methods used by the Dark Ones. Only Modred stopped just short of killing Ian."

"I wonder why," said Blood. "After all, killing should hardly bother him. And Ian tried to murder him, so I suppose it would have been self-defense."

"Modred is a complicated man," said Kira.

"He couldn't come with you?" said Blood.

"He *wouldn't* come," said Makepeace with a smile. "He didn't want to put a chief inspector of Scotland Yard through the discomfort of getting a hospital visit from a professional assassin."

"Is he *really* Morpheus?" asked Blood.

"Yes," said Makepeace. "Though that part of his life is over now."

"I've actually seen Morpheus," said Blood. "And I've lived to tell the tale. I wonder how many people can say that? Still, it's a tale I'd probably be better off not telling. I'll have to fudge up some sort of fantasy for the superintendent. The truth might be a bit tough to explain." He looked at Billy and grinned. "Especially the part about how a two-thousand-year-old thirteen-year-old saved the day with a bit of acrobatics and a flick knife, of all things. No one would believe it."

"Hell, *I* don't believe it," Merlin said "Next time you pull a stunt like that, young man, I'll kick your arse up between your ears."

"I think that would be a bit *too* acrobatic, even for me," said Billy with a grin.

The grin disappeared instantly, to be replaced by a scowl as Merlin muttered "You know what I damn well mean! It was foolhardy and reckless."

"'Ey, it worked, din't it? So bugger off!"

"*What* did you say?"

"You 'eard me, old man, I said bugger off!"

"Why . . . why, you miserable, misbegotten little toad, I ought to—"

Blood burst out laughing, and the rest of them all followed suit as Billy scowled at them. Nobody could tell if it was Merlin or Billy doing the scowling. Maybe it was both of them.

"I can see," said Wyrdrune, "that this is going to be the start of a beautiful relationship."